ia Kibbie

Edited by Benjamin White

Published in North America and Europe by Running Wild Press. Visit Running Wild Press at www.runningwildpress.com Educators, librarians, book clubs (as well as the eternally curious), go to www.runningwildpress.com for teaching tools.

ISBN (pbk) 978-1-947041-32-5

ISBN (ebook) 978-1-947041-44-8

Printed in the United States of America.

Chapter 1

"But surely, good Lancelot." Queen Guinevere's mellifluous voice floated over the lute she strummed gently in her lap, skirts spread wide upon the carpet of flowers in the castle's garden. *"You say such things in friendship."*

"Have you no esteem for me?" Lancelot grabbed her hand, and the strumming of the lute stopped.

"Of course I do. You are my good husband's most courageous knight."

"And his closest friend," Lancelot reminded her. *"And yet... as much as I love him like a brother, I cannot deny my love for you. Please, my queen, give me but a morsel of your affection, a kind word — and I shall leave you in peace."*

James froze and stared at the small wireless that sat on the shelf above the bed. His pencil hovered expectantly over the columns of numbers in his accounting book. "Oh, no, Gwen, don't fall for that rubbish!" He begged the voice on the radio.

"Oh... I... I... oh, Lancelot," Queen Guinevere cried just as a dramatic crescendo of music swept her words away. *"Stay tuned,"* the announcer advised, *"for the astonishing final episodes of this ageless love story. Part six of 'Legends of Camelot' will air next Tuesday at half past nine in the morning."*

James arched his back away from the sofa and grunted his annoyance. He slapped down the accounting book and stuck his pencil behind his ear. There it rested against his auburn curls that accented his temples where fine hairs formed tiny arcs like the decorative plaster molding that graced the flat he shared with Arthur. The 19th century accents had once been beautiful, but the ceiling was dingy now, stained with London smog and cracked in the bombings. Still, they kept the space cheery and bright with gauzy curtains, potted plants with lush, cascading vines, and a large mirror that hung from a gilded chain over their small fireplace.

1

"We interrupt our scheduled broadcast to bring you the latest on the coronation. Massive crowds are gathered along the route—"

James sprang up and snapped off the radio with a flick of his thin white wrist. He turned to the window and drew back the curtain to search the wet street for Arthur's hulking form in the sea of umbrellas. Nothing. He squinted at the cloud-darkened sky and then let the curtain fall back into place. "Well, it wouldn't be a coronation without a bit of English summer rain." He shrugged. "Let's hope they packed the—"

He was startled from his reverie by the tea kettle's sudden, sharp whistle. James cursed bounced over the bed. He raced across the large open room toward the little turquoise stove nestled in the corner next to the equally tiny sink.

A series of loud bangs erupted from the room below as Mrs. Wylit pounded on her ceiling with a broom handle. James pulled the kettle from the stove and winced as he set it down on the small wooden table with a tea towel beneath it. He leaned down and called through the Victorian-era ventilation grate, "I'm so sorry, Mrs. Wylit. I know you hate that sound."

She did not reply, but he could faintly hear her cursing and the smack of the broom as she roughly tossed it back into the corner of her own flat.

James poured the hot water into their white and gold-trimmed teapot and tiptoed back to his accounting figures as the leaves steeped. After a few minutes, the columns of numbers, which represented the profits of Mr. Conner's tailor shop, swam before his eyes. He tossed the book aside again and went to the window to watch for Arthur.

Just as he pulled back the curtain, he heard the downstairs door swing open and then shut with a bang. Arthur's usually heavy footsteps echoed up the front staircase to their landing with uncharacteristic spryness. Mrs. Wylit yelled something up the stairwell, but James couldn't make it out.

The door of the flat banged open, and in came Arthur with his head bowed to avoid conking it on the frame. One of the reasons they put up with Mrs. Wylit was because of their flat's high ceilings, a necessity for Arthur, who stood nearly six-and-a-half feet tall. Arthur carried a nondescript parcel in his massive hands, carefully wrapped with brown paper and tied with string, its surface spattered with raindrops. He set it down on their little table with the utmost care before he bent to remove his rubber overshoes. By the time he'd un-buttoned his Mackintosh, James was at his side with a cup of tea, fixed with a sizeable pour of milk and a fistful of sugar cubes.

"Oy, mate," Arthur greeted loudly, directing his performance at the metal grate in the kitchen that fed down into Mrs. Wylit's sitting room. "Bit o' rain, but nothing severe."

"Did you bring a paper? I want to look at the cricket scores," James played along as he handed Arthur the teacup.

"Look at this blooming flat. Don't you ever pick up after yourself?" Arthur winked one of his emerald eyes and James winked back. Arthur took a gulp of tea, and then used his free arm to sweep James up to his height, planting a silent but sizeable kiss on his cupid's bow mouth. Once lowered back to the floor, James took their cups to the sofa, far enough away from the grate that they could talk softly and presumably not be heard. Arthur followed with the box.

"You were gone for ages." James reached out with a stocking foot to nudge Arthur's backside. "I was going to make a proper breakfast for you today, but you ran off on me."

Arthur's mouth curled up in a half-smile as he put the box carefully on the bed, and set about moving two of James' potted plants from their place on top of the small bookshelf opposite the sofa. The sofa was where the rest of the world thought James slept every night. If anyone knew the truth, they would go to jail, and the weight of it hung around them even in this happy moment. "Careful, those two are temperamental." James took another sip of his black tea. "What are you doing?"

"You'll see." Arthur started for the box on the bed, and then stopped to put a sausage-shaped finger to his chin in thought. "Better have you blindfolded," he decided, and rummaged through the small bureau for a few moments. Giving up, he peeled the case from a pillow.

James set his cup to the side. He made a face as Arthur put the pillowcase over his head. "Is this a kidnapping, then? Arthur, what's going on?"

"Be patient," Arthur scolded. James heard him bang around in a drawer, and then came the rustle of the paper. Then came the unmistakable groan of a cardboard box, and a small thud.

"What on earth are you doing?"

"Blimey," Arthur muttered over more rustling. James felt Arthur's hulk sink down next to him on the sofa. Gently, the pillow case wisped over his nose and uncovered his eyes.

"Good Lord." James' hands flew up over his mouth to soften his exclamation. He turned to Arthur and found him beaming a radiant smile. His green eyes snapped with excitement.

"Arthur, you didn't!"

"Do you like it?"

James put his fingers to his chest and laughed. "Arthur, it's a television." He admired the small sleek box with the gently curved screen, graced with two shiny silver dials.

"A television? The nutter who sold it to me said it was a box of encyclopedias. Better return it then." Arthur made as if to stand up.

James laughed and dragged him back onto the couch. Arthur came willingly — there were few people physically formidable enough to force Arthur to do anything, but James had his ways. "Surprise." Arthur gave James another kiss.

"That's why you've been hauling lumber like a mule for the last month." James crossed his arms as Arthur stood up to plug in the new set and adjust the receiver. "All of those extra jobs suddenly make sense."

Both of them had inherited money and heirlooms from Lady Barlow, but everyone struggled after the war. Most of their money and valuables were locked away in the bank, and they withdrew judiciously. Arthur worked construction, his immense stature a boon to his supervisors, and James balanced the tailor's books and minded the counter a few times a week. They could live comfortably on their small monthly budget, as neither had extravagant tastes. *Well,* James thought, *except for the new telly.*

"Didn't want us to miss history." Arthur switched on the set. An image flickered to life — a wide, sweeping shot of Whitehall with Big Ben proudly in the background. He adjusted the other knob, and the voice of the commentator broke in. "Queen Salote of Tonga, sitting with Sultan Ibrahim of Kelantan." As the open-topped carriage rolled past the camera, the stoic Sultan sat still as a statue, but Queen Salote waved cheerfully, a beaming smile wrapped around her face. Though many of the other carriages in the procession had pulled up their hoods to protect their precious cargo from the rain, Queen Salote's conveyance remained open as she continued to greet the adoring crowd.

"Oh, she's brilliant. Do you know, Arthur, she's almost as tall as you are." James' focus was on the other side of the screen in the crowd as Arthur sat down beside him on the sofa.

Arthur squeezed James' shoulder, and grinned at the way the flickering images transfixed his lover's attention. He got up and freshened their tea, then rescued two apples from his coat pockets.

"Long live the Queen." He handed James the fruit.

"Long live the Queen." They tapped their apples together in a makeshift toast. Arthur set down his tea and put his arm around

James, who nestled down against his barrel chest. "Oh, this is perfect," he said. "So much better than fighting the crowds."

"Mad out there," Arthur confirmed, stroking James' ear with his rough knuckle. "I saw—"

The door to the flat flew open, and they both jumped landed on opposite ends of the sofa. There, in the door frame, stood their landlady, Mrs. Viola Wylit, her frame (bony in some places, blobby in others) forever encased in a worn pink chenille robe, gray-streaked dark hair tied up with her usual blue scarf, a smoke hanging from her slack lips. The stench of a thousand cigarettes wafted in and James had to physically restrain himself from holding his nose. She had a foil-covered round object in her hand, which she slapped unceremoniously on their small table. She used the freed hand to draw the cigarette away from her lips. "Did I hear you two cabbages toasting our new Queen up here without me?"

"Mrs. Wylit, please, we've spoken about this." James stood up and moved for the door. "You're not allowed to unlock the door and come in as you please."

"My own house," she muttered, but closed the door after ashing her cigarette on the tiles and Arthur's drying overshoes. She rapped with her bony knuckles. Her hands were strangely dry and withered for a woman that couldn't be over 40. "Excuse me, good afternoon, Mr. Wilde, may I please be admitted on this joyous day of celebration?"

James opened the door and made a show of waving her inside. "Why, Mrs. Wylit, so lovely to see you. Do come in."

"Bloody hell! That's a television!" She wobbled over to the sofa, entranced by the royal procession as they crossed Trafalgar Square. "Oh, look, there's our lovely Queen Horseface herself."

"She's a very nice-looking queen," Arthur argued around his teacup, and shot James an apologetic glance over the back of the sofa.

"Beautiful even," James insisted with a wink.

Mrs. Wylit huffed, but did not tear her gaze from the screen. James freed their only ashtray from a drawer and brought it to the coffee table in time to catch her next batch of discarded ash. She caught his arm, but kept her gaze fixed on the television. "Be a dear and fetch me a cuppa, there's a good lad."

James sighed and put the kettle on again. Arthur winked at him, then settled back to watch the procession with Mrs. Wylit.

This time, James was careful not to forget about the kettle and let it heat to the point of whistling. He brought the tray and poured Mrs. Wylit a cup of tea and freshened Arthur's as the Queen's procession arrived at Westminster Abbey. Mrs. Wylit patted the sofa cushion at her side and James plunked down between her and Arthur as she lit another cigarette.

From the folds of Mrs. Wylit's robe came a silver flask, one that had decorative initials carved upon it that someone had crudely scratched out with a pen knife. She poured a generous dollop of spirit into her tea, and reached over to do the same to James' cup. "Please, Mrs. Wylit, the day's rather young."

"How much have you had already?" Arthur asked in that quiet, impressive way of his, that said more than the literal words he spoke.

She sniffed. "This isn't a house where we judge people. This isn't... a *judgemental* house. Is it?" She raised a curved eyebrow and glared at James a moment.

"Of course not." James held out his cup.

"Coronation day, after all," Arthur added, and accepted a dram of her wretched liquor as well. "And, did you hear, Hillary and Norgay reached the summit of Everest."

"Who's done what now?" Mrs. Wylit sipped her spiked tea, her gaze glued to the queen as she strode forward down the aisle toward St. Edward's Chair.

"How exciting." James took breath to calm his voice. "Proud day for the Commonwealth." He wanted to ask if Arthur had bought a paper with the headline yet — he'd been clipping articles about Hillary and his progress all along — but that seemed too personal of a thing to know about, well, a flatmate. To Mrs. Wylit, and the rest of the world, they were two lads sharing the rent.

Little-black-and-white Queen Elizabeth moved slowly across the screen, encumbered by her dress, overwear, and enormous train. They watched in reverential silence as she hefted the orb and scepters. Proud tears of happiness gathered in James' eyes and a lump swelled in his throat, but he swallowed it all down. Mrs. Wylit smoked furiously, and angled herself toward the little set, rough elbows pressed into her knees. At last, St. Edward's Crown touched the royal forehead, and the spectators chanted, "God save the Queen."

"God save the Queen! God save the Queen!" Mrs. Wylit, James, and Arthur repeated along with them, and then raised their voices in a celebratory whoop. They clinked their tea cups. James couldn't be sure, but he thought he saw Mrs. Wylit scrub a tear away from her sallow cheek with the heel of her chapped hand. He coughed discreetly as she lit another cigarette off of the butt of the previous, but the mood was celebratory, and somehow he didn't mind her intrusion. One glance at Arthur's benevolent smile said the same.

"What's in the tinfoil, Mrs. Wylit?"

"Go see for yourself." She waved her cigarette hand dismissively as Elizabeth shouldered the burden of rule and greeted her husband, the Duke of Gloucester, who stepped forward to swear his oath to her.

Arthur hauled his T-shaped frame from the sofa, which gave them quite a jostle, and opened the foil package. "Mmm," he said, and brought it to the coffee table. Inside was a lemon tart, the top layer of pastry cut in the shape of a crown.

"Oh, it's smashing, it really is," said James. "You must have saved your sugar rations for weeks."

"Stopped putting it in me tea." Mrs. Wylit shrugged and blew smoke from her nostrils with a disinterested wave of her hand. "Had to substitute a few ingredients. I've arsed it up, I'm sure."

"Nonsense. Tart fit for a queen," Arthur said with his sideways smile as he brushed back his thick black hair that insisted on falling over his broad forehead.

"Do you eat with your eyes?" Mrs. Wylit elbowed James with her sharp arm. "Go on, then, for God's sake."

James offered to cut a piece for her out of courtesy, but knew she'd refuse it with a curse. Mrs. Wylit was typically too pissed to cook, but when she did, it was heavenly. However, all he'd seen her eat in the past two years was a handful of licorice. She watched them devour their slices with a certain amount of satisfaction, as she swigged from her flask and lit another cigarette. The Queen took communion on the little screen glowing under the window.

"Any predictions, Mrs. Wylit?" James asked, his tone jovial and carefree, but with an undercurrent of true curiosity threaded through it.

James and Arthur, in private, called Mrs. Wylit the Drunken Oracle. When she was particularly bladdered, she had a tendency to make odd predictions. It would have been silly, harmless fun perhaps, if they didn't come true more often than not. For example, in a drunken rage, she'd once told them that King George would die before St. Valentine's Day, and he had, at age 56 on February the 6th.

Mrs. Wylit took a long drag from her cigarette and let the smoke roll from her nostrils like a dragon. "God Almighty, she'll reign for decades," she proclaimed as the rest of the smoke escaped. "She'll go well past the millennium, chaps."

"Considering how young her father died?" James scoffed over his second piece of tart.

"Was right about George, wasn't I?" She poked her cigarette at him again. "And I knew that little cold of yours last winter was pneumonia, didn't I? Now eat your damned tart."

As they finished, the bell downstairs rang. "Now who the hell is that?" Mrs. Wylit lurched to her feet and stumbled over the end of the table. "You blokes expecting anyone? You know what I've said about houseguests." She punctuated her outburst by stabbing her cigarette into the ashtray.

"Not expecting anyone," Arthur patiently said. "Let me go get it."

Mrs. Wylit melted back onto the sofa and James rolled his eyes. With a shake of his head, Arthur went out into the hall and clomped down the steps to the front door of the old brick row house.

As James helped himself to another piece of the tart, Arthur started back up to the second floor. The spring was gone from his step, and he took the wooden staircase with heavy, plodding legs. Arthur's gait was so markedly different from how he'd gone down the stairs that James put the tart down and met him at the door. His face contorted in concern as Mrs. Wylit stared into the telly.

"What is it?" James whispered as Arthur shut the door and faced him. Tears gathered in Arthur's large green eyes.

Arthur handed him a telegram. "Mr. Marlin," he said, voice husky with emotion. "Mr. Marlin's died, James."

Chapter 2

Mr. Conner approached James as he wrapped up a length of fabric and set the bolt back on the shelf. The tailor tapped the small ledger book against his palm, his usually placid mouth turned down in concern.

"Mr. Bennett rang while you were out." James folded another length of fabric, set it to the side, and wound up a measuring tape. "He's coming in tomorrow at nine to be fitted for something called a Teddy Boy." James' smile evaporated as he glanced at his employer's expression. "Sir?"

"James, there are several errors in your entries yesterday." Mr. Conner flipped open the ledger to reveal his markings in red pencil. "You were off by a fiver at least."

"I'm so sorry, sir." James sank onto a cloth-covered bench with a sigh. "I was... distracted, I suppose."

Mr. Conner's frown melted a bit. "The coronation, perhaps?"

"No. Well, yes. But that's not all." James sighed again and shook his head. He moved instinctively from the bench to straighten a rack of ties. "I received some bad news, sir."

"Oh?" Mr. Conner closed the ledger book and tucked it under his arm.

James kept his gaze averted, and tried to concentrate on the ties so not not to betray his tearful eyes. "I've lost someone... who was very important to me."

"I'm sorry to hear that." Mr. Conner nodded his sympathy. "A family member?"

"N...no. Not exactly." James turned away from the ties.

"Oh. A... friend, then?"

James crossed his arms over his thin frame. He felt weepy and small. "It's... well, it's hard to..." Flustered, he bit his lip. "Pied Piper," he said finally. "I was sent away with my class when the Nazis began

11

their bombing runs on London. This man, the one who died... he took care of me. He protected me."

"You went away with Pied Piper?" Mr. Conner's greying eyebrows rose. "I had no idea."

"Yes. I was twelve at the time. Mr. Marlin was, for all intents and purposes, in charge of the manor house where we stayed. He, well... he made it bearable. Better than bearable. The man was..." He shook his head and silenced himself, overcome for the moment.

"It must have been terrible, leaving home like that." Mr. Conner squeezed James on the shoulder with a brief but caring hand. "He must have been very important to you."

"He was. He—"

Right then, the bell on the shop's door rang wildly, and Mr. Conner's son, Corbin, burst in with his usual self-important fanfare. He did the thing that annoyed James the most — letting the heavy door slam shut behind him with a solid *bang*. "Father! Did you hear Arvel Bennett's coming in tomorrow for a Teddy Boy?" Corbin stopped short at the door of the storeroom when he saw the redness in James' cheeks and eyes, and the concerned posture of his father. "What's the matter with you? Crying on the job now? That ought to bring the customers racing in. Come see the blubbering buggerer." He gave a cruel laugh and slapped the doorframe.

"Corbin, that's quite enough," Mr. Conner scolded. "James has had a death in the... well, family, I'd say."

Corbin huffed and went behind the counter.

"The funeral is tomorrow." James bit his tongue against the acidic things he wanted to say to Corbin, the things he wanted to say to him every damned day. "I'm afraid I won't be in to help with Mr. Bennett."

"I'm sure we'll manage." Mr. Conner put his hand on James' shoulder again for a moment of reassurance. "Take as much time as you need." He followed James' watery green gaze to Corbin's back as he busily stacked shirts on the shelves. "Don't mind him; his mother spoiled him growing up. That's why he's full of piss and vinegar these days."

Mr. Conner was a wonderful man, and a skilled tailor, but he had blinders on when it came to his son, who was nothing but a schoolyard bully in a body too big for such behavior. Still, it wasn't the worst he'd been called, not by a long shot.

"You could use some fresh air. Why don't you give the windows a wipe? When you're finished, you may be excused for the day."

After he'd finished, James bid the Conners goodbye and took the tube to his mother's in Catford. He knew she'd be home from work at the phone company by the time he arrived. Sure enough, he spied her through the front windows of her prefab house. He instantly recognized her silhouette; her tightly curled hair was unmistakable, the same brown-red as his, perhaps even a few shades more vibrant. She colored hers to battle the booming population of grays that infiltrated her scalp. The tin-roofed cottage, built after the bombings to combat the lack of housing in other parts of the city, was constructed by German and Italian prisoners of war as temporary shelters. His mother had gotten one after their building had burnt to the ground during a bombing raid. Luckily, she'd been staying with her aunt after Cousin Ted had died at Tripoli. James had lived there after returning from Willowind House until he'd headed off to university.

He hadn't been back often. James and his mother got along well enough, but didn't have a burning desire to spend time with one another. Something had changed when she sent him off on Pied Piper, put him in the care of others, left him there at the train station. *She must have known I'd be devoured by those bullies — Morgan and the rest,* James thought. *Thank God Arthur was there. Blessed Nim. And Mr. Marlin. Poor Mr. Marlin.*

Well, it was easier for her, wasn't it? Better not to have to worry about a child in a city painted with a target for Nazi bombing runs.

Better not to have to worry about him being targeted by the other children, coming home day after day coming home with his cap stolen or his uniform torn, or "fairy-boy" scrawled in ink all over his books. *Yes, it must have been difficult for her,* he thought bitterly, *raising a son like me.* These days, she still claimed to lose sleep over him. Was she worried, as she proclaimed to be, about the possibility of his imprisonment for breaking the law, or worried about her own reputation? He'd never quite been sure.

Still, she'd loved him once, hadn't she? And here she was, opening her door for him, tea and biscuits already set out in her tacky terra-cotta kitchen which bled right into her sitting area in the tiny cottage. "Hello darling," she chirped, and ushered him inside to sit at the cheap, wobbling kitchen table. "You look exhausted. Here." She handed him his cup and poured one for herself.

He sipped. "How's the switchboard, Mum?"

She clucked, and sank into a chair opposite, then lifted her black rhinestone cat's-eye glasses to her face to get a better look at him. "Busy, darling, terribly busy — it never stops. And the tailor shop?"

"Well enough." He grimaced at the thought of Corbin.

"Any more trouble with the landlady?" His mother pushed the small plate of biscuits toward him.

He dipped it in his tea — it was stale — and washed it down quickly. "She's a nutter, I suppose, but she's our nutter."

"What a lovely, lovely coronation," his mother barreled on as she swiped up some of the crumbs from the biscuit plate and touched them to her tongue. "Did you do anything special to celebrate?"

"Watched it on the telly. We've got a telly now, and it's just brilliant."

"Oh, it must have been expensive!" This, coming from the woman who owned every insipid ceramic animal figurine ever produced. Every available inch of flat space in the cottage was crammed with doe-eyed china dogs and cats and babies.

James shrugged, and hardened his jaw. He knew where the conversation led. Eventually, the meandering road would come back to Nim's jewels, Arthur's antique armor and sword, and what she thought they should be doing with their inheritance.

James was relieved when she swirled her tea and changed the subject. His mother looked into the swirling vortex of tea instead of his gaze. "And how is... erm... your friend..."

He stared at her expectantly, chin raised, until she looked at him with the distant sorrow of her brown eyes magnified in her lenses.

"Arthur." She set the spoon in the saucer with an irritated clank.

James fed her a saccharine smile that felt like a grimace. "He's my *boyfriend*, Mum. If they'd let us marry, he'd be my fiancé. Or maybe even husband by now."

"Oh, James." She broke a biscuit in two, then three pieces, only to let them fall in the saucer.

"What? You're the one who kept asking. And asking and asking and asking. I'm sorry it wasn't the truth you wanted to hear." James leaned back in his chair and crossed his arms over his gray twill vest.

"I'm sorry, James, please," she begged, and he relaxed with a gruff sigh. "You're right, I wanted to know the truth. And do you remember what I said? I don't want to see you," she looked for the right word, "*convicted*, and I told you I would love you the same as always.

As if that was something to treasure, he thought, but his flinty heart softened as she unclasped her handbag and withdrew a handkerchief to dab at her eyes.

"I've been terrified for years that someone else would find out about the two of you. Tell the police. Or worse. You have to understand how scared I am for you every day. You young people think you're invincible."

"Mum, I'm aware of the risks," he argued.

"If only your father hadn't abandoned us." She sniffled and frowned at the mascara marks on the handkerchief. His mother reached out and he gave her his hand. She squeezed it with a watery smile. "What kind of heartless swine would leave a woman with a little baby crawling around on the floor in his nappies? It wasn't easy, you know, raising you all alone, darling. I feel as if I wasn't the mother I could have been, what with the war—"

"Mum, it's all right," he said, and he meant it, though the look of pure relief when she dropped him off at the platform haunted him.

She squeezed his hand, and then let it go. "So," she started over. "How is Arthur? How are things?"

"Jolly good, actually. I've been over a year at Mr. Conner's, and he's given me a raise. Of course, I'd rather sell some of my poems and stories, but you know how it is."

"I'd love to see you use some of your education. A degree in literature, and working for a tailor—"

He plunged on, deaf to her. He'd heard it all before. "For Arthur, plenty of construction work, more than we need."

"Even after he sent so much to his parents?" His mother pointed at him with her teaspoon.

There, she did it — it happened any time they were together. She had to give her opinion about the money. "His father is loads better." James leaned away from her again. "Do you know he can walk outside without children screaming about a monster? That he has *eyelids* now?"

"James, it was merely a question. Of course, I want Arthur's father to have the best treatment available. For God's sake, the man lost his face fighting the damned Jerrys." She gulped her tea and lifted part of a biscuit to her painted lips.

"It's only that we've talked about this. Nim gave Arthur and me the inheritance. I know we were lads, but she meant it for us. And now that we're men, we'll manage it as we see fit." He stood up and went to the back bedroom. "Did you find my black suit?"

"Yes. It's pressed. I hung it up in the loo," she called after him. "Tell me again who's passed away?"

"Mr. Marlin. He was Nim's head of household." He pushed open the cheap door to the loo and rescued his suit from the shower curtain rod. It was nicely pressed, the shirt fresh and crisp.

She met him in the hallway, and put her hands on his shoulders. They were the same height. "I'm sorry for your loss, dear," she said, with the same sincerity as Mr. Conner. "I know how important he was to you after Lady Barlow passed away. Had you been in contact much?"

James folded the suit carefully over his arm. "We wrote like mad for the first few years. Then he retired and returned to the village to be with his family, and, well... we always sent a Christmas card. I had no idea he was sick." There were the tears again, but he refused to cry in front of her.

"Perhaps it was some kind of accident." His mother brushed a sweaty auburn curl away from his forehead.

"Miss Ivaine, Lady Barlow's lady's maid, sent us the telegram. All it said was that he had died, and when the funeral would be."

She took his free hand, and they walked toward the door. "And where did Mr. Marlin hail from?"

"Meopham."

"Ah, Kent's lovely this time of year." She rubbed his shoulders again. "Travel safely, darling. Be aware... of your surroundings. Of who's watching." She let the weight of the last word hang in the air. Despite the gravity of her warning, it cheered James a little — perhaps his safety was all that was on her mind, not her own struggle having a pouf for a son. "And do give me a ring when you get home," she added.

"I will, Mum."

Right then, the black rotary phone on the kitchen counter rang.

"Speaking of. Wait a moment, don't go yet, darling." She bustled into the kitchenette, the summer humidity forming a T of sweat on the back of her striped pussy bow blouse. His mother picked up the receiver. "Hello?" Then... "Hello... hello? I can hear you breathing, you know. Say something for God's sake... Ugh. Bastard. Pervert!" She slammed the receiver down.

"Mum, what in the world—?"

She hurried back to him, and stroked his arm again like he was frightened animal. "It's nothing, love. I've had a rash of prank calls. Some blighter calls and doesn't say anything. Lord, it happens at least twice a week. Since... February, perhaps."

"Mum! Have you called the constables?" James made as if to go to the phone himself, but she stopped him, yanking his elbow.

"Darling, it's nothing really. Some men... well. You know. Tossers. Besides, I don't trust the police, knowing what they'd do to you and Arthur."

"Now I'm going to fret all day about you," he said, though he let her lead him back to the door. Her comment about the bobbies left him warm.

She kissed his cheek. "That's sweet of you, dear. Please ring me when you get back, yeah? And again, so sorry. And..."

He raised an auburn eyebrow, arched it high in anticipation.

"Tell Arthur I've said hello."

He kissed her cheek again. "Cheerio, Mum."

"Be careful on the tube," she called after him as he trotted down the small walk through her spotty lawn. "And don't forget to pack a brelly and your overshoes."

By the time he reached the end of the lane, he heard her cursing the heavy-breathing caller again, her voice shrill through her open windows.

Chapter 3

One of the principal pleasures in Arthur's life was to watch James when James didn't know he was being watched. Now, for instance, as James read on the train to Meopham, curled up in a seat by the window in the otherwise deserted compartment, Arthur abandoned the newspaper he'd brought and sank into the trance of his love.

Some gazes of desire are hungry, starving even — or predatory; aggressive. The way Arthur looked at James, the way he'd always looked at him — ever since they'd evacuated to Willowind House over ten years ago — was the way a country tourist might examine a painting on the wall of the Louvre. A man might stand there in the bustle, surrounded, encased in beautiful rooms full of beautiful things that he could always and forever admire, but would never fully comprehend. An uneducated observer, lucky to have walked through the front door of the museum in the first place, would suddenly be awestruck by the beauty within.

The way James crinkled his freckled nose when he read something particularly interesting - how the sun haloed his auburn hair freshly cut in what the barber had called the "college contour" — his eyes, nearly the same emerald shade as Arthur's — his nimble hands and fingers — everything about James, when he wasn't aware Arthur was watching, was as perfect and unchanging as a work of art.

Oh, they'd had their squabbles, to be sure. A few rows that could have awakened the dead (but did not wake Mrs. Wylit, for they were late enough at night that she was pissed beyond repair and had lapsed into unconsciousness). James was rubbish at milestones and important dates — Arthur only half-jokingly suggested he have their birthdays tattooed on him somewhere. When James was writing, he was not present; even after he'd stopped for the day, and put the typewriter away, Arthur could see the wheels spinning behind his eyes, the words weaving in and out of the clouds in his mind like so much smoke. It could be infuriating at times, speaking to James and knowing that the words were barely sinking in, that fictional people occupied his mind.

But no matter the strife, Arthur came back to these quiet moments where he put James on a pedestal like a last-of-its-kind archaeological relic, something to be preserved at all costs because of the exceptional beauty it brought to the world.

Arthur watched James place his marker back in his book. It was his beaten paperback copy of *Idylls of the King* by Tennyson. Their autographed first edition was locked away in the vault with the rest of the treasures Nim had bequeathed them at the time of her death. Arthur had once noted James always turned to that particular text when he was troubled.

James put his chin in his hand and leaned on the armrest as the fertile fields of waving wheat rolled past as the train cut through the lush, fruitful countryside of Kent.

"What's the matter?" Arthur leaned forward on the edge of the seat facing James. His legs were so long their knees practically met.

James didn't look at him, his eyes distant. Their glassy green surface reflected the puffy clouds of the glorious summer day outside. "We should have kept in touch," he murmured as he played with his full lower lip. "He was one of the best men I ever knew."

"Wish we could have said goodbye, as well." Arthur folded the newspaper and slid it into the inside pocket of his own suit, one that Mr. Conner had to fashion especially for him to accommodate his height. "I pray he knew how much he meant to us."

"Quite." James sniffed, and artfully snuck a tear away from his cheek with his sleeve.

Arthur leaned forward and caught one of James' long, nimble hands to stroke the knuckles. James stole a glance at the glass of the cabin door to the hallway outside. He gave Arthur's palm a furtive squeeze and then pulled away.

"Why are you so afraid?" Arthur asked, though he knew in his heart that this was not the time or the place for this conversation. Perhaps it was the rawness of his grief for Mr. Marlin, but he couldn't help himself. He wanted James' comfort, not his fear of being discovered. "There's no one on this train we know."

"What do you think would happen if either of us were arrested? It's the law, Arthur. Nothing we do is going to change that." James rubbed his eyes and deflated back into his chair.

"If anyone bothered us, I'd make them regret it." Arthur leaned back as well. His head nearly brushed the luggage rack above.

"You can defend yourself. No one would dare get into a scrap with you. Look at me. I'm as dangerous as a tea towel."

"I'll always protect you." Arthur resisted the urge to lean forward again to touch his boyfriend, take him by the hand or the knee, to make some kind of physical connection.

"I know you will." James shook his head with a sigh. "I'm sorry. I don't want a row. I'm really knackered and need a kip, I suppose. Besides, that man in the long brown coat..." He cut himself off and waved the words away like so much smoke. "Mum's got me paranoid."

"What man? And what's this about your mum?" Arthur put his elbows on his knees to catch every word. The suit, which he rarely wore, strained against his muscled shoulders, even with the tailor's smart alterations.

James rubbed his chin with a little groan. "I had to pop by Mum's yesterday for my suit. She's got me looking over my shoulder. She's had dozens of these eerie hang-up calls. Some bloke calls her and breathes into the phone. Makes you wonder about what kind of perverts are out there."

"You mean besides us?" Arthur crafted a little sideways smile that he knew James liked.

James allowed a little laugh to slip out. "Anyway, when I got home with the suit, right before you came home for supper, I saw a man sort of... lingering about on the corner near the house. I noticed him because he had on this old-fashioned long brown coat. Seems like it would have been rather hot for summer. It was like something you'd see a gangster wearing in a film. He had on a fedora as well."

"Was it Al Capone's ghost?"

James smiled again; he couldn't help it. "No, not nearly so thick. He was sort of pale and spindly. I don't know. There was something familiar about him. I couldn't quite make out what it was."

"Perhaps he's a customer of Mr. Conner's?"

James snorted — it was meant to be rude, but Arthur found it adorable. "Not the way he was dressed."

"So why did he make you so nervous, pet?"

James slapped his hands down on his knees and rolled his eyes. "You're going to think me daft."

"Come on, then."

He shook his head.

"James."

James bit his rosy bottom lip. "I swear I saw the same man get on the train with us this morning. Same brown coat and everything. But I can't be sure — it was only for a moment," he hesitated, looking up for a reaction from Arthur. "There, I've said it, now have your laugh."

Arthur did not laugh. Instead, he stood and brushed some lint from his suit. "Better have a look, then."

"Oh, really, Arthur," James pretended to protest. But his bitten-lip smile was enough to send Arthur out into the car to search the train. He went up and down both directions, even lingered awhile in the dining car, but saw no one who fit the description James gave. On the way back to their cabin, he did notice a middle-aged man, thin, like James had said — but his coat was bundled up against the window and he slept on it for a pillow. His hair was salt and peppered, rather too long to be fashionable, and his clothes were rumpled. He reminded Arthur of what a professor should look like, right down to the gold-rimmed spectacles carefully tucked in his breast pocket. Harmless and bumbling. And an easily beaten opponent, should anything happen.

James' expectant green eyes caught him as soon as he returned to their cabin. When Arthur shook his head, James relaxed back into his seat with a grateful whoosh of air from his lungs. "Silly of me," he said. "But you know how it is... what if he's some kind of detective? Watching us?"

"I'm worried about these calls to your Mum. She called the bobbies?" Arthur settled back down in his chair and removed the newspaper from his coat — Hillary and Norgay were on the front page.

"Not yet. She told me she doesn't trust them. Because of how they'd treat us if they knew."

Arthur lowered the paper a few inches. "That was..."

"I know. Quite nice of her to say. I think she's getting used to the idea of you. She's not used to the danger, though."

"Well," Arthur sighed, "we aren't, either. Keeps us sharp, doesn't it?"

"As a needle."

It wasn't long before the train slowed and stopped at the platform of Meopham Station. Arthur carried his suit jacket over his arm as they exited into the station and out onto the street. A rare sunshiny day was a treat, but sweat prickled his brow as the rays sunk into their black suits. Out of the corner of his eye, he caught James craning his neck to scan the crowd of people who had stepped off with them. "Looking for your shadow?"

James blushed and nodded. "Never mind. You're here with me — what have I to fear?"

A kindly woman, likely from the village, pulled over in her sleek little Ford Prefect and offered them a lift to the church. Their clothing, apparently, marked them as funeral-goers.

"No, I didn't know Harold Marlin." Their new chauffeur smiled appreciatively as Arthur steadied her sacks of groceries in the cramped back seat. "But I know his daughter, I believe — Mrs. Alice Benwick. Her mother died when she was rather young. Her father went to work for the Baroness Lady Barlow over at Willowind House in Lincolnshire and she stayed with her aunt here in Meopham. Married one of our constables, Kerr Benwick, good man, too gentle with the drunks if you ask me."

"Mummy," said the tow-headed child in the backseat with Arthur and the grocery sacks. "Why have you picked up a giant on the side of the road?" Arthur turned to the little boy and tried to smile his innocence.

"He's going to grind my bones to make his bread," the child shouted, rather enthusiastically, considering he referenced his own death.

"Ugh, bone bread? That sounds wretched. I like toad-in-the-hole." Arthur winked, and the child giggled.

"I'm so sorry, sir." The mother shook her curly red head. "Ricky, don't be rude."

"It's all right." James grinned into the rear view mirror at Arthur in the back. "He's got quite the imagination."

"If you have a chance, stop by the George." The woman pointed to the steep-roofed inn built of whitewashed brick as they passed. "Try the steak and kidney pie." Not long after the inn, the churchyard came into view. The woman pulled off to the side and let them out before she continued on her way with a cheery beep of her horn.

St. John the Baptist was a stone church with the flat-topped steeple, skirted by a pastoral burying-ground dotted with mossy stones. Though Arthur had thought their arrival early, a small group of soberly-dressed people already gathered around a hole in the ground near a large oak; the fine weather, apparently, had encouraged a graveside service. One of the mourners was a bobby in his dress uniform, no doubt Mr. Marlin's son-in-law. Arthur strode forward and followed the little path until the way necessitated turning onto the lawn. James followed hesitantly behind. Arthur wanted to say something reassuring about the presence of an officer of the law, but didn't know what to say.

As soon as they arrived, the white-haired priest began with the fair summer breeze rustling his white robes and purple stole. "My friends, we are gathered here today to bid farewell to Mr. Harold Marlin and wish him a safe journey as he goes to God's waiting arms. Please join me as we begin with 'All Things Bright and Beautiful.'"

Arthur rumbled along quietly. He knew full well he was tone-deaf; James had told him so on several occasions. Arthur's eyes climbed over the faces of the other mourners in search for someone they knew. A decade had passed, a war had ended, the rebuilding after was all but complete — it might as well have been fifty years. The two of them were so young back then...

One group of mourners was a collection of men in their mid 60's. They had arrived together, and were unaccompanied by women or families. One of them had the sleeve of his jacket pinned to his side, as he had no arm to fill it. Mr. Marlin's war mates, to be sure. Arthur thought perhaps he recognized a woman in a dark dress with a small hat pinned into her dishwater hair. A veil fell over half of her face. She was accompanied by three impeccably dressed and frighteningly well-behaved children, as well as a portly, pleasant-looking fellow with sandy hair. *Could that possibly be Miss Ivaine?*

Another woman with long dark hair, her locks streaked with gray at the temples and twisted back into an elegant, but old-fashioned, chignon, sniffed into her handkerchief and leaned into the bobby. He put his arm around her and kissed the top of her head. When she looked up at the priest, Arthur was able to see the color of her eyes. They were the same steel-gray as Mr. Marlin's had been. On the other side of Mr. Marlin's daughter stood a young man. He had the Marlin family eyes, though his hair was textured and blonde, which must have been a Benwick trait.

The hymn ended, and the priest continued. "Harold Marlin was a son of Meopham, raised here by his mother and father, both of whom were household domestics. Harold worked for the grocer before meeting his lovely wife Katherine, whom he lovingly called Kit. Their daughter Alice is here with us today, along with her family. Harold served with distinction in the Great War, and was awarded the Distinguished Conduct Medal for his courage during the Battle of the Somme. Sadly, a few years after he returned home, the village lost Katherine to illness. Harold took a position in the household of Lord and Lady Barlow, and served the Baroness until her death in 1942. He remained there until his retirement, when he returned to Meopham. He was known as a man of few words, but of deep wisdom. His grandson, Lance, wishes to speak."

Mr. Marlin's grandson stepped forward to stand at the head of the casket that rested on the lush grass near the open grave, decorated with a spray of flowers. He coughed into his fist and said, "Good afternoon. I really met my grandfather when I was twelve years old. Of course, he came home from Willowind House from time to time, but much of his life was dedicated to the care of others. When he retired and moved home to be with us, I, well, I didn't much care for it to be honest." He cracked a grin through the tears that threatened to spill from his eyes. The smile revealed perfect white teeth and accentuated his square, dimpled jaw.

There were some sad chuckles from the audience. "I thought, 'Who is this man, this quiet old man come here to move into my bedroom?' Like Father Haley said, he was a man of few words, but of a tremendous capacity to love. Well, I couldn't *help* but love him; he took me fishing."

Alice Benwick laughed through her tears, and her husband squeezed her tight again.

"He had a wonderful way with young people. I don't know where he learnt it — he left my mother with relatives when she was wee, only four or five years old. I know it was hard for Mum, growing up with cousins, without her father. But he had to leave the village, I think — he missed my grandmother too much." Lance Benwick looked at the ground for a long time, and composed himself with a series of long breaths. Arthur felt his own throat go tight at the sight of this barely-concealed grief.

After a time, Lance continued. "Anyway, the point is that my grandfather was a good man, a brave man, a man who always put the needs of others before his own. He taught me how to stand up for myself and take pride in my work. The strangest thing..." He sniffed, and took another pause to catch his tears again. "The strangest thing is that now that he's not snoring up the whole house, I can't sleep. I was so used to it. Dad, you're going to have to start snoring."

"Don't you dare," Alice laughed through her weeping, and gave her husband a playful tap on the chest.

Arthur resisted every pulse that ran through his muscles. His instinct wanted to grab James' hand. James could barely contain his own tears, his cheeks a violent red over his trembling jaw. It was evil that right now, in this moment, he could not comfort his boyfriend because of who might witness it. Arthur's eyes flicked over to the bobby, a man who so sweetly comforted his wife in her grief, but who would arrest him for loving James. They could be locked away for years, or forced to take drugs that would effectively castrate them. And that was better than being caught out on the street by ruffians who knew their secret. Men had been killed, stomped to death, for expressing their love. Sorrow, hate, and even shame boiled in Arthur's chest, and he clenched his meaty fists at his sides.

"I'd like to end with a poem. Tennyson was always Granddad's favorite. He told me Lady Barlow introduced him to his work." He withdrew a folded piece of notepaper from the jacket pocket of his dark suit, and read:

"Sunset and evening star,
And one clear call for me!

And may there be no moaning of the bar,
When I put out to sea,
But such a tide as moving seems asleep,
Too full for sound and foam,
When that which drew from out the boundless deep
Turns again home.

Twilight and evening bell,
And after that the dark!
And may there be no sadness of farewell,
When I embark;
For tho' from out our bourne of Time and Place
The flood may bear me far,
I hope to see my Pilot face to face
When I have crost the bar."

Lance returned to stand with his family. Psalms were read, prayers said, responses chanted, and at last, Mr. Marlin went to his rest as the gravediggers lowered the casket into the hole with ropes.

The immediate family followed the priest into the church to light candles as the war mates stood about and murmured somber re-membrances. The woman in the veiled hat dragged two of her children along by the hand as she hurried over to Arthur and James. The sandy-haired husband followed with their youngest in his arms.

"Arthur, it must be you." She let go of the children and embraced him.

"Miss Ivaine?" A sudden recognition lit up his face and chased away the dreadful crimson of suppressed weeping.

"Yes, yes!" Lady Barlow's former lady's maid dabbed at her eyes with a wadded-up handkerchief after she embraced James as well. Motherhood had filled her out perfectly, Arthur thought — she'd been skin and bone back at Willowind House. "Though I'm blessed to call myself Mrs. Edwardson now. Oh, it's lovely to see you both again. Look how much you've, well, grown."

"Martha." Her husband hefted the suddenly squirming toddler.

"Yes, of course." She tucked the rosy-cheeked little girl into her hip. "Gilbert, this is James Wilde and Arthur Pensinger. They were with the class of children evacuated to Willowind House during the war as part of Pied Piper. Mr. Marlin — God rest him — and I helped care for them there. These two were quite the favorites, let me tell you. Lady Barlow adored them." She beamed her gapped teeth. "I'm so glad you could come. I was hoping to see you. I'm so pleased you're still..." She glanced at her husband, and it drove an icy needle into Arthur's heart, the horrid, necessary charade. "Best mates," she finished.

James reached out to tickle the little girl's chin. "You have a lovely family."

As they caught up and enjoyed a good chinwag, Arthur noticed Lance Benwick exit the church without the rest of Mr. Marlin's family. He strolled through the churchyard with absent steps, a cigarette at his lips as he glanced at the names carved into the mossy headstones. Meanwhile, the former Miss Ivaine launched into a long narrative about her children's recent bout with chicken pox. James listened with intent politeness, but Arthur's mind and body drifted away. He and Mr. Edwardson grunted at each other about football and cricket for a few moments before falling silent. Then, movement caught his eye again, this time from across the road. Someone was standing idly on the walk across from the cemetery gate, half-obscured by a hedge, smoking in an attempt to look nonchalant, perhaps. Arthur couldn't be sure — the sun was at an angle now, and right in his eyes — but he could have sworn the loiterer was wearing some kind of long coat.

At last, they said their goodbyes. "I'd offer you a lift back to the station, but our car's rather full."

"Oh, no worries." James handed back the affectionate toddler. "It's a beautiful day for a walk."

They exchanged post addresses and finally James and Arthur were alone together once again. James turned with a sigh to watch the gravediggers fill in the hole where Mr. Marlin would wait until Judgment Day. "Goodbye," he whispered. Arthur put a hand on James' shoulder, and they turned to go.

Lance Benwick stepped out from behind a tree, and blocked their progress. "Arthur and James?" He dropped his cigarette and ground it into the earth. "Please tell me you're Arthur Pensinger and James Wilde."

Arthur nudged James behind him with the almost-imperceptible movement of his hand and forearm. "Yes," he said, "we are."

"Brilliant. Meet me at the George Inn tonight, oh, say half-past six. It's important, all right?"

"We're headed back to London," James argued with a cock of his head. "Why—"

"Please meet me. It's about me Granddad. I can't get away now — family — but we need to talk." He turned and strode back up to the church. They watched, dumbstruck, as he disappeared inside.

Chapter 4

That night, at half-past six, James and Arthur stepped over the threshold and entered the George Inn. The pub was cheery, with white brick walls, gleaming wood floors, and a rustic fireplace. The cool dim interior was a respite from the sun, which had no intention of setting anytime soon. However, a quick glance about showed there was no sign of Lance Benwick. A few men perched on bar stools, locals, enjoying a chinwag over a pint. Across the room, a family sat at one of the larger tables for supper.

Arthur and James chose a small table by the bank of windows where they could keep an eye on the traffic. Both were sweaty and tired; it had been a long afternoon. Meopham was quaint and charming, certainly, but once they'd visited all the shops and taken a long walk through the green, they were both exhausted and overheated, despite the ice cream they'd enjoyed.

"Hullo, lads." A middle-aged gentleman in an open vest sauntered their way. "What'll it be?"

Arthur leaned back in his chair to look at the menu board. The flimsy piece of furniture griped in protest. "A pint o' bitters and the steak and kidney pie."

"Aye," James grunted in assent.

The man nodded and went back behind the bar to fetch the drinks.

"Should've ordered two pies." Arthur groaned and clutched his uninhabited stomach.

James unbuttoned his suit jacket and hung it over the back of the chair as Arthur had done when they came in. "Do you think he was having a laugh?"

"If he doesn't come, I'll be wound up." Arthur mopped his broad brow with his handkerchief.

"It'd be too bad if he were a git," James said as the barman set down their pints. Each raised his and drank away their thirst.

"Why d'you say that?" Arthur directed his question at James, but his eyes travelled across the restaurant as several pies left the kitchen, bound for the family table. "Should've ordered two pies..."

"Well, you saw him." James leaned in on his elbows to whisper.

"Right. I did. And?" Arthur spread his hands wide.

"He looks like Tab Hunter." James dipped his lips in his pint again. "You know, from *Island of Desire.*"

"Oh, he doesn't," Arthur argued, despite the fact that James was absolutely right. It was hot, he was tired, hungry, and his contrariness couldn't be contained.

"He absolutely does. Spitting image." James put his napkin in his lap.

Arthur opened his mouth to protest, but as he sucked in breath to do so, a boy from the kitchen appeared at his elbow with the pies. The barman followed shortly with a few slices of bread and butter. "You look hungry enough to eat your mate here," he said with a robust laugh. "Here, some bread on the house. Let me know if you need anything else."

"'Nother round," Arthur requested around his mouthful of steaming hot pie.

"Yes, definitely." James grabbed up his knife and fork. "Ta." The barman laughed again and retrieved two more pints.

They had finished eating (truth be told, it hadn't taken long, and it was far from pretty) when the inn's heavy wooden door opened. James nearly choked on a piece of kidney, eyes wide, but Arthur was too engrossed in the crust of his pie to notice anything was amiss until the stale smell of cigarettes and whiskey floated over to their table. He sniffed widely, then spun around in his chair and sputtered. Pie crust fluttered down on the front of his suit.

"Mrs. Wylit?" James gagged, and coughed violently.

Their landlady struggled between two large suitcases and a leather satchel, her handbag clenched in her teeth. She dropped the load to the floor with a clatter, panting, and straightened with a groan. Seeing them, she gave a tired salute. "Oy, Arthur, your mate's about to choke to death; care to do anything about it?"

Arthur leapt from his chair and pounded on James' back. James pitched forward nearly into his plate.

"Bob's your uncle!" Mrs. Wylit celebrated as James coughed up the piece of kidney, and then chugged his bitters, face crimson.

"Are you all right?" Arthur demanded incessantly until James could speak.

"Is he all right?" The barman hustled over and peered into James' face. It was scrunched up, eyes squeezed tight, tears streaming down his face.

"I'm fine, I'm fine," James croaked after a while. "Really, I'm fine."

Mrs. Wylit turned to the family who sat frozen, open mouthed, completely gobsmacked. "There, everyone, see? He's all right now, cheers, yes, everything's hunky-dory. Good sir." She addressed the barman as she gave the suitcases a kick, moving them slightly out of the way of the front door. "Whiskey, neat, and a glass of water if you please."

"R... right away, marm." He backed up slowly, perhaps afraid if he turned his back on her she might pounce, like a wild animal. When safely away, he lunged behind the bar.

Mrs. Wylit snagged another chair from an empty table and shoved it across the floor toward them. She sagged into it with an exhausted, doleful sigh, and lit a cigarette that came from behind her ear. "Tell you what, lads, I'm knackered. Quite the day, you wouldn't believe." She crossed her legs, revealing a pair of stems youthful enough, but clad in stockings marred here and there with small holes — cigarette burns, no doubt. It was the first time in ages they'd seen her presentably dressed and wearing hard-soled shoes. She had on a navy skirt and small jacket with a red striped blouse underneath. Summer wear from close to ten years ago, the last time she'd had anything new, perhaps. Still, with her hair pinned back and her figure revealed to the light of day, she looked several years younger than when she'd popped up for the coronation.

"There's a pretty sight." She grinned as the barman set her drink down on the table. She handed him a crumpled note. "Thanks, luv. Better bring along a pint as well." Smoke curled from her nostrils as the nearby family recovered enough to pick up their forks again, eyes still fixed on their table. For their part, James and Arthur stared unabashedly at her as well. "What?" She tossed back the whiskey.

"Mrs. Wylit, what on *earth* are you doing here?" James took another pull of his drink to soothe his irritated throat.

"Ta, dearie." Mrs. Wylit accepted her own pint from the barman and drank deeply before she put the cigarette to her lips again. The words came out smoky. "I had another of my... well, I suppose one can only call them 'visions.'"

"Were you pissed?" Arthur eyed his fork as his stomach rumbled.

James' eyes went wide at Arthur's question. They didn't often, if ever, acknowledge Mrs. Wylit's drinking.

"Of course I was," Mrs. Wylit jerked the ashtray closer to herself. "That's when they come, isn't it? The house was... well, with you blokes gone there was nobody to set off the damned kettle or clomp 'round like a herd of horses over my head. I couldn't sleep with all that quiet, so I got up to have a little nip, you know, something to help me ease off." Her hair, curled for once, bobbed around her ears as she shook her head. "Strongest vision I've ever had. I was standing in a field, and a man with a long white beard spoke to me. He told me that you two were going on a journey, and that I should help. So I went up stairs, packed your things and came here to find you. I didn't have to look for long, thank God."

"I *thought* that was my suitcase," James hissed under his breath in an attempt not to shout. "Mrs. Wylit, you're *not allowed* to go into our flat when we're not at home."

"Well, of course not." She took a mouthful of bitters. "I wouldn't have done it if the old man hadn't demanded. Wizard sort, he was."

James' head swiveled slowly to meet Arthur's gaze as he did the same. Both their faces were wide-eyed and pale and conveying the same bewildered terror. *This is the moment. She's lost her mind completely.*

"Now, he didn't explain how long the journey was, or how far you were going." She sharpened the ashes of her cigarette into a point against the lacquered surface of the ashtray. "I only grabbed a few things and I may have forgotten any socks. You'll have to buy some on the way, I suppose. When you do, I'll have to get myself a decent pair of stockings." She looked at the runs on her legs and clucked in disapproval.

James struggled in his indignant throat to make words, but only strange half-syllables came out. Then his face froze with his mouth half-open, eyes fixed on something behind Arthur's shoulder. Arthur jerked about in his chair and grumbled, "What fresh hell...?"

Lance Benwick stood inside the inn's door. He stared down at the pile of suitcases on the floor, and then took in the scene at their table. His face twisted in bewilderment at what must have been the very distressing sight of Mrs. Wylit lounging with one of her feet in her lap, rubbing her toes as a cigarette dangled from her mouth. He recovered in a moment and ran a hand through his wheat-colored hair before he stepped over to the table. "I hope... I'm not interrupting."

"Not at all," James dried his hands on his napkin before extending one to shake. Arthur rose to his full height and did the same. "This is, erm, our landlady, Mrs. Wylit."

"Viola Wylit, pleasure to meet you. Would you care for a smoke?"

"No, thank you, that's very kind," Lance replied with a confused half-smile. "I'm so sorry I'm late — I had trouble getting away. Are... are those your suitcases, Mrs. Wylit?"

"Well, mine, and Arthur's and James'." She drained her pint and motioned to the barman for another. "I had to bring them all up on the train. Bloody near killed me — op!" She raised her hand to her lips and waved a little apology to the family, who were determined to finish their meal and leave.

"Let me help you." Lance retrieved the bags and stacked them neatly on a nearby table. He helped himself to a chair and thanked Mrs. Wylit as she shuffled aside to give him some room. Once settled, the barman appeared with a pint for him. "Ta, Lenny."

"Sorry to hear about your grandad, mate. Sixty-one was too young." The barman patted Lance on the shoulder and returned to his post, though Arthur was sure he was listening in. Mrs. Wylit, whether she meant to be or not, was going to be the talk of the village tomorrow morning.

"Well, I'm sure you're wondering why I've asked you here." Lance put his hands palms down on the sticky table. He did not wear a wedding ring, and the nails were short-trimmed and clean.

"Mrs. Wylit? Perhaps you should..." James tried, and then trailed off.

She stared at him through a halo of smoke. "Perhaps I should..."

James looked pleadingly at Arthur, who shrugged, a diminished, helpless gesture.

Lance continued after the awkward pause had passed. "My granddad told me all about the two of you and the time you spent at Willowind House during Pied Piper. When he retired in '45, I was twelve, the same age you chaps were when you evacuated. We always read your letters together. He talked about... well, about those nasty boys who used to bully you, and how the two of you stood up to them together. He held you up as an example of courage when I was dealing with bullies of my own."

James and Arthur shared a pale, panicked glance. How much more had Mr. Marlin told his family about the two of them?

"After so many years, the two of you grew up. I grew up. Grandad stopped talking so much about the old days, you know. His time with you at Willowind was wonderful, he said, but he had so many painful memories from the past. Well, you know he was at the Somme. Losing my grandmother, all of it. His heart was weak, and the doctor said it was best that he not dwell on upsetting things or discuss them with anyone. So, imagine how surprised I was when he called me to his bedside the day he died, and began to speak about the two of you again."

Lance paused to whet his throat with ale, and they stared at him in perfect, frozen silence. Unattended ash drifted down from Mrs. Wylit's cigarette.

"He'd had an attack, and he was in and out that evening, confused — he kept saying he heard the Baroness ringing for him." Lance paused again to shove a tear aside from his cheek with the heel of his hand, a nonchalant motion. "At one point, I was alone with him, trying to get him to drink some tea. He seemed coherent suddenly, and he said to me, he said 'Lance, find James and Arthur. Tell them Matthew is still alive. Tell them to find Matthew and bring him back. He's completely alone now, and he won't last. He needs to see his mother's grave. He needs to know how much she missed him.' I tried to ask more questions, but he wasn't making sense after that. He died the next day. Without telling me anything more."

Lance took a breath to compose himself, then lifted the glass and sucked in more of the bitters. He placed the glass back on the table and looked back and forth between James and Arthur.

"So," Lance said, "who is Matthew?"

Chapter 5

James handed Mrs. Wylit a glass of water. She sloshed it down the front of the smart little red and white striped blouse she'd taken such care to wear. She tried again, and managed to get some of the liquid into her mouth. "Give me a ciggy," she slurred, and patted his cheek affectionately.

"You'll burn the sodding house down." James set the glass of water on the low coffee table to his left and eased Mrs. Wylit back onto the sofa cushions.

"I can't sleep on a bleeding sofa." Her eyelids drooped over her bloodshot, glazed-over orbs.

"Something tells me you will," James hissed back with an impatient sigh. "Besides, it's not as if we can be choosy about the accommodations. Lance's family has relatives from out of town for the funeral. It's shameful we're here at all, imposing on these poor people."

"Don't scold me, laddie." She burped, and her eyes closed. After a moment, her breathing went deep and steady.

"Good God." James looked to the heavens for patience. After a few moments, he stood up and turned to tiptoe away.

She flailed out and snagged his pants leg with claw-like fingers. "Maggie." She tugged on the fabric, her eyes still closed. "Bring me Maggie. Bring me my Maggie." Mrs. Wylit opened her arms and beckoned for something.

"I don't—" What was Arthur's favorite phrase, a tribute to the deliciously hilarious Dorothy Parker? *What fresh hell is this?*

"Give..." She wiggled her fingers and drew her arms toward her.

James fumbled with a discarded cushion and pushed it into her chest. Mrs. Wylit smiled, hugged it close to her, and promptly passed out.

"Thank God." James backed away from the sofa, turned, and rammed his shin on the coffee table. He bit his lip to stifle the curse, and limped through the dark hallway to Lance's bedroom.

Arthur sat in Lance's desk chair, and Lance sprawled on the bed of the homey little room, painted green, the floor protected by an oversized rag rug. James was impressed with the selection of books on the small shelf next to the cluttered desk: Fitzgerald, Hemingway, Ellison, Vonnegut, Whitman, some detective novels. There was one book he'd heard of, but hadn't read yet — *Strangers on a Train* — and he meant to ask Lance if he could borrow it. On the other side of the room from Lance's bed were two crates and a steamer trunk, peppered with dust bunnies. Four furniture-leg marks stood out in the dust on the floor as if a bed had been above the stored items.

They'd stumbled home to Lance's cottage more than a bit tipsy with the rubber-legged Mrs. Wylit, but the conversation with Alice, Lance's mother, had sobered them within minutes. She never would have let them stay if she hadn't heard about James and Arthur's history with her father. Mrs. Benwick seemed much less knowledgeable than Lance about the time her father had spent at Willowind House during Pied Piper, but she knew Mr. Marlin had spoken of Arthur and James often and fondly.

They had no excuse or explanation for Mrs. Wylit, but something in her incoherent babbling tugged at Mrs. Benwick's heartstrings, and she had reluctantly offered up the sofa.

"Did she finally settle in?" Arthur asked as James snuck into the room and closed the door. They kept their voices low out of respect for the rest of the slumbering household — Mr. and Mrs. Benwick, and his aunt and uncle in the guest room.

"At last. I thought I was going to be up for hours with her," James groaned. Lance shifted over and offered him a place to sit on the bed. It creaked and sagged as he settled in on top of the homey quilts.

"You two must have a few war stories, renting a flat from her." Lance shook his blonde head.

"Loads." Arthur played with a loose string at the ankle of his blue-striped pajamas. "Smokes like a locomotive."

"She's always barging in unannounced, and she's got a particular problem with the kettle whistling." James drew one foot up and dangled the other. "If I let the kettle whistle, she'll bang on her ceiling with a broom. Once I forgot two days in a row, and she came upstairs with a mop. I thought she was going to club me over the head."

"Why did she come up and find you in Meopham?" Lance asked.

Arthur held out his broad hands. "Apparently, we needed luggage. Even managed to grab our toothbrushes."

"Yes, because a wizard told her to," James said. They laughed as quietly as they could, and Lance dug his face into his elbow to muffle himself.

In the matter of a few hours at the pub, in between talking about Mr. Marlin's cryptic last words, remembering him fondly, and corralling Mrs. Wylit, a magical switch had flipped. James was amazed; people rarely warmed up to him so quickly. Arthur, on the other hand, had mates from work — acquaintances, more — who were always inviting him to the pub. James was friendly with a few of the customers from the tailor shop, and Mr. Conner's daughter, Margo, was always very kind to him. But he hadn't had a friend, besides Arthur in, well... forever.

"It's such a strange, sad story," Lance mused once they'd calmed down. He shooed Arthur out of the desk chair and leaned over it to open the small window. "You lads don't mind?" He held up his pack of cigarettes.

"Not at all." Arthur settled down on the bed next to James, far enough apart as to avoid suspicion. The frame groaned beneath his weight.

"As long as you don't plan to chain smoke them like Mrs. Wylit," James added.

"I promise." He lit a match, and James watched the flame pop up, perfectly reflected in Lance's deep gray eyes.

"A strange, sad story..." James bit his lip. "You mean Mrs. Wylit? Or..."

"Matthew, of course." Lance aimed his smoke for the window.

"Nim — that was what Lady Barlow wanted us to call her — said her youngest son Matthew was weary of the world, and he died. I always took that to mean that he committed suicide. Mr. Marlin never made any indication to me that Matthew could still be alive somewhere." James absently stroked the hair on his forehead. "But if it was his dying wish that we find him, then I suppose we must."

"Why did he... want to kill himself? Did she say?" Lance puffed out more smoke, took one more drag, and pressed his cigarette down into the ashtray.

Arthur and James looked at one another, and then back at Lance. "She didn't say," James lied.

Lance opened his mouth as if he was going to say something, but then closed it. "Hell's bells, it's nearly midnight." He indicated the shiny chrome alarm clock on the desk next to the bed. "We ought to try and get some sleep, don't you think?"

James agreed, and Arthur glanced uneasily at the creaky bed beneath them. It sagged where they sat.

"Sorry, mate." Lance half-smiled apologetically. "I'm afraid the bed would be a joke for you. Dad moved Granddad's bed into the guest room for Aunt Bea — she can't bear to share with my uncle. Blanket-stealer first-rate. But James and I can fit here. I'll go fetch some blankets and things for you."

He returned shortly with a few quilts and another pillow. Arthur stood and accepted them, then moved the desk chair to the corner and made a nest for himself on the rug. Lance folded back the thin summer blankets of the bed and slipped between them. James climbed into the bed as well, and glanced at Arthur, who gave a tiny nod. Lance propped himself up on his elbow and leaned over James to switch off the desk lamp. James' world was suddenly dark and saturated with Lance's smell, which he had just come to know — aftershave with hints of musk, lemon, and lavender, mixed with a hint of smoke.

"Well, goodnight lads." Arthur made himself as comfortable as he could on the rug. "Wish we were still a bit pissed."

"Aye," Lance agreed. James snorted a laugh.

They lay in silence for awhile, and James scrunched himself over as far as he could to make sure he wasn't crowding Lance. Arthur was seconds from sleep when Lance spoke up again. "J-James?"

"Yes?"

"Arthur, are you still awake?"

"Mmmph," Arthur grunted from the floor.

"I feel as though I ought to tell you." Lance exhaled, and put himself up on his elbow again. James could see his outline in the dim light of the moon that glimmered outside the cracked window. "My granddad told me about... erm, well, he told me about the two of you. In that... you're in love, I suppose you'd say."

Terrified silence. James froze, an icy log in the bed. He wanted to squeeze his eyes shut, to protect his head with his hands.

"I thought you should know that I don't believe there's anything wrong with it," Lance said. "So don't feel like you must hide yourselves when you're with me."

"W-what?" Arthur sputtered from the floor.

"Really? Y-you're sure?" James' tongue was dumb with surprise.

"Of course I'm sure." Lance snuggled down into the bed. "Look, when I heard what happened to Alan Turing, a man whose work saved the country, someone who should have been honored as a hero, it broke my heart." He gave a heavy sigh, and went on. "I think most people have had feelings for someone of the same sex at one time or another. It's that society won't allow us to admit it."

Another long silence. Then, Arthur said, "I think you're right, Lance."

"Well, goodnight then. James, if I start snoring, turn me on my side, mate."

"Cheers." An irrepressible grin spread over his face. "Goodnight, Arthur."

" 'Night, love," Arthur said, and James' grin spread wider as a joyful tear was freed from his eye.

James was too happy to sleep, but his curiosity about what Mr. Marlin had said, turned back to the sorrowful thoughts of his passing. The conflicting feelings swirled through his mind, and he lay awake long after Lance's breathing became long and even.

James turned on his side and found Lance sleeping on his as well. Now they were face to face. There was enough light from the moon outside to make out his features.

Arthur's wrong, James thought, *he could be Tab Hunter's brother.*

He studied Lance's slackened face until he, too, fell asleep.

The next morning, James awoke to someone kissing him as the sunlight turned the insides of his eyelids red. He jerked up as his eyes opened and he knocked a flailing hand into a solid mass of body.

Arthur grunted in surprise and reared back.

"Sorry!" James' hand snapped to his mouth. "I thought—" *you were someone else,* his mind finished, but his mouth was wise enough to close before those words came out.

"It's all right, the door's closed." Arthur backed away from the bed. He was dressed already in his specially altered brown trousers and a white buttoned shirt. James noted a small round burn near the right cuff — collateral damage from Mrs. Wylit doing the packing.

"I'm sorry. You gave me a start." James breathed through his smile. "Shall we try again?"

Arthur grinned and leaned in for a kiss. "Better. Now, up with you. Your turn in the loo."

As James made his toilet, there was a knock on the door. "Erm, one moment, please."

Someone on the other side grumbled, "What is this, a roadside inn? Are we running a restaurant?" James couldn't be sure, but it sounded a bit like Lance's father. Ice squeezed his heart.

James hurried to finish. He had just packed away his things when Mrs. Wylit burst in. The door's flimsy lock, which perhaps hadn't worked in the first place, gave way immediately. She was shriveled, corpse-like, squinting in the morning sun that streamed in through the small frosted window. Her clothes from the previous night were rumpled and damp.

"I need a wee," she announced.

"By all means." James danced out of her way as she shambled to the pot and hiked up her skirt. He turned to leave, but she grabbed his arm in mid-squat. "Mrs. Wylit!" he hissed in scandalized fury.

"You be careful," she said, "you be careful, lad. Don't let something shiny and new blast apart your past."

"What does that mean? What are you — oh God." He managed to pry her fingers away as she let loose her stream. Then, he paused. She was so pathetic, sagging on a stranger's loo, everything about her wrinkled.

"Mrs. Wylit — no, no, I think now, since you've... well, you've gone to the loo in front of me, that I'm going to start calling you Viola, all right?"

Mrs. Wylit burped.

"Right. Well then, Viola, you're going to have to let me help you a bit, I think. Did you eat at all yesterday?"

"Sod off." Her eyes drooped shut as she slouched on the toilet.

James steeled himself with patience and left the bathroom to retrieve her bag from the side of the sofa. He returned and did his best

wide-eyed. "I'm dispensing with formalities," he said. "She's packed our suitcases and vomited on our shoes and... and, well, you know!"

"Viola." Lance leaned forward on his elbows to shoot Mrs. Wylit a butter-melting smile that caught James in the spread as well. "That is a very beautiful name. Almost, but not quite, as beautiful as..." He reached out and took the bread from James. "...this piece of toast. There has never been a piece of toast as perfect as this in the history of this sceptered isle. I should like a piece of toast as perfect as this, but, alas, I am not the chosen one. But you, dear Viola, are in fact that special."

James couldn't be sure, but he thought he saw Mrs. Wylit's lips curl up at the ends. She snatched the toast from Lance's hand. "Vi," she corrected, and shoved the bread in her mouth.

Chapter 6

After breakfast, Lance, Arthur, and James parked Mrs. Wylit outside with another cup of tea and her cigarettes. They returned to the house to say an awkward goodbye to Lance's aunt and uncle, and then disappeared back into Lance's room to avoid his father's glare.

"You're sure it's not wrong to go through his things?" James' body jerked when Arthur put a reassuring hand on his back, an automatic reaction to being so suddenly exposed. He took a breath and forced his shoulders to drop.

Lance diffused the moment effortlessly. "You're safe, remember?"

"Sorry." James smiled up at Arthur, who continued to rub his shoulders. "I forgot. It's hard to just let go of all these years of... fear, I suppose."

"Doesn't help your dad's a policeman," Arthur added.

"I understand. But in answer to your question, I'm sure it's all right." Lance crossed the small room to kneel before the crates and the steamer trunk, each coated with a fine layer of dust. "Granddad loved the two of you. He saw how happy you made Lady Barlow in the end. Besides, he wanted us to find Matthew. I don't know where else to start. You lads have any other ideas?"

They both shook their heads.

"Ought to get started. Don't have all day. Need to take the train back." Arthur cracked his neck.

"Or to wherever the journey takes us." James half-smirked as he knelt down next to Lance to help him with the first crate. "Mrs. Wylit seems to think we'll be gone awhile. My suitcase is stuffed."

Together, James and Lance opened the lid on the first wooden box. Arthur opened the other, and systematically they lifted Mr. Marlin's things from their orderly places and spread them out with gentle, reverent hands. There were framed pictures of steel-faced Victorian relatives, the family bible, a brass-handled trench knife, and a velvet box, lined in satin, in which rested his war medals. In another small box they found a locket, which Arthur handed over to Lance immediately, knowing his large fingers would never open it.

"Careful," James advised as Lance attempted to run his fingernail through the seam.

"Better let you do it." Lance took James' hand and opened it to drop the chain into his palm.

James' quick fingers clicked the locket open. The picture inside, yellowed with age, was of a soldier with a youthful face and an oval chin, so boyish beneath his sharp cap. They puzzled over it a moment until Lance said, "It's Grandad. This must have belonged to my grandmother."

They uncovered tiny, lacy dresses, likely ancient familial baptismal gowns, a portrait of Mrs. Benwick as a child, and Mr. Marlin's uniform, wrapped in crumbling tissue. Books, official papers, and a set of solid silver candlesticks emerged as well. "A parting gift from Lady Barlow, I should imagine," said Lance.

At last, all of Harold Marlin's worldly possessions lay on the rug or on Lance's bed. The only item that might be of any use to them was Mr. Marlin's black leather address book, full of his spidery, perfect handwriting, a lifetime's worth of friends, acquaintances, and family. James pointed out their names and the address of the flat they shared above Mrs. Wylit, one of the final entries in the book.

"I suppose someone in this book might know something about what happened to Matthew." James turned the pages with gentle fingertips. "But there are so many names to go through."

Lance put a warm hand on his shoulder, and then stood up to light a cigarette near the window. "Perhaps Granddad was... out of touch with reality. In the end. Perhaps he simply wished that Matthew was still alive. He did love Lady Barlow, you know. Of course those who serve are always proud of the house they care for, but there was something very special to him about the Baroness."

"She was an incredible woman," James said, and Arthur nodded in assent before he hung his head to hide the sudden tears in his eyes. "Arthur and I owe her so much. If Mr. Marlin thought it important that we put these matters to rest, then we must *put these matters to rest.*"

"You really think he was losing his grip at the end?" Arthur stood and brushed the dust from his trousers.

Lance stood as well. "I don't know. I don't think so, but I can't be sure. The doctor never said anything about dementia when he visited in the final days." He sighed, and tapped Mr. Marlin's black address book in the palm of his broad, smooth hand. "I suppose this is where we'll have to begin, then."

Mrs. Wylit's voice growled up from the hallway, muffled slightly by the closed bedroom door, although the impatient cadence cut through the pocked wood. "I know it's all unexpected, Alice, I do, and I promise we'll be going soon — but for now I need you to stop chirping in my ear. At least you have your son is all I'm saying."

"Mrs. Wylit!—" Lance's mother's exclamation cut off as Mrs. Wylit burst through the bedroom door with Alice at her heels.

"I need to go to the shops." Mrs. Wylit hugged her arms over her chest. Her yellowed nails tapped madly on the crook of her arm. "I need cigarettes."

And a bottle of whiskey, James thought darkly. "We're right in the middle—"

"Now." The wild hunger flashing in her bloodshot eyes urged him to cease his protestations.

"All right," James relented. "You two have a look through the address book and try to decide where we're headed. I'll take her into the village."

"I'll do it," Arthur stepped forward to loom over Mrs. Wylit's frizzy head. "I can handle her if... well, you know."

"No, I want James to take me." Mrs. Wylit pointed a claw at her desired companion.

"Beggars can't be choosers." Mrs. Benwick backed up out of the doorframe and allowed Arthur to steer Mrs. Wylit outside by the shoulders.

She struggled. "No, you send James with me, I want James!"

"Careful, Vi, you'll hurt his feelings," James called after them.

Mrs. Benwick shot her son a look of pure, venomous annoyance. "Tonight, I want a peaceful house," she said, her voice cool, but low, and dangerous. "I think we're owed a bit of rest after burying your granddad."

"Mrs. Benwick, I am so terribly so—" James tried, but she shut the door.

Lance turned to him, and scratched the back of his head, eyes squinted in a rueful expression. "We've got to shove off, or she might murder me."

"I ought to apologize to you as well." James knelt down to avoid Lance's gaze, and folded up Mr. Marlin's uniform with delicate fingers. "I can't believe Mrs. Wylit followed us up here."

"Well, I think she's a holy fool." Lance dropped his knees to help pack things away. "Or the jester in a Shakespearean play. Speaking the truth when nobody else can."

The bedroom door shuddered and burst open again. Mrs. Wylit made it one step inside before Arthur's meaty forearms wrapped around her waist and lifted her off her feet. "You're not looking hard enough," she shouted before being carried away back down the hall and out the front door. "Look for the yellow!"

She shouted on about yellow until the slamming front door cut her off. Lance jumped up and shut his door against the barrage of "bloody this" and "bloody that" emanating from his father's chair in the living room.

"We'd better hurry." Lance picked up the family bible and prepared to replace it in the box. As he did so, the ancient cover flapped open, and a small yellow envelope fell free from where it had been tucked in the pages.

Lance and James stared at it where it fell on the edge of the rug, one corner on the dusty wooden floor.

"L-look for the yellow," James whispered, wide-eyed, and then knelt down to snatch up the envelope.

As he picked up the envelope, James turned to look at Lance, who was kneeling to position himself beside James. James bonked his eyebrow right into Lance's knee, lost his balance from the balls of his feet, and fell sideways onto the floor. He saw stars for a moment before Lance's concerned face swam into focus.

"Oh, now I've gone and done it." Lance gathered James up by his elbows and hauled him to his feet. "Sorry, mate, entirely my fault."

"It's nothing." James cupped his hand over his eye. His eyebrow stung, a dull ache beneath the surface. "Clumsy of me."

"Let me see." Lance took James' wrist and led him a step closer to the window's summer light. "Move your hand."

James dropped his fingers. He blinked with a series of rapid grimaces. The eye watered a bit, but seemed undamaged. "It doesn't hurt."

"I don't think it'll bruise," Lance said.

And then, simultaneously, they each realized that Lance still had his warm hand attached to James' cool, slender wrist.

Lance let go immediately and James stepped back and cleared his throat. James's cheeks prickled with heat. "Stay still this time, I'll get it." James bent and scooped up the envelope, which could have started its life as a creamy white, but had aged to a tell-tale yellow.

"What did I tell you? Holy fool." Lance took it from James' outstretched fingers. The flap was unsealed, and Lance lifted out a bundle of thin papers. He unfolded them one at a time and set them out on his desk for James to see. They were letters, clearly, but the penmanship was haphazard, and each page was marred with savagely scratched out words and paragraphs.

James lifted one of the letters between his fingertips and squinted at it. "Dear Mother, I regret to inform you that I plan to end my life... Though I love you... Father never understood..."

Lance tapped the desk and James set the delicate paper back down. Frowning, Lance stroked his square chin and studied the letters a moment before slowly rearranging their order on the desk. "Do you see it?"

"They're drafts. Each one longer than the next. This one seems the most finished, do you agree?"

"Let's see if we can make it out." Lance opened his middle desk drawer and removed a magnifying glass to aid their toil.

Dear family,

I have lived in this world for fifteen years. Many of them have been miserable, but not all. I remember the happy times as a child. I remember Father picking me up and swinging me around, or playing soldiers with me all afternoon. I remember a time before Mother was afraid to kiss me or brush my hair, before she was accused of sissifying me. Life was happy. Life was beautiful. It is precisely because I remember what a happy life could be like that I have decided that I can no longer live in the misery my existence has become.

What kind of life can I expect to live? One of secrets, of shame? Shall I be an actor in a play, portraying a role for the rest of my life? Pretending to love some poor wife, forever keeping my true feelings in the shadows? Or should I loudly and publicly proclaim who and what I really am, and go to prison or to my death?

If these are the paths offered to me, I choose to steer off the road and over the cliff into the sea.

Mother, I know you tried to protect me as long as you could. I love you for that. But once Father knew, your protection wasn't enough. I know you felt as trapped as I, limited by the laws and Father's indignation. I know this will cause you pain, but it's for the best. I can't help but feel as though I never should have been born. I know you never said as much to me, but your late age at the time of my birth, with my siblings so much older, speaks for itself. I was an accident. I should not be here. I do not belong on this earth.

I do wish to extend my unending gratitude to Mr. Marlin and Mrs. Galhad for their kindness. There were countless times Mr. Marlin found me crying in the garden or in my chamber, and dried my tears. Of course, he knew nothing of why I suffered, but he offered silent solace and companionship. There were many nights that I sat up in the kitchen with Mrs. Galhad, drinking warm milk until past midnight and talking about everything in life. She, too, knew nothing of my secret, but offered a listening ear and unending patience. Strange how a young man's servants should be closer to him than his own family. To Mr. Marlin and Mrs. Galhad, I am truly sorry for any trouble I caused you. For you both, it is better this way.

The moment that John and I were discovered in the forest was the moment my life crumbled away to nothing. I know it is too much to hope that whoever is reading this will carry my message, but please, please tell John how much I felt for him, and how sorry I am that he was dragged into this horrid predicament because of me.

I hope that death will not be painful, and that it will not take long to drown. I have put stones in my pockets. The river is deep, and the currents swift. I hope when we meet in heaven that we are able to love and understand each other once again.

Goodbye.

Matthew Barlow

"Crikey." Lance squinted through the magnifying glass.

"It's Matthew's suicide note," James said. Lance glanced up in surprise at the sound of his utterance, its cracked quality. James swiped the heel of his hand against his face hurriedly, then sniffed and coughed casually. "These must have been his attempts before he got the words right."

"Here I was, ready to make a little joke — lad's rather hyperbolic, I mean, fifteen, you know — a little gallows humor, perhaps — but you're upset." Lance squeezed James' shoulder with his free hand, and his gesture of reassurance made his eyes leak further.

"I'm all right." James sighed and accepted Lance's handkerchief. "I feel like all I've been doing is crying these past few days. For God's sake, he was your granddad, wasn't he? But this..." He sniffed again and gestured to the note. "Don't you see? Matthew... Matthew was like Arthur and me. I remember Nim told me as much. And all of his pain, written out here, God, it's... it's like I wrote it myself, do you see?"

"I do. I understand." Lance kept his large palms on James' shoulders, and squeezed them again to emphasize his promise.

"There were so many times when I... when I thought about..." He took a breath and tried again. "When I thought about doing the same thing to myself, Lance. Arthur was the same way. Even as little children we contemplated it. Throwing ourselves in front of a train, diving into a river, drinking poison — and we were children! If we hadn't found each other during Pied Piper, with Nim's help, and Mr. Marlin's protection, this same thing might have happened to us."

Lance shifted his weight awkwardly and dropped his arms. He bit his lip. "Don't... don't think about it, James. Look, ah... well, you did find each other, and Granddad said Matthew is alive, so perhaps he never went through with it all."

"I'm sorry. I'm being childish." James wiped his face and gave Lance the handkerchief back.

"It's all right." He accepted the damp cloth back and tucked it in his pocket. "It's that I can't stand to see you like this. It's breaking my heart." He knuckled James' face with a gentle fist. "So chin up, yeah? Look, if you ask me, Matthew was dead set on making it appear as though Mr. Marlin and Mrs. Galhad knew absolutely nothing about his secret. I mean, what that says to me is that they did know. They must have known, based on how close they seemed to be. I bet Matthew took them into his confidence."

"I think you're right." James' voice returned to its usual cadence. "Well, unfortunately we can't ask Mr. Marlin. But perhaps we could ask Mrs. Galhad. She might know what happened all those years ago."

"Right. Let's see." Lance stepped over to the bed and picked up Mr. Marlin's black book to flip through the entries. "Here." He tapped the book with a triumphant finger, and read the entry to James, "Louise Galhad. Church Lane, Welby. Lincolnshire."

Chapter 7

Arthur knew that the bottle in the brown bag Mrs. Wylit had in her hand when she left the shop wasn't cough medicine, but he didn't speak up. James, he knew, would have said something. Despite his small stature, James always spoke up when it counted. Arthur wasn't as brave or as forthcoming, at least not when it came to causing a scene. It was bad enough being the tallest person in the village tagging along after the perpetually rumpled Mrs. Wylit like her guard dog, with all eyes glued to them as they went from shop to shop.

"Did you get everything you needed?" he asked as they strolled down the lane in the vague direction of the Benwick cottage. Arthur was in no hurry to return — stalling Mrs. Wylit would give Lance and James time to figure out their next move, and prevent Lance from being slapped to death by his mother.

"For a tall man, you do like to drag your feet." Mrs. Wylit hustled him forward. "Come on, will you? We need to get back there."

"So they can toss you out properly? The last time wasn't enough?" Arthur grumbled as Mrs. Wylit scurried ahead with her parcels, a trail of smoke behind her. "You're not going back there, you do know that, don't you?"

Mrs. Wylit stopped, and let Arthur catch up to her. "James and that boy," she started, then groaned, and put her fingers into her temples a moment. "Why is it so bloody *bright* out?"

"It's daylight." Arthur stepped aside on the walk so a couple of old ladies could pass by with their shopping bags. The gray-hairs stared unabashedly at them as they shuffled past. "Morning." He nodded to each of them. When they finally turned away, he leaned closer to Mrs. Wylit, who dug fruitlessly in her purse for something. "Why don't we go sit on the green? It's a lovely day."

"Lovely and burning me eyeballs out of me skull." Mrs Wylit rammed a pair of scratched tortoise-shell sunglasses onto her face.

"Now, we really ought to go back. You know I can't tell you, well, you know I can't tell you exactly *why*, but—"

"Hush." Though Arthur had been mired in the stares of other people all morning, and should have been immune to one more person, something caught his eye. There was a man standing in front of the book store, looking at the sales rack out on the walkway. However, as Arthur's eyes adjusted for the sun's brightness, and the distance, it was clear the man was watching him, as well. The man was wearing an old-fashioned long brown coat, much like the one James had mentioned. He couldn't say for certain, but it was too much of a coincidence for it not to be the same man he'd seen loitering about after Mr. Marlin's funeral.

"Come." He took Mrs. Wylit's arm in a steely grip. She squawked in protest, and tried to light a cigarette and shuffle along next to him at the same time as he strode toward the bookshop up the road. Her protestations drew many looks, and easily alerted the man in the brown coat. As it became clear that Arthur was intent on approaching, the man stepped into the book shop. Arthur dragged Mrs. Wylit inside, past the brick storefront's hand-painted sign and flower boxes spilling over with begonias, vinca vines, and purple and pink petunias.

The bookshop was cramped, the walls lined with built-in shelves and the floor dangerous with haphazard piles and half-unpacked crates. Near the front was a large wooden counter topped with an ancient cash register. Behind it sat a young woman with fine white-blonde hair. She didn't acknowledge them and instead gnawed on her fingernail, eyes wide, fixated on a copy of *Other Voices, Other Rooms*. The author's rather sensual portrait on the back of the dust jacket made Arthur look twice before scanning the small shop for the man. Nothing.

"Did a man just come in?" Arthur demanded, without greeting or explanation.

"Oh, I've been wanting to read that one." Mrs. Wylit thrust the tip of her cigarette in the shopgirl's direction.

The girl started, and slammed the book down so that the cover was pressed up against the wood of the counter. "Yes, what? Oh, this? Someone in the village ordered it, it's not mine."

"Did a man just come in?" Arthur repeated. "A man in a brown coat?"

"A man in a brown coat? Erm... well, I don't see anyone in here." The shopgirl craned her slender neck to look around the shop. "Why would anyone be wearing a coat? It's delightful out. Though my gran says rain this afternoon."

"Is there a back door? A loo?"

"Right through there." She pointed to a small dark hallway that led off of the main shop.

"Stay here." Arthur sidestepped the piles of books and darted down the hallway with long strides.

"I ought to evict you for dragging me around like this. I think you've bruised me." Mrs. Wylit's words grew fainter as he moved down the cramped hall with the peeling plaster. He shoved open the flimsy door to the grimy restroom. Empty. At the end of the hall was another door. Arthur shoved it open and found himself in the alley next to a rubbish bin. The old cobbled alleyway was empty save for a scabby cat that regarded him with contempt from a low wall.

Arthur cursed, and went back to the front counter, where Mrs. Wylit was enjoying a good chinwag with the shopgirl. "Now, what you've got to read next is *Orlando*."

"Oh yes. I can't wait to get into that one." The girl brought the cigarette that Mrs. Wylit had undoubtedly given her to her mouth in a jerky, unpracticed motion. She tried to inhale and coughed.

"Hold on, luv, let me get you something to wet your—"

Arthur's hand closed around Mrs. Wylit's wrist as she reached into the parcel bag for the bottle. "No. We're leaving now."

"I was only being personable," Mrs. Wylit protested as Arthur dragged her out into the sunshine again. "*Now* where are we going? Who was that you were chasing?"

"I don't know." They crossed the lazy street, headed back toward the Benwick cottage. "But he saw me notice him. And he did a runner. I need to tell James."

"Oh, so now we're going back because *you* want to." Mrs. Wylit flicked her cigarette into the flowerbed of a nearby home.

They returned to find James and Lance on the front steps of the little house, sitting in front of the packed luggage, their knees close, heads bowed in confidential whispers. Something circled Arthur's heart and gave it a sudden, sharp squeeze; he burped, and blamed it on the greasy breakfast. The feeling slid away. As he opened up his mouth to tell James about the man in the brown coat, Lance leapt up from the stoop and tossed Arthur's suitcase at him. He caught it with a small grunt.

"Great reflexes, mate." He gave Arthur's shoulder a playful punch. "Did you play rugby?"

"What, and endanger everyone on the field?" James stood as well, and smiled up into Arthur's face, cheeks pink with humor and pride. His smile melted down the sides of his mouth when he saw Mrs. Wylit's laden grocer's bag. "Good God, Vi, how much liquor did you buy?"

"There now. You've made a rhyme." Mrs. Wylit struggled to light a cigarette with her free hand. "It's provisions for our journey, of course." She tipped the bag lower so he could see the apples and biscuit boxes inside. "Lot of thanks I get, trying to keep you healthy and fed."

"*Our* journey," said Arthur in his rumbling baritone. "I suppose that means you're coming with us."

"Well, of course." A stream of smoke swirled from her nostrils as she hefted the bag again. "You're only boys, aren't you? Who will feed you, sew your buttons back on and such?"

"I work for a tailor." James raised a dry eyebrow as he lifted his suitcase from the worn grass.

"You need guidance." She raised her fingers to her lips and withdrew the cigarette momentarily, perhaps to prove her point. "Consider me your north star."

"Well, come on if you're coming, Miss Polaris." Lance shouldered his small bag and took the provisions from Mrs. Wylit's shaking hands. "We have a train to catch."

The party was in high spirits. It was a short ride to Rochester, then on to King's Cross, where they'd change trains and ride up to Grantham. Lance kept them entertained with stories the entire way about his apparently abysmal athletic talent. Arthur, who rarely laughed for long periods of time, had to borrow James' handkerchief at least three times to mop his streaming eyes. He thought Mrs. Wylit might die, the way she giggled and then coughed and wheezed. "Some medicine for my throat." She opened her purse to fish out the surprisingly ladylike round flask, the one with the knifed-out engraving.

The cosy train cabin, with the curtains to the hallway pulled shut, and the gentle, womb-like rocking of the coach was nothing short of heaven. Arthur reflected on being there; being there with James, just being *who* they were. And it was safe.

There was a delay at the Rochester station. Mrs. Wylit, exhausted from uncharastically enjoying life decided to put her feet up for a kip. The boys left the train to stretch their legs. Arthur and Lance strolled along the front of the yellow brick building while James went to a nearby phone box to call his mother and Mr. Conner.

A swaggering group of young men, three of five wearing Teddy Boy suits, strutted up the street toward the station. They smoked and swore, and periodically fished combs from their jacket pockets to slick back their hair. Their laughter was edged, fraught with an insatiable hunger for position. Arthur thought it sounded like animals snapping at each other's heels.

Lance lit a cigarette, still talking, but Arthur slowed to a stop and watched as the Teddy Boys approached the station. The gang drew up by the red glass-paneled phone box where James spoke. His gestures were animated, exasperated; he must be talking to his mother, Arthur thought. One of the youths, his hair curled into what seemed like an impossibly perfect v-shaped pompadour, slowed as he passed the phone box. He pointed with his cigarette at James inside, and the group of them howled with laughter. Their guffaws increased to a cacophony as their leader mimed James' movements for his friend's enjoyment. Then, making a fist, he banged on the side of the callbox. James jumped, and perhaps yelped in surprise. This sent the Teddy Boys into fits. James shrunk to the far side of the call box, the phone still cradled in his ear, his face turned away.

Arthur had stomped several long strides forward before Lance caught up to him and grabbed his arm. "Never mind those cretins. The world's full of 'em. We can't have you end up in gaol, mate. Lord, you'd knock their teeth out their arseholes. Have mercy."

Arthur let Lance's words lower his hackles, but he still made for the callbox and James. As they passed the Teddy Boys at the station doors, one of them sniggered, "Right old harry hoofter, eh boys?" Rage threaded through his veins. Arthur's meaty fists clenched, but he went to the callbox instead of ramming his right hook into the bully's smug face. As he neared, James stepped out of the box and closed the door.

"Are you all right?"

"Fine," James replied, but there was no mistaking the drawn lines on his face as he frowned, rosy cheeks now soured and pale. "Mr.

Conner says I can take as much time as I need. His daughter can help until I get back."

"And how's your mum?" Lance eagerly changed the subject as they returned to the train.

"Well. She's quite well, actually." They settled back into their cabin. Mrs. Wylit snored against the window. "She's been getting these strange hang-up calls from some pervert. On the daily. But yesterday and today she hasn't had one, so she's quite cheerful."

"We used to get those in the village all the time." Lance rummaged about in Mrs. Wylit's grocery sack for a box of biscuits. "Someone calling and breathing like that. It turned out to be my Sunday school teacher. Well, they got rid of him after that. His wife turned him in."

Their conversation woke Mrs. Wylit. She was grumpy at first, but then sat back, as contented as a woman watching her own children play in the yard at dusk. They got on the subject of films and began doing their best impressions of different silver screen stars. It was a lovely way to pass the time, until, out of the corner of his eye, Arthur saw movement in a crack of the curtains, followed by a commotion in the hallway. Through the gap in the fabric, he saw the leering eyes of the leader of the Teddy Boys from the Rochester station. His face twisted into a roar of cruel laughter.

"James." Arthur's voice snapped them all to attention.

James, responding to Arthur's conspicuous irritation and rising temper, turned and saw the gang of young men peering through the crack in the cabin curtain. Yapping like hyenas, they dashed off down the hall, presumably to another car.

Their sanctuary broken, they rode in gloomy silence to King's Cross.

As they disembarked onto the crowded platform, Arthur handed James his suitcase, and turned to Lance. "Are you with me?"

Lance nodded, and passed off his bag to Mrs. Wylit, who sagged beneath the weight of her luggage and his.

"Don't," James advised to their backs as they turned to walk away. "It's not worth it."

"Meet us at the next platform," Arthur called over his shoulder.

They found the Teddy Boys strutting off the platform and into the station, making rude comments about a woman's blouse as she hurried along with her baggage away from them.

"Oy!" Arthur thundered. "Over here."

The gang turned, and grinned when they saw who it was. "Where's your pet fairy?" The leader flicked his cigarette at Lance's feet. Others on the platform, sensing danger, gave them a wide berth.

"If you've g-g-got s-something to s-say, t-then..." Arthur's rage brought back his long-buried stutter from childhood, and his throat choked itself off. He swallowed. It felt like hot gravel in the back of his mouth.

"Then say it to us," Lance finished for him.

"Piss off, twats," the pompadour-crowned one snarled. He stepped forward to shove Arthur, but he might as well have pushed a tree trunk. As he stumbled back, Lance stuck out his foot and tripped him.

The ensuing brawl was short. Lance and Arthur fought together as if they'd trained side by side; even as the punches were flying, Arthur thought to himself how uncanny it was. They seemed to know the other's moves as they were happening instead of reacting to them. Even though they outnumbered their opponents, the Teddy Boys fled after a fraction of a minute.

Lance and Arthur appeared on the platform to catch their train to Grantham with minutes to spare, with bloody noses and grinning mouths. When they were secured in their cabin, the curtains closed and clipped shut with Mrs. Wylit's hairpins, James wrapped his arms around Arthur and would not let go for a long, long time.

Mrs. Wylit fussed over Lance's nose, and he at last accepted a swig from her flask. "There are few things that are truly satisfying in this world." Lance passed back her liquor. She took a mouthful of liquid fire, swallowed, and said, "*That* was one of them."

Chapter 8

James flinched away as an old brass key attached to a small block of wood came flying at his face. Arthur reached out and snagged it from the air.

"There we are." Mrs. Wylit stumbled over the heel of her shoe, a bumbling gesture at odds with the noble medieval facade of the Angel and Royal inn that rose behind her, the gilded face of a placid seraphim hovering overhead.

"I'm going to pretend you didn't just lob that at my face." James heaved a tired sigh that seemed to rack his whole body. The train from King's Cross was delayed, and the afternoon was unbearably muggy. They'd arrived in Grantham in the evening — too late to take the bus to Welby.

"Too bad my mother isn't here." Lance ground out his cigarette on the walk. He'd smoked more on the journey, James noticed. Out of boredom while they were waiting, surely, but also as a response to kind of underlying irritation. Well, this *was* his first time dealing with Mrs. Wylit. James half wished he smoked if it would make wrangling her easier.

Lance went on, "She loves these old carriage inns." He gestured through the archway to the courtyard within, where, long ago, carriages had come to unload their rich passengers and stable the horses for the night.

"We could have easily stayed at the guest house we passed near the station." James hefted his suitcase in his limp, tired arm.

"Not so." Mrs. Wylit pulled out a cigarette and raised an eyebrow at Lance. He leaned over and lit it for her, careful to avoid igniting the wisps of hair that escaped her pins. "Something like seven kings and queens have bedded down in this old place through the years. Let me see." She counted them off on her yellowed fingers. "King John, Edward III, Charles I, George IV, Edward VIII... I can't re-

member them all. But history is about to be made again." She leered
at them with a sly little smile. "King *Arthur* is going to add his name
to the royal registry tonight."

Arthur could not contain a guffaw of laughter. James sighed, entirely exasperated with Mrs. Wylit's tiresome antics.

"Anyway, I could only afford one room." Smoke shrouded her
face as she exhaled. "So we're all together. I told 'em you're all my
nephews, so if anyone asks..." She shrugged. "All right. Come along,
I'm knackered."

The room was small, with only a double bed, but it was theirs
— a private washroom even. Lush red carpet matched the bedspread
and the heavy drapes, accented with gold and creamy white.

Arthur fell face-forward on the bed with a mighty thump and
a satisfied sigh. Lance jumped on as well and shoved his elbow into
Arthur's ribs. "Shove over, you hog." Arthur responded by putting
him in the kind of good-natured headlock that male friends often
share.

"Lance, you're on the floor." Mrs. Wylit tossed him the cushions
from a nearby armchair. "Let James and Arthur..." she wiggled her
finger indistinctly at the bed, "you know."

"And you, Vi?" James asked, his cheeks red at her implication.

"Be a dear and throw a blanket over me where I fall." She lit
another cigarette. With a groan of dismay, Lance leaned over and
cranked open the window.

After a hasty fish-and-chips and a pint (several for Mrs. Wylit)
they collapsed to sleep. Arthur waited until he could hear Mrs.
Wylit's snores, and no noise from the floor next to the window where
Lance lay. Then he pulled James into his huge embrace, and promptly began to snore.

The street through the open window was quiet. James lay in the
dark for some time. *Why can't I sleep?* He suppressed a moan of ag-
gravation. At last, he was back in Arthur's arms. It felt like ages since

they'd been free to really touch each other. Shouldn't his boyfriend's embrace lull him to blissful sleep? James was exhausted from travelling and his restless night in Lance's bed.

Lance. The name made his stomach flip into a knot. He ignored it, pretended it was too much vinegar on his fish and chips. James peeled himself out of Arthur's arms and wiggled down to the end of the bed to go to the loo. When he climbed back onto the bed the same way he'd left, he turned to carefully fold himself in to Arthur's arms again. Something through the window snagged his attention. He squinted. Across the street from the Angel and Royal was a corner building with a mortgage broker's office. Standing in front of it, beneath a streetlight, was the figure of a man wearing a warped fedora hat that shaded his face into blackness. A long brown coat in an old-fashioned cut hung from his thin silhouetted shoulders.

James' throat eked out an audible choking sound. He kept his eyes fixed on the man beneath the streetlight, and slid off the bed toward the window.

He stumbled and fell back on the mattress as his foot sank onto something soft. Lance grunted and sat up with a book in one hand and a small extinguished torch in the other. His eyes travelled from James' astonished face to the window. "What is it?" Lance reached up to clasp James' wrist. "What is it, what's wrong?"

"It's him," James hissed. Arthur and Mrs. Wylit continued to snored as he threw his black suit jacket over his pajamas and slammed his feet into his shoes.

Lance watched the man under the streetlight shuffle his feet, and rub his arms as if he were cold. "James, who *is* that?"

"No time — please come with me!" James yanked open the door to the room and dashed out into the dim hallway.

Lance burst out after him, shirtless, his shoes in one hand, a bathrobe slung over his shoulders. As they ran, he managed to hop on each foot long enough to shove them on. James led him to the end of the red-carpeted hall, to the stairwell, and eventually through the lobby where the desk clerk glanced up sleepily to utter a muffled question.

As they burst out the front doors, James uttered a bark of frustration. "Where'd he go?"

The street was empty as far as they could see. James took off across the street to investigate the mortgage broker's and the streetlight. There was no alley, and no sign of where the man could have gone. "Damn." James pounded his fist against the light pole. "I can't believe this. He's gone."

"Easy, mate." Lance put his arm around James' agitated shoulders and led him back across the street. "What's going on?"

"That man, the man in the coat—" James sputtered, the words bursting out in unintelligible spurts.

Lance pulled the door to the lobby open and ushered James inside. "Sit down, sit down," He eased James down into one of two red plush armchairs positioned near the dead fireplace.

"What's the matter?" The clerk put a sleepy chin in his hand. "Need to call the bobbies?"

"No, thank you," James said immediately. That was the last thing they needed.

"Right, then." The clerk sat back in his chair and put his legs up on the counter. By the time Lance returned from the room where he'd tiptoed in to fetch James a glass of water, snores floated through the air from behind the front desk.

"He's louder than Mrs. Wylit. I didn't think that was humanly possible." Lance handed James the water and shrugged on the bathrobe that he'd slung over his shoulder. This deprived the lobby of his shirtless spectacle and curly reddish-gold chest hair.

James smiled, but it felt weak. He swirled the water in the glass after taking a sip, staring at the tiny whirlpool he'd created.

Lance settled into the chair opposite James', and waited a respectful moment before posing his question. "Do you want to tell me what happened, mate?"

James spat out a self-pitying little laugh. "You won't believe me. It's total rubbish. I know it is. I can't explain why I'm so paranoid. And now I've dragged you into the little spy novel I've created in my head."

"Spy novel?"

He nodded. "It sounds daft when I say it aloud."

Lance slid free of the red plush chair and onto one knee. "James Wilde," he proclaimed, one hand over the part of the bathrobe that covered his heart, "I swear on my good name that I will not laugh at whatever it is you have to tell me." He regained his seat. "All right, seriously," he went on, "please tell me what's going on."

"I woke up for a wee, and I looked out the window. I saw a man standing under the streetlight in front of the mortgage broker's."

"I saw the man you saw," Lance validated. "Who do you think he is?"

James sighed impatiently and tapped his fists on his knees. "Let me start over. All right, now, my mum — she's been getting these strange phone calls. Someone rings and then breathes into the phone."

"Right. And?"

"She told me about the calls, and that must have shaken my nerves. I can't explain it — but after we heard about Mr. Marlin and were planning our trip to the funeral, I saw a man loitering about not far from where Arthur and I live with Mrs. Wylit. He was wearing an old brown coat, from before the war I should think, and there was... something about him." James studied Lance's face a moment, the downturned mouth and concerned brows. "You think I'm nutters."

"No, no, not at all. Please, keep going."

"Well, I saw him again." James took a sip of water. "I saw him get on the train that Arthur and I took to Meopham. That's when I told Arthur about it. And then he went through all the cars and looked, but he didn't see an old brown coat like I'd described."

Lance rubbed his lip with his thumb. "I'm not sure of how seriously to take most of what Mrs. Wylit says," he said, "but she mentioned something to me while you and Arthur were buying the tickets at the station. Something about Arthur chasing a man dressed for winter into a bookshop."

James' eyes popped into green saucers rimmed in white. "What? Arthur never said anything to me. When did this happen? While they were at the shops?"

Lance's straight shoulders lifted in a little rueful shrug beneath the blue terry cloth. "I'm not sure, mate. You'd have to ask him."

"Why didn't he tell me?" James leaned forward, his elbows on his knees, and clasped his fingers into a worried ball. "It's not like him to keep a secret."

"Maybe he didn't want to worry you." Lance squeezed James' shoulder with his warm hand.

"I suppose..." James rubbed his face. "I'm still going to ask him."

They sat for a minute, listening to the clerk's oddly syncopated snoring. Then, "Do you two really tell each other everything?"

"Arthur and I?" James straightened his back to look Lance in the face. His friend's usual bright humor had melted away, and Lance pensively picked at the lint on the arm of the chair. "Well, yes. Of course. We haven't had a secret from one another since we were children." He paused to ensure the desk clerk was as deeply asleep as he seemed. The drool and slackened jaw made a safe bet. "Isn't that true for couples?"

"Not my mum and dad." Lance did not meet James' glance. "They lie to each other all the time. I used to call them out as a child, but they'd be angry with me. Both of them can dish out a real ear bashing. You see, well, it's like, Papa doesn't know Mum spends money on snake oil products to make her look younger. He thinks that money's going in the collection plate on Sundays. Or my dad will say he has to go in to work on paperwork at the station, and then go off for a pint with the lads." He shook his head. "I suppose I consider all that normal. But you and Arthur... never tell a lie? Never even a little fib?"

"Well," James spread his hands. "I'll admit that once he bought me a jumper for Christmas that I wasn't... overly fond of. But of course, I didn't let him know that. Oh, and once he got a haircut — tried a new barber, you see — and well, the lad was just starting out, and it was... lopsided. But we both pretended that it wasn't."

Lance pshawed, and hiked up his heel to rest it on the cushion of the chair, wrapping his arms around his leg. "That's nothing. Are you barmy?" They laughed. "No, what it sounds like to me... is that you and Arthur, well... it's special."

A string inside of James, already taut, felt plucked. His cheeks were hot. "It is," he said, averting his eyes from his friend's steady gray gaze.

"Now, I see why it would bother you that Arthur didn't say anything about chasing a man in an old coat." Lance dropped his leg down again and scooted their chairs closer together. "Besides, I know the two of you have to be... careful about drawing attention."

"Look, I don't want you to... well, I mean, it's not like we aren't argy-bargy once in awhile." James traced his finger around the rim of the glass. They listened to the faint sound and slipped into separate thoughts.

Around the corner from the front desk was a grandfather clock, and it suddenly struck midnight, giving them both a start. "It's so late," said James, rising. "Don't you think we ought to try and sleep?"

"Think you can?" Lance flipped his wrist to look at his watch.

"In all honesty, no." James cracked his back on one side, and then the other. "But I can lie there in the dark. Count my blessings, as my mother always says. You should get some rest."

"I'll be lying there staring at the ceiling, too." Lance reached out and snagged the sleeve of James' suit jacket, and tugged gently until he sat down again. "After that stunning feat of athletics, it'll be hours before I'm tired again."

James' lips curved up in the hint of a smile. Lance winked at him and he laughed. "All right. So, here we are, serenaded by snoring — shall we play cards? There's a deck in Vi's purse, I promise you that."

Lance laughed, but shook his head. "I had something else in mind. If it's all right with you."

James' stomach bounced in a trampoline-like jerk. "W-what did you have in mind?"

"I was eleven or twelve when my granddad started to tell me about the two of you and Pied Piper." Lance absently smoothed his hair. "But he only told me little bits at a time. Eventually I think I pieced together the whole story, but one thing I've been dying to know — well, what I want is to hear the... well, the whole thing, I guess. From start to finish. From you. Because I've only heard it from Grandad's view, what he saw, what he thought. I never thought I'd have the chance to actually meet you, to be mates, to hear it all." He looked at his watch. "I mean, I'm so dreadfully awake. Would you..."

"Tell you?" James blinked rapidly and leaned back, as his mouth scrambled for the words. "Well... I — well, I suppose I could do that, yes. I mean, Arthur and I have talked about it over the years, told our side of things to one another. If you're sure you really want to hear it. Of course, I think it's incredible because it happened to me, but I'm afraid I'd bore you, Lance."

"You won't," he insisted. He must have caught James' glance at the clerk, for he said, "He's dead to the world. This whole place is asleep. I think we're safe. Please, say you'll tell it."

James took a drink of water. "Well, I hope I can tell it properly."

Chapter 9

James glanced at his mother every few moments as they walked briskly towards the train station. Her expression was blank, though she raised her lace-trimmed handkerchief to the corners of her eyes from time to time. Once, she caught him looking, just as another family with their children trotted past, toting small luggage. The two young girls wailed openly and their mother streamed silent tears in a continuous torrent.

"Come along," James' mother said as the suffering family passed. "We don't want you to miss the train."

The station teemed with children and parents. Siblings clasped hands in iron, unbreakable grips; mothers wept and smashed their babies into one final embrace before releasing them to the school teachers that would accompany their children on the journey. James and his mother found Mrs. Balin at the prearranged place on the platform. A young woman in a pale dress stood at her side. Her long, giraffe-like body towered over his teacher's pinched old frame. Several of James' classmates had already arrived, and stood in proper lines, arranged alphabetically by last name. The girls cried and the boys joked about, buffeting each other with their luggage.

"Morgan, I told you to stop that at once!" Mrs. Balin scolded before turning back to James and his mother as they approached.

"James Wilde," she said to the young woman, who crossed James' name off of a list affixed to a clipboard.

"Hello James, a pleasure to meet you," the young lady said. She had a warm smile that made her plain features glow with the subtle tint of hidden beauty, like a flower growing through a crack in the pavement. "I'm Miss Pelles. Here's your identification card." She knelt and pinned it to his jacket lapel. "And your gas mask." Miss Pelles lifted a cardboard box on a string over his head and let it swing around his neck like a grim pendulum. "Go ahead and say any goodbyes you need, ma'am," she said to James' mother. "We're still waiting on a few before we board."

"Thank you."

James turned to his mother. He felt Morgan's cruel eyes climb over him and search for a way to ridicule his behavior.

"Behave yourself." She put her hand on his shoulder and squeezed with gentle pressure. "You know I love you very much, dear. Do your best to stay out of trouble, now, promise Mummy you will."

"I promise," James said. He cast his green eyes down and to the side, worried that if he caught her gaze he might cry. It would be hideous if he cried. He could already hear Morgan and his friends snickering behind his back.

"I know you don't want to leave," she went on, though he prayed she would be gone already. The cry of a train whistle muffled some of her words, God be praised. "But perhaps this is a chance for you to make better friends with some of the boys, you know? You'll have lots of time to play together and really get to know one another."

James' heart clenched and he swallowed the bile that threatened the back of his throat. Trapped on a train with Morgan and the boys. Trapped at some country house in the middle of nowhere with Morgan and the boys. A wave of nausea crashed against the shoreline inside of him.

He managed to nod. His mother smiled and squeezed both of his shoulders. "It's for the best," she went on. "It's not safe here, you know that. The Germans could attack any day now. It's only a matter of time. I'd come with you, but I must stay and protect the house and keep working as long as I can. You understand, don't you?"

He nodded again, reached up, and removed her hands from his shoulders.

An errant shadow crossed her features, or perhaps it was a flicker of pain. "Goodbye, darling." She turned and marched away down the platform. James' mother looked back once to wave, and it struck him, how her shoulders and facial features relaxed in relief, now that he had been deposited with Mrs. Balin. Relieved he would be safe, away from danger. *Or*, he thought, *she's glad to be rid of me. She's ashamed.*

As soon as he fell in line with the other boys, the taunts began. "Is your father coming to see you off, fairy-boy?" Tommy chuckled, bumped Morgan with his elbow, invited him to laugh as well.

Morgan pushed his reddish curls under his cap and wiped his nose with his sleeve. "Can't be," he sneered, "hasn't got one, has he?"

Kenneth, moving quickly despite his girth, snatched James' suitcase and undid the clasps to spill the contents. Books and clothing scattered over the platform's grimy floor.

"Oy, don't do that!" Miss Pelles cried from her post. She handed Mrs. Balin the clipboard and rushed to catch some of James' sketches before they blew away in the warm September breeze.

Together, they stuffed everything back into the case and snapped it shut. "Keep your hands on your own things," she scolded Kenneth.

"He started it!" Kenneth lied, pointing at James. "He touched mine first. He's trying to steal from me."

"I saw it," Morgan verified.

"Nobody is touching anyone else's luggage." Mrs. Balin thundered from the head of the line. "Now stand up straight and be quiet."

The children obeyed. Just as the hubbub died down, their final classmate arrived.

"Lord, his mum's as big as a cow." Morgan stage-whispered to the rest of the boys. "How is she getting so many rations, I wonder?" Mean-spirited snickers rippled through the crowd.

Arthur was the biggest boy in the class, by far. He was twelve, like the rest of them, but could have passed for fifteen, or perhaps even older. His massive shoulders gave his body the shape of an upper-case T, if he ever stood up straight. Most of the time he stood hunched, deflated, almost, as though his body wished it was a normal size. His mother was a hefty woman to be sure, but handsome, with jet-black curls and pale green eyes just like her son. Her face was red and blotchy, her cheeks still damp with tears.

"Gather your things, children." Mrs. Balin shouted over the din of a passing train. "It's time to board."

Arthur's giantess mother crushed him into a long hug. "I love you so much. Your papa loves you so much, sweetheart," she blubbered. "Do be careful. Listen to everything your teacher says and you'll be all right. Pray every night, and write as soon as you get there."

Arthur nodded, patted his mother on the back before she broke their embrace. She whipped a handkerchief from her cavernous frock's pocket and mopped her face with it.

"I didn't know the hulking idiot could write," Morgan snarked to his friends. They laughed under their breaths.

Mrs. Balin and Miss Pelles ushered the children down the platform and onto the train. Arthur's mother waited until the locomotive lurched away, waving her handkerchief madly until they were out of sight.

"Children, file into these cabins here," Mrs. Balin ordered, indicating the train car compartments. "No jostling, no pushing. Simply file in and fill the seats as you go. Do not leave this car."

Despite her warning, the class immediately split into cliques and piled into seating compartments with their friends. Arthur lumbered into one of the half-full compartments with a few of the unpopular girls (Mary with the buck teeth and glasses, and her only friend, the unwashed Patricia). Mrs. Balin heaved a sigh and pushed open the door to where she and Miss Pelles intended to sit. The compartment was partially occupied with other adults cowering at the sight of so many energetic school children. "You'd best sit with us," she said to James. "It will prevent problems."

James had no way to refuse, so he put his little suitcase on the luggage rack and settled into his seat, farthest from the window, with his book. Some of the adults shared glances. "The others pick on him so relentlessly," Mrs. Balin explained as though James were deaf, or as invisible as a vacated spirit. "It's better to keep him close so they don't whip themselves into a frenzy, you know."

"Oh, I see," said Miss Pelles in a murmured tone of sympathy. She plopped down next to James, removed her hair combs, and ruffled her maple locks. As she gracefully replaced the combs, she said, "Don't worry about a thing, James. We're going to take wonderful care of all of you. Did you know we're going to Lincolnshire? It's absolutely beautiful, stunning, really. And this weather! Just grand. It'll be like a holiday, you'll see."

James wanted to like Miss Pelles. But once she heard him speak, saw the way he walked, she'd hate him, just like everyone else. Oh, she wouldn't be openly cruel like Morgan and the rest, but she'd avoid him, only speak to him when necessary, and blame him for the way he was bullied. It was better to kill hope in the womb. "Yes, miss," was all he said, and turned his attention back to his book, back to escape, to pirate adventures on the high seas.

"*Treasure Island*." Miss Pelles admired, nodding. "Well, if it's adventure you love, then think of this as a grand adventure."

"Yes, miss."

Mrs. Balin clucked and drew Miss Pelles away from James into adult conversation, which, of course, centered on the fighting in Norway.

A few hours passed. Every now and then, James leaned forward and stole a glance out of the window. The dreary city had transformed into lush countryside; the train barreled through field after field of magnificent green, dotted with unconcerned cows and the silhouettes of distant farm houses. Once in awhile, they passed a herd of sheep blanketing the greenery like clouds come to earth. In the golden light of early autumn, James couldn't help but notice the scenery, and had to admit it was beautiful.

An old man with a pipe grunted and rustled his newspaper. "Fancy a sit by the window, sonny?" he called across several laps.

"The boy is fine where he is. Aren't you, James?" Mrs. Balin barked.

"Yes ma'am," James murmured. Then, "Mrs. Balin? I need to..." he indicated the door.

"Go ahead," she dismissed with a wave of her hand.

James put his book and his gas mask on his seat and let himself into the hallway. He stole along the corridor to the loo, hoping Morgan and his friends wouldn't catch sight of him. As he passed their compartment, he snuck a glance through the window. Morgan's gang was asleep with biscuit crumbs on their faces. Good. As he passed the next compartment, he caught Arthur looking at him with a fixed, unbroken stare. Usually, the mammoth boy kept his eyes to the ground, but they inexplicably caught James' gaze, green to green.

James broke the connection and trotted along to the end of the car. He stole glances over his shoulder as he went.

After finishing, he adjusted his cap over his auburn hair, and brushed the strands to the side so they would lay over his forehead the way he liked. He took a breath, tiptoed out into the corridor and concentrated on slipping back to the adults' car like a willowy shadow.

Without warning, the door to Morgan's compartment shot open, and the bully leapt out with a roar, his gas mask pulled over his face, alien and insect-like. The mask-muffled shout shattered the calm quiet of the train's berth. James gasped and a hand flew up to his throat. He fell back against the wall and clutched the railing in surprise.

Morgan ripped off the gas mask with a howl of laughter. His friends piled out into the corridor. They brayed like donkeys, slapped their knees, cheeks red with mirth. "Look at the chinless wonder, boys!" Morgan roared, throwing his arm around Tommy. "Have you ever seen a poof scream like that?"

James took a breath and steadied himself, and then attempted to slide around the gaggle of guffawing boys.

"Where do you think you're going?" Kenneth hooked an arm around James' slender neck and doubled him over, then drove his fist into James' gut. The air wooshed out from between James' lips and he fell to his knees, clutching his midsection.

At last, the ruckus in the corridor alerted Mrs. Balin, who threw open the door to her compartment. "Boys." she shrilled. "Get back to your seats."

Morgan and his henchmen leapt away from James and scurried to comply. They banged the door shut behind them, and left their prey in a ball on the ground. "Come along, Wilde, don't dally," Mrs. Balin scolded.

James, using the corridor railing for leverage, hauled himself to his feet. Arthur stood at the door of his compartment, his bulk filled the small space and cast a bold shadow against the sunlit windows. He watched James get up, and did not look away until he'd disappeared into the compartment in a storm of Mrs. Balin's sharp words.

Chapter 10

Arthur had never imagined a house like the one he and his classmates shuffled toward. They lugged their suitcases and rations down the gravel drive. He had never seen *warm* gray stone before, but that was what the place seemed to be made of. Aside from the color, the rest of the structure was imposing: rectangular windows all in perfect, symmetrical order, blank and gaping, a sharp and depressing slate-colored roof, and a portico adorned with impressive columns at the top of a sharp stair. Even against the sweet September evening sky, it seemed lonesome and haunted with overgrown gardens and lawns and a courtyard scattered with last winter's leaves.

"There it is, children." Miss Pelles chirped, her hands full with the timid digits of two particularly homesick girls. She seemed to think that taking the same tone used to entice five-year-olds would work with young people who were nearly thirteen. "Look at it, isn't it beautiful? Carolean architecture, I believe. Late 1600s. Wasn't that a long time ago? It has an Italian garden and a fountain out back and loads of space for you all to play and bask in the sun and fresh air. So much better than the drab city, isn't it?"

As they approached, Mrs. Balin ushered them into two lines, boys and girls, a phalanx of refugees tripping timidly up the drive. When they neared the bottom of the great stone staircase, the enormous door at the top swung open, and three figures emerged. One was a pot-bellied gentleman clad in a butler's fine weeds, and the other two were female, one gray-haired woman with powerful forearms, and the other a stick-thin girl in a maid's uniform.

Mrs. Balin held up a hand for them to stop, and the children obeyed, clutching their suitcases while regarding the keepers of the mansion.

"Welcome to Willowind House," the balding butler greeted, his posture and pronunciation perfect. "On behalf of the Baroness Lady

Barlow, myself, and the rest of the staff, we are pleased to have you here as our guests."

"Thank you very much, sir." Mrs. Balin smiled, and it forced her blunt and weathered features into a face resembling a turtle with indigestion. "The children and their families are ever so grateful for your hospitality."

"I am Mr. Marlin," the butler said. "Allow me to introduce our cook, Mrs. Galhad, and my lady's maid, Miss Ivaine."

While the man spoke, Arthur's eyes wandered up to the second story windows where a sudden movement caught his attention. As a cloud passed over the sun, he made out the figure of a bent old hag peering down through the glass, the wispy curtains clutched in her gnarled hands. Her owlish eyes stared back into his gaze, and a chill raced through him. Arthur dropped his head to break the spell.

Once the introductions and drippy, yet obligatory thank-yous had been dealt with, the children were marched into the main hall, a massive foyer with a black and white checkered floor. Through an arched doorway, Arthur could see a grand staircase leading up to the second story.

Mr. Marlin led them through another set of intricately carved double doors. Their shoes echoed over the marble floor and disturbed the grave-stillness of the house. The room they entered spanned almost the length of the back of the house, and was lined with row upon row of dusty windows providing sunlight and views of the back garden, now wild and overgrown, the fountain dry and lifeless. "I thought this would do for a classroom, and a place to take your meals," Mr. Marlin said.

"Plenty of light." Miss Pelles admired the forest green and brown paneled walls and complicated plaster ceiling.

"Rooms on either side of this one have been cleared," Mr. Marlin went on. The calm softness of his voice appealed to Arthur, as did his gray eyes, which seemed to focus on everything and nothing simultaneously. "One for boys and one for girls. The chapel is down this way." He indicated the doors at the end of the right side of the long, empty saloon. "Mrs. Galhad, will you be so kind as to show Miss Pelles the kitchen?"

"Right away, sir. This way, if you please." Miss Pelles and Mrs. Galhad disappeared through the far left doors.

"Mrs. Balin, please inform me if there is anything further you require." Mr. Marlin clasped his hands behind his back. "Mrs. Galhad will see to your provisions, laundry, and water for washing."

From somewhere in the distant depths of the house, the muffled tinkle of a bell reached Arthur's ears.

Apparently, the sound alerted Mr. Marlin as well. "If you will excuse me." He disappeared back into the main hall, leaving the class alone in their new quarters.

"All right, children," Mrs. Balin barked, "boys, your quarters are to the left, girls to the right. There should be cots, mattresses, and bed clothes stacked there for you. Help one another set out the beds and prepare them. I'll go speak to the cook and Miss Pelles about scrounging up some tea."

The boys filed into what had once been a drawing room, decorated with heavy red damask draperies that flowed over white panels. In the dim light permitted through the curtained windows, gold gleamed on mirror frames and small furnishings. Most of the furniture had been removed, and the fine carpet rolled away, replaced with two stacks of cots, a pile of mattresses, and several boxes of sheets. The room's museum-like intricacy was oppressive, and Arthur was afraid to touch anything.

"All right, boys, let's get this room ship shape." Miss Pelles called cheerfully as she emerged through the opposite door from a stairway that led from the kitchen. Morgan and his friends fell on the stacks without hesitation, and put their cots next to each other near the fireplace. The rest of the boys lined up their beds adjacent to the classmates they were friendliest with. Arthur and James held back and waited to see what was left. With quick, curious glances, Arthur looked around the room, scanning the chaotic activity of children settling into new surroundings. James, on the other hand, stood with his head bowed and his arms crossed, gently tapping an innocent dust bunny with the toe of his shoe.

"Oh my, you're a strapping lad, aren't you?" Miss Pelles patted Arthur's swollen bicep. "I'll be happy to have your help around the vegetable garden... Arthur." She read his name from the tag on his coat. "I'm sure you're quite strong. Why don't you help James with his bed?"

Arthur nodded, nearly imperceptibly, and did as she asked, fetching two cots and mattresses. James retrieved the sheets and handed a set to Arthur without looking at him.

"Oh, the strong silent type." Miss Pelles winked at them. "The girls go mad for that, don't they, gentlemen?"

Morgan made a sound of dismissal. "He's always silent, Miss." He took a tone of concerned confidentiality while Tommy handed out pillows to his mates. "Never says a word, so don't take it personal. He's an imbecile."

Tommy, Kenneth, and some of the other boys tittered, but Miss Pelles hushed them. "Make those sheets tight. I don't want to see a single sloppy bed," she warned.

Arthur and James made their beds, which had been shoved farthest from the fireplace and closest to the door leading back to the saloon. The two outcasts smoothed their blankets and passed inspection.

The schoolchildren helped carry a long wooden table into the saloon and outfitted it with chairs. They also brought in smaller tables and other fine, but mismatched, furnishings to serve as their classroom. Mrs. Balin opened a crate sent by the government and began to assemble the blackboard while Miss Pelles unpacked the primers and paper.

At long last, late in the evening, they sat down to supper. Though the bowls were heaped with a chunky, vile-looking stew, the children were ravenous. Mrs. Balin forced them to wait, however, and the table was surrounded by lolling, covetous eyes as fingers itched to snatch up spoons.

Mrs. Balin rose next to her chair. "Children, you have all been very brave today. We expect you to continue this and be on your best behavior while Britain fights off those nasty Germans. Now, I know Miss Pelles has referred to this trip as a holiday. Of course, there will be time for fun and games, but we will continue our studies as well. The best way we can work to defeat our enemies is to carry on as if life has not been disrupted. His Majesty's armies need intelligent boys, as well as dependable and capable girls to hold the country together while the men are away. Do you understand?"

"Yes, Mrs. Balin," they chanted. All but Arthur, who simply mouthed the words.

"Now, understand these rules," she droned on. Arthur's mouth watered as the grisly soup's steam reached his nostrils. "Lights out will be at 8:30. No talking or mischief of any kind will be tolerated. You will be awakened at 6:00 to wash up. Breakfast is at 6:30 and lessons begin promptly at 7:00. Keep your bed, your clothes, and your bodies clean. You will also be assigned certain chores about the house, whatever Mr. Marlin needs us to do. This is to help pay the gracious Baroness back for use of her estate-" she cut herself off sharply, "Jane, if you touch that bread, I'll thwack your knuckles until they bleed!"

Jane put her hand back in her lap, and bowed her head with a whimper.

"Speaking of Lady Barlow," Mrs. Balin continued, "I have been informed that she is elderly and infirm, and is, for the most part, confined to the upstairs of the mansion. It is imperative that we do not disturb her in any way when going about our daily business. Do not wander away from the designated areas we have been assigned, and keep the shouting during recreation time to a minimum. Is that understood?"

"Yes, Mrs. Balin," came the dirge of childlike voices.

"Good. Now, let us say grace."

Arthur's stomach roared so loudly that the girl to his left shot a disgusted glance his way. She put her hand in his with intense reluctance as they bowed their heads.

"Bless, O Father, Thy gifts to our use and us to Thy service; for Christ's sake. Amen."

"Amen." the schoolchildren cried, and took up their spoons.

An hour later, Arthur lay on his bed while his feet dangled from the bottom edge. The room was dark, save for a twinkle of moonlight that seeped in through the heavy draperies. A lantern burned near the door to the loo. The dark air filled with little noises and rustlings as the boys tried to get comfortable on their hard cots, wrapped in scratchy sheets. They were used to city sounds; the ear-shattering peace of the nighttime countryside provided no comfort.

Arthur knew sleep would not come. He did not try to coax it. Yes, the country was too quiet, the bed too small, the linens dreadful (not to mention, his rations weren't nearly enough to fill his stomach) but his insomnia came from a different place. Whenever he closed his eyes, he saw his father's face, twisted, monstrous, disfigured by the gout of fire from a Nazi flamethrower. Nothing had been the same since Papa had come home from Norway. The scarred face, the scarred heart, all of these things were strange to Arthur. His powerful, vigorous father, reduced to a trembling invalid, his features unrecognizable, his laugh slaughtered and buried. It was as if Papa had died trying to defend the iron mines and they'd sent someone else back in his stead.

A gentle sniffle wafted over from his left. There was only one bed between Arthur and the wall, where James lay, folded into a protective ball, covers yanked up under his chin. The moonlight fell over his heart-shaped face as he shifted, turning towards Arthur's cot, near sleep but not fully in its grasp. Tears streaked his face and glimmered as his features relaxed gradually into slumber.

Arthur stared at him until he drowsed and slept; one face replaced with another.

Chapter 11

Days marched by, marked by schedule and routine. Lessons continued much as they had at school back in London. James' marks were nearly perfect, as usual, though he'd learned some time ago the importance of making purposeful errors. It kept Mrs. Balin from the terror of not having anything more to teach him, and prevented classmates from thinking him too stuck up. It was best not to call attention to yourself when your name was James Wilde, the class queerie.

They ate, they washed up, they learned, they read, they recited, they prayed in the chapel, they slept. They took turns tending the victory garden, washing dishes and sheets, and cleaning the blackboard and classroom floor. A little mail would arrive here and there, and when Jane's parents sent a tin of biscuits it was a momentous occasion. For the most part, each day was like the next, save the temperature, which dropped a degree or two with each turn of the sun as the earth prepared for winter. It was a rare thing to see the Baroness at her window, and sightings of her were recorded as though she were a mythical beast. The girls suspected she was a witch. The Baroness looked the part—folded skin, talon hands, and cavernous eyes. Whenever she noticed the children pointing at her window, the curtains whispered shut. Sightings were uncommon.

Part of the daily monotonous ritual was that James would be accosted by Morgan and the boys, whether at recreation time, out in the garden, or before bed. The strain was enormous; there was no respite, no mother to run home to, no sweet solitude of his bedroom in their flat. Every hour he had to be vigilant.

Each day, as they filed out the east door for recreation, they passed a fourteen-foot replica of Polykleitos's *Doryphorus,* the Spear Thrower. The girls always averted their gazes, forming visors with their hands to protect their tender vision from the statue's exposed stone manhood. Most of the boys were too busy anticipating football to notice the house's accoutrements, but James always took a moment to look at the statue's classical beauty, strength and humanity portrayed in stone. Every few nights, he dreamt that he was Pygmalion, praying to Aphrodite for a magical kiss to bring the statue to life. A spear-thrower could protect him from Morgan and his gang.

As soon as Mrs. Balin was out of sight, and Miss Pelles was distracted by the girls and their games, Morgan and his friends encircled James before he had a chance to pull out his book or sketchpad and disappear into the tangled garden.

Kenneth tore James' book from his grasp and tossed it in the dirt. "You're sick!" He waggled a finger in James' face. "Staring at that naked statue like that!"

"He looks at it every day." Tommy roared through his snaggletoothed jester's grin. His blonde curls whipped in the brisk autumn wind. "I've seen it. It's disgusting! What in God's name is the matter with you, anyway?"

"Well, he fancies it, that's why he's always studying it so." Morgan laughed and slapped his friends' shoulders.

Their taunts fell on James as he stood with his head bowed and waited for the blows to come. When they shoved him to the ground, he was surprised to see, through the forest of legs kicking at him, that Arthur had rescued *Treasure Island* from the hedge and held it against his massive chest, the tome dwarfed to the size of a prayer book.

"Gentlemen."

The even, measured voice was cool and calm, but still managed to cut through the bullies' mad laughter as they prodded and stomped on James with their feet. The boys snapped to attention, their hands behind their backs in a posture of innocence.

"Please join the other children near the oak tree." Mr. Marlin held out a directing hand.

"Yes sir," they chorused, and raced away, leaving Arthur hulking to one side and James in the cold dirt. As he picked himself up and dusted off his trousers, James noticed Arthur drift away to join the others, wary of the adult intrusion, the book tucked under his arm.

"What is your name, young man?" Mr. Marlin asked, fixing his cool gray gaze on James' scuffed knees.

"James Wilde, sir." He tried to stand up straight, but the pain in his side made it difficult.

"Lady Barlow requests a young man to come upstairs and read to her," Mr. Marlin said. "She would like to extend her invitation to you."

James hurriedly brushed grime from his elbows, or tried to. "M-me, sir?"

"Yes. Will you come this way, please?"

James gulped and nodded. He followed Mr. Marlin back into the mansion and up the grand staircase. They twisted and turned through a series of ornate hallways before they arrived at a bedchamber door. Mr. Marlin knocked gently. "The boy is here, my lady," he said.

A time-ravaged voice rasped, "Send him in, Mr. Marlin."

The butler nodded his balding head. James licked his lips and put his fingers on the cool door handle.

The exquisite chamber had ivory damask walls and an enormous green and gold oriental rug. Lavish cream silk bed hangings rippled in a gentle draft, and polished wood gleamed everywhere. A monstrous armoire loomed next to a pristine vanity which displayed bottles of ancient perfumes and a jewelry box inlaid with opals and mother of pearl. The air was stuffy and medicinal.

The Baroness, Lady Barlow, sat in an overstuffed chair near the window, and the chair from the vanity stood opposite, a small table between them. Several books were stacked in a tower on its shining surface, along with a silver plate of tea and watercress sandwiches. James eyed them, hunger mixing with his dread-tinted curiosity.

"Come." As the crone's gnarled hand rose from her lap and beckoned him closer, her rings flashed in the sunlight that streamed in through the lacy curtains.

James did not respond immediately. He continued to take in the room, the finery, the sight of palatable food. Mr. Marlin put a gentle hand on his back and guided him forward. James snatched his cap from his head in a moment of sudden remembrance, and patted his hair down as best he could before he sat opposite the Baroness.

"Will there be anything else, my lady?" Mr. Marlin asked, bowing forward slightly.

"No, thank you." She fixed her watery blue eyes on the thin boy before her. Mr. Marlin quietly shut the door behind himself.

They regarded each other for some time in silence. James tried with all his might to be the picture of politeness, but he couldn't help staring. The old woman was draped in a cavernous blue dressing gown, her bony feet enveloped in soft slippers. Her silver hair, however, was perfectly coiffed into an old-fashioned chignon on the top of her head, and a large diamond brooch hung at her wrinkled throat.

"What is your name?" she asked, raising her ring-heavy hand again.

He swallowed noisily and wished away the dirt on his clothes. He forced his body into proper posture. "James Wilde, ma'am," he said. "M-my l-lady," he tried instead.

"Will you take tea, Mr. Wilde?"

It didn't take him half as long to answer that question. "Yes, please." He coughed, and used a napkin to clean his soiled hands, praying it was the right thing to do. "May I serve you, my lady?"

She smiled, weathered lips climbing over her brown, nubby teeth. "Indeed you may. Two sugars, if you please." She took the cup and saucer with shaking hands, and steadied them on the chair's arm.

The tea was different than what the children were given, delicate and citrusy, and the sandwiches were divine. The plate was empty before James knew what had happened. "Thank you very much, my lady."

"Mr. Wilde, I am not long for this world," she said, handing him back her teacup to be refilled. "Let us not stand on formalities. We live under the same roof, do we not? May I call you James?"

"Yes, of course," he replied with a nod. "And I shall call you..."

"Nim, please." She smiled. "It's a fond name my husband used to call me. Now, James, if you would be so kind as to read to me, it would be much appreciated. My eyesight fails me."

Nim requested he begin with a poem. "It should be on page 37 of the blue book on top of the stack." James leaned forward and picked up the slender volume. He thumbed through it until he came across the right page. "'Crossing the Bar,'" he read aloud.

"That's the one." Nim settled into her chair and put her gnarled hands on her lap. "Begin."

His voice quivered at first, and she stopped him after a few lines. "Young man, you're reading to me like you've a flock of butterflies in your stomach."

"I'm so sorry—"

She held up a time-worn hand. "Do not apologize. I've been watching you, child. I know your intelligence. What you're capable of. Now, if you please. Give me the poem like you're giving me a gift."

He began over again, stumbling over his words, but his voice smoothed over time, like the surface of a pool minutes after a stone's splash. Her face was so pleased and she was so relaxed by his recitation that he grew ever more confident, inflecting emotion into his words, using his chords as an instrument in a way he'd never done before. "'*I hope to see my Pilot face to face when I have cross'd the bar*,'" he finished.

"Very good. Lovely." James felt the first genuine smile in days, perhaps weeks, creep over his face. "I think we ought to have a bit of Shakespeare now." Nim settled back in her chair with her cup and saucer in her lap. "Read me Juliet's balcony speech."

He did, relishing in the words, giving them dramatic emphasis, gesturing with his hands and affecting Juliet's voice. "Thou knowest the mask of night is on my face, else would a maiden blush bepaint my cheek!" The old woman smirked, her foggy eyes sparkled with delight when he finished.

"And now *Hamlet*, if you please. Something about solid flesh."

He switched books and flipped the pages until he found his place. "Oh, that this too too solid flesh would melt," he began, "thaw, and resolve itself into a dew, or that the Everlasting had not fixed His canon 'gainst self-slaughter." His voice wavered a moment as the Bard's words cut him unexpectedly, dredged up a carousel of horrible memories: the taunts, the beatings, the invisibility. "Oh God, oh God," he struggled, swallowing back his tears. "How w-weary, stale, f-flat and unprofitable seem to me all the uses o-of this w-w-world." He sniffed. "Tis an... unweeded garden..." Bloated tears escaped the corners of his eyes and raced down his cheeks. He searched helplessly for his handkerchief before he noticed Nim dangled one in front of his face, a fine thing of embroidery and lace. He accepted it and wiped his eyes.

"I'm sorry, my lady." He took a watery breath.

"Close the book, James," she said, her voice a whispery crackle of dead leaves over pavement. He obeyed. "Now, tell me what troubles you."

"Nothing," he mumbled, avoiding her gaze.

"Why, that cannot be so." Nim raised her tea to her spotted lips. "When you spoke Hamlet's words of wishing to escape the mortal coil, of a pale and meaningless world, you felt something, else you would not have wept."

He said nothing, but the traitorous tears continued to smear from his eyes.

"Those boys," Nim said, "led by the red-headed one. They're quite cruel to you, aren't they? I have seen them, nearly every day, mocking and threatening you."

He took a deep lungful of air and forced himself into a state of trembling calm. "I'm *different*, Nim," he said, "and they hate me."

"Different because they think you fancy boys?"

He nodded.

"And do you?"

He paused. Then nodded.

She nodded as well, closing her eyes. They disappeared into the folds of her face a moment before she opened them again. "My son," she said, "my youngest boy, Matthew, was like you. I tried to protect him, but... he found the world just as weary, stale, flat, and unprofitable as Hamlet. And he went away to heaven, do you understand? Well, you're twelve years old, dear. Old enough to know death."

"Yes ma'am," he replied, a meek murmur.

"I miss him very much," she admitted after a long pause. "He was just a few years older than you." She fixed her gaze out the window and seemed to solidify, to sink into herself, turn to stone, her knobby hand under her chin, teacup held loosely in her other hand.

He had long dried his tears and finished his tea before she spoke again. "Hand me my cane, dear." She pointed a yellow-nailed hand toward a gold-headed staff that leaned against her bed. He retrieved it for her, and she climbed to her feet with a series of weary sighs. The old woman hobbled over to the vanity, and he followed with the chair, replacing it so she could sit.

"Look in the drawer by the side of my bed," she suggested. "You'll find something there I think you'll like."

James obeyed, his quick fingers pushing aside a pile of clean handkerchiefs and coming up with a small gold-painted box. "Chocolates!" he cried, unable to contain his enthusiasm.

"Bring the box here, and we will share a piece," Nim said. He returned with the box. She removed a plump bonbon from the tissue paper within and instructed him to split it with a letter opener. "Must make them last," she said. "Men and their wars. Don't they realize we need our chocolate?"

It was heaven on James' tongue. He could not muffle the moan of ecstasy that escaped his lips as the cocoa sweetness dissolved over his taste buds. Nim ate hers with relish as well, little flecks sticking to the corners of her puckered mouth.

"Now, let's look at some pretty things." She opened the lacquered jewelry box, and James' eyes widened. Nim withdrew piece after piece of antique jewelry, lovingly polished and cared for, glimmering gems in every color of the rainbow. "This was my engagement ring," she revealed. Her shaking hands struggled to open a velvet box lined in silk. The ring was enormous, a bulging sapphire flanked by diamonds.

James' eyes bulged accordingly. "That was the *engagement* ring?" he blurted.

She winked at him with a little grin. "The wedding band," she revealed, holding out her hand to him. James took it and drew it closer to his face, inhaling her scent, a mixture of old books and lavender. The diamond blazed in the light of the falling sun outside.

"Now this." She held up a jeweled pin shaped like an insect, inlaid with emeralds, "was a gift from the President of the United States of America."

"Which one?" James asked as his fingers curled eagerly over the precious bug.

"I am afraid I don't quite remember," Nim said. Gently, she lifted a magnificent choker of pearls with a massive rosy stone in the center, ringed with more diamonds. She wound it around James' white throat. He sat up straight and threw his shoulders back, scrutinizing his reflection in the mirror. Nim clasped the piece and then took up her comb, smoothing down his hair, using a bit of rosewater on the end of her handkerchief to smear away the grime on his cheek.

"An emerald would bring out your eyes," she said, "but this brings out your color beautifully. Simply lovely, isn't it?"

At the mention of his skin, he glanced at Nim's reflection at his side, and her deathly pallor struck him in comparison to his young, vibrant glow. "Are you well, Nim?" he asked.

She sighed, and the bruise-purple half-moons under her eyes seemed to sink deeper. "I am very old, my dear." She unclasped the choker from his neck and laid it next to her other treasures, "and we are marching through a dark and costly war. I fear the winter." She clucked as his eyes misted. "Please do not start all that again. We all must cross the bar. I am the one who is dying, not you, so keep your chin up! Ah, see here, this ruby comes all the way from the darkest regions of India..."

Chapter 12

"I hope the war comes." Morgan violently stabbed a stick into the ground. He and Tommy and Kenneth jabbed the earth with their staves, bayoneting invisible enemies. Arthur lingered nearby, one eye on them, the other on James, who lounged on a stone bench in the sun. He drew furiously in his sketchbook.

"I hope I meet Hitler. I'll punch him right in his stupid mustache," Morgan said.

"I'll jab him in the bum with a bayonet." Tommy mimed the motion with his stick.

"I wish we were older," Kenneth lamented, kicking a dirt clod. "I'd like to join the army. I'd join this second, I would."

"Would you?" the calm, cool voice floated over to them. It cut through the dying hum of the last of the bumblebees and flies buzzing about the fallen apples—too rotten to bake—that littered the ground of the neglected orchard. The boys jumped and whipped up their heads to behold Mr. Marlin standing straight as a soldier on the gravel path before them.

"Good afternoon, sir," Morgan said, his voice saccharine, pleasing.

"Would you?" Mr. Marlin repeated. Arthur took a few steps forward, trying to catch his words before they blew away in the breeze.

"Would I what, sir?" Morgan asked.

"Would you jump at the chance to go to war?"

"Yes sir!" Kenneth barged in. "Send those Germans crying home to their mothers."

Mr. Marlin's gray eyes flashed with sudden flint. "What is war, gentlemen?" he asked.

Morgan, Tommy, and Kenneth glanced at each other. "It's when armies fight," Morgan answered, "and one of them wins. And only the brave soldiers go to protect their land."

"*What* is war?" Mr. Marlin asked again as Arthur edged closer.

The boys shared uncomfortable glances, shifting from foot to foot. "When two governments..." Kenneth tried before his voice drained away.

Mr. Marlin took a step forward and bent at the waist, low and confidential. "The mud turns red with blood," he said. "The horses scream when they die. Men trapped in the barbed wire in No Man's Land, hanging there until the crows come for them. Your brothers, drowning in their own lungs. Chlorine gas. The whistle blows, and they drive you up, up and over, out of the trench and into the jaws of hell."

The boys stared at him with saucer eyes. Kenneth's mouth wagged before he remembered to clamp it shut.

"Now, speak up, boys," Mr. Marlin said. "*What is war?*" They stood in stupid silence.

"War is hell," Mr. Marlin finished, straightening his back and turning away. Morgan and his friends shared a quick glance, and ran. Arthur watched as Mr. Marlin approached with measured, purposeful steps, his heart rumbling in his broad chest.

"Young man," the butler said, "Lady Barlow wishes to speak with you."

Arthur put his hand on his chest and raised his eyebrows in unspoken question.

"Yes." Mr. Marlin extended an arm toward the house.

As they stepped into the marble hall, headed for the staircase, they met Mrs. Balin and her stack of papers, headed, perhaps, for the kitchen and a cup of tea. "Mr. Marlin," she cried. "Oh, are you taking Arthur upstairs with you?"

"Yes ma'am," he replied.

"I'm sorry, but this one... he stutters terribly," Mrs. Balin said. Arthur flushed scarlet, and his eyes spat emerald fire. He wished he could shrink, diminish, desiccate.

"The Baroness *does* wish him to read to her, doesn't she?" Mrs. Balin pressed.

"I do not know, ma'am. Lady Barlow requested that I fetch Arthur."

Mrs. Balin fixed Arthur with a dubious glare, but left them with a dismissive goodbye.

Arthur's cheeks burned, pulsating heat with each step up the staircase. Shame clouded his eyes, and he had no appreciation for the finery of the Baroness's bedchamber.

"My lady, Mrs. Balin informs me that Arthur has a stutter," Mr. Marlin said, putting an apologetic hand on Arthur's thick shoulder.

"That has no bearing, whatsoever," her ancient voice creaked. "Perhaps, I wish for him to listen as I reminisce about times long past."

"Very good, my lady." Mr. Marlin let himself out.

"Arthur," the Baroness invited, stretching out a hand that was bone and vellum. Arthur moved toward the vanity chair offered to him and settled across from the old woman, terrified that the delicate, ornately-painted seat would break into pieces under his weight.

"Arthur," she repeated. "Arthur *Pendragon*. The Once and Future King."

He raised his chin inch by inch, and looked her in the eyes, fierce green to tired blue.

The Baroness leaned forward. She was clutching a small blue-bound book in her tenuous grasp, and stretched it to him. Arthur took the book and read the flaking gold leaf imprinted on the title. *Idylls of the King* by Alfred, Lord Tennyson. "Read," she said. "To me, or to yourself. It is time you claimed your name, my dear."

Arthur thumbed the book open, its pages dwarfed in his meaty hands. He moistened his thick thumb and turned past the dedication to the first of the poems. "L-l-leodogran, the K-k-ing of Cameliard..." he began, voice grazed just above a whisper. With every word, the slight stutter receded until it evaporated completely. It had been gone for some time, but he'd been too frightened to return to speech again.

With each stanza, his voice grew and rumbled deep at times and lilted in others, as if his throat could not decide if he were man or boy.

"For many a petty king ere Arthur came ruled in this isle, and ever waging war, each upon other, wasted all the land; and still from time to time the heathen host swarmed overseas, and harried what was left. And so there grew great tracts of wilderness, wherein the beast was ever more and more, but man was less and less, till Arthur came."

The poem rolled over them both, undulating around them, a tide, a sea of words and cadences. Arthur was lost in it, and was rudely awakened when presented with the blank page as the poem ended.

He glanced up at the Baroness. She reclined in the chair, her eyes closed, her pale lips curved into a secret smile. Perhaps she was asleep.

"I knew you could speak," she said. He jumped, and clattered the tea things on the table. Only then did he realize there was tea, sugar, and watercress sandwiches. "Pour me a cup of tea with two lumps, Arthur, and tell me about the Once and Future King."

The delicate china pieces were like a child's playthings in his sausage-round fingers, but he managed to fix the cuppa the way she liked it. "Arthur was a great king," he said, marveling at the strange, unfamiliar sound of his maturing voice. "He had the Knights of the Round Table. The table was round so no one was above the other. But one of his knights, Lancelot, he fell in love with Queen Guinevere. And, um, when he died he went to Avalon."

"Have you read much?" she asked.

His mouth filled with saliva looking at the sandwiches. "No ma'am," he said. "Just picture books when I was a little 'un, ma'am."

"Well, fall upon the sandwiches, boy, I can see you eyeing them," Lady Barlow laughed. "And as you eat, let me regale you with tales of Arthur. You see, his legend has been with us as long as there have been people on this isle. Perhaps even before! Arthur kept enemies from these shores. He was chosen. He proved his worth drawing the fabled sword from the stone, and was befriended by the great wizard Merlin." With each feat the old woman described, Arthur's eyes grew wider, and one sandwich after another disappeared.

After he'd washed his bread down with his tea, the Baroness regarded him down her long, graceful nose. "Arthur, please read to me the second to last stanza of the poem once more."

He obeyed.

"Ah, there it is," she said, lifting one talon into the air as though she could snag his words from the aether. "There at the banquet those great Lords from Rome, the slowly-fading mistress of the world, strode in, and claimed their tribute as of yore. But Arthur spake, 'Behold, for these have sworn to wage my wars, and worship me their King; *the old order changeth, yielding place to new*'."

"The old order changeth, yielding place to new," Arthur whispered, an echo.

"It's time, Arthur," the Baroness said. "Seize your name. Seize your destiny." She leaned back and pulled the bell rope at her side. Seconds later, Mr. Marlin knocked and entered. "Mr. Marlin, bring up a plate of bread and jam," she said. "Arthur must gather his strength."

Chapter 13

Then Arthur as a lion, ran unto King Cradelment of North Wales, and smote him through the left side, that the horse and the king fell down; and then he took the horse by the rein, and led him unto Ulfius, and said, Have this horse, mine old friend, for great need hast thou of horse. Gramercy, said Ulfius. Then Sir Arthur did so marvellously in arms, that all men had wonder. When the King with the Hundred Knights saw King Cradelment on foot, he ran unto Sir Ector, that was well horsed, Sir Kay's father, and smote horse and man down, and gave the horse unto the king, and horsed him again. And when King Arthur saw the king ride on Sir Ector's horse, he was wroth and with his sword he smote the king on the helm, that a quarter of the helm and shield fell down, and so the sword carved down unto the horse's neck, and so the king and the horse fell down to the ground.

"Sir Arthur did so marvelously in arms, that all men had wonder," Arthur whispered, his hefty finger holding his place on the page. The tome in his hand was Le Morte d'Arthur, given to him by the Baroness for further study.

This he now closed, and swapped it for *Idylls of the King.*

And near him stood the Lady of the Lake,
Who knows a subtler magic than his own—
Clothed in white samite, mystic, wonderful.
She gave the King his huge cross-hilted sword,
Whereby to drive the heathen out: a mist
Of incense curled about her, and her face
Wellnigh was hidden in the minster gloom;
But there was heard among the holy hymns
A voice as of the waters, for she dwells
Down in a deep; calm, whatsoever storms
May shake the world, and when the surface rolls,
Hath power to walk the waters like our Lord.
There likewise I beheld Excalibur

Before him at his crowning borne, the sword
That rose from out the bosom of the lake,
And Arthur rowed across and took it—rich
With jewels, elfin Urim, on the hilt,
Bewildering heart and eye—the blade so bright
That men are blinded by it—

Arthur paused, shifted his weight on the stone garden bench, and

moved downward in the poem to his favorite line. "The old order changeth, yielding place to new," he breathed, his lips moving without a single stutter.

"Look at him!" came Morgan's shrill cruelty from across the yard as he laughed and pointed, elbowing Kenneth and Tommy in the stomach. "The big oaf's mouthing the words. What a moron!"

"They ought to lock him up somewhere away from normal people," Kenneth said.

"He can't read for anything." Tommy sniggered behind his hand. "Why is he pretending to?"

Movement from the left. Without warning, James shot out from behind the hedge, his sketchbook clutched to his chest with white fingers, cheeks pink from the morning chill. "Shut up!" he yelled right into Morgan's face. "You shut up, do you hear me?"

Each of the bullies' faces flashed raw surprise. James hadn't resisted them in years.

"Morgan, you're absolute *rubbish* at maths!" James raged on, his body vibrating with wrath, "and no one says anything about it. And *you* can't spell a damned thing." This he directed at Kenneth. "You leave Arthur alone. He hasn't done anything to anyone, and we're all sick of listening to you talk about him that way."

"Don't tell me to shut up, you little fairy." Morgan roared and lifted his fist.

James braced himself for the blow, but it never came. A long, low wail rose from the trees in the direction of the village nearby, alien, mechanical, haunting. Arthur's flesh trembled at the sound. It was the air raid siren.

They stood frozen, their heads snapped in the direction of the undulating wail. After a few moments, Miss Pelles shot out of the side door and raced over to the dead fountain, around which the children had been playing or lounging about during their recreation time. "Everyone, inside immediately!" she shouted, gathering girls by their elbows and shoving them towards the mansion. "Head to the kitchen!"

Some of the girls leaked instant tears as Miss Pelles herded the students back inside through their classroom, the boys' dorm, down a hall, and into the dim kitchen, where the lingering smell of last night's stew assaulted their nostrils, bitter and greasy. Mrs. Balin was there with Miss Ivaine and Mrs. Galhad, propping open the door to the cellar. They filed down the slippery, ancient stone stairs and huddled down beneath shelves containing jams, jellies, and pickled vegetables. The adults knelt on the other side, their backs to a vast rack of dusty wine bottles.

They had only settled when the dull thuds began, moving ever closer. The girls clung to each other, and many of the boys drew their knees to their chests; they hid the fear on their faces. Miss Pelles crossed the narrow space between the adults and the students and wormed between two of the more hysterical ones, putting her arms around them. "Now now, don't go to pieces." She forced her words through a plastic smile. "Look, we're in the middle of the country, there's no way they'd waste bombs destroying an old country estate, now would they? No, they're attacking the towns nearby I suspect. We should be perfectly safe.

The children responded to her soothing tone, inhaling deeply to contain their sobs.

"Now, Mrs. Balin," Miss Pelles whispered in an effort to further lighten the mood, "what do you say we open one of those wine bottles and have a nip, eh?"

Mrs. Balin pretended she hadn't heard any of what Miss Pelles had said. "Pray, children," she suggested, and knitted her own fingers together.

As the planes came closer, Arthur could hear the whistle of the bombs before the impact. The jars and bottles rattled on the shelves with each hit. Sweat gathered at his hairline and under his arms, and his fingers ached as he clutched the King Arthur books closer to his chest.

He heard a small, watery sigh from his side. There sat James, his knees drawn up, hands clasped around his ribcage. His eyes misted, but his mouth was set in a firm, grim line. His chin wavered as his fears threatened to unhorse him. Still, he kept his face up, illuminated in the light of the small lantern the cook held, his eyes hard and determined.

The whistles and thunderous booms came ever closer. They could make out the whine of the plane engines, undulating as they flew closer and then away again. Arthur looked his death in the maw, and then fixed his eyes on James, who forced himself to look at nothing, to show no fear. The girls whimpered, Miss Pelles tried to joke, and the bombs fell.

A strange calm crept over Arthur, and desires came to him in soft waves. He wanted to *hold* James. He wanted to cover his small body with his broad one in case any jams came flying off the shelves, in case there was a fire. He wanted to weave their fingers together. He wanted to kiss his cheeks to make the tears go away.

There was a brief respite now, but James knew there would be another wave coming. There were more thuds in the distance. He crawled over to Miss Ivaine, who kissed the cross on a chain around her birdlike neck. "Miss, where's the Baroness?" he demanded with whispery urgency. "Shouldn't she be here, where it's safe?"

"She's upstairs with Mr. Marlin, love," the maid replied, putting a thin hand on his shoulder. "She's far too old to climb down those stairs, and carrying her would give her too much pain."

"But if a bomb hits—" James turned, and locked his frantic green eyes with Arthur's. They shared a silent understanding, green to green.

Before Arthur was aware that he had moved, he found himself on his feet. He turned and thundered up the cellar stairs, pushed the door aside and burst into the kitchen. He ran, rounded corners, thumped up staircases, and flung open the door to Lady Barlow's bedchamber.

She sat by the window, as she always did, this time wrapped in a soft white blanket that billowed around her. Mr. Marlin sat close by, reading to her from Beowulf.

"My lady, it's not safe up here!" Arthur cried without introduction. "We must go downstairs—the bombing..."

"Arthur," Mr. Marlin began.

The Baroness held up her hand, and he silenced himself. "My sweet boy," she said, turning in her chair as he knelt at her side. "I shall never come down from this room again. I'm very old, you see."

"But the house could fall down on top of you." Arthur cried.

"Death comes for us all at one time or another, dear," she replied, stroking his hot cheek with the back of her gnarled finger. "But you should return to your classmates."

"No. I'm staying. I can protect you. We can protect you," Arthur said, indicating himself and Mr. Marlin. "I won't let anything happen to you, my lady."

The Baroness turned to Mr. Marlin, a slow smile crept through the lines on her face. "It's time, Mr. Marlin," she said. "He is ready." Mr. Marlin nodded, and rose from his chair, crossing the room to a tall object draped in white near the armoire that Arthur hadn't seen when he'd rushed in. Mr. Marlin took hold of the sheet and whipped it away just as a particularly loud impact echoed over the countryside from the German bombing run.

It was a suit of armor, with a chest-plate, greaves, gauntlets, and a helmet with a visor. The metal was pewter-colored, inlaid with intricate curling vine-like patterns of gold. It was so brightly polished that Arthur could see his face in the curves. The whistling, and the growl of the nearing propellers continued, but it became an unimportant, muffled drone in his ears. The armor was mythical. It was beautiful.

"This belonged to my ancestors, generations back," Lady Barlow said. "I've had Mr. Marlin pull it down from storage."

"Stand here, son," Mr. Marlin suggested. Arthur obeyed; his eyes never left the metal that called his name. Mr. Marlin removed the chest and back plate from the dress dummy and slid the piece over Arthur's head. He buckled it into place with leather straps, and then affixed the gauntlets to his arms over his school jacket. Next came the greaves, and finally the helmet. Mr. Marlin guided him over to the vanity mirror so Arthur could see himself.

Yes, he was a schoolboy with armor strapped over his knickerbockers and jacket, which might have looked ridiculous if his figure wasn't so grand and imposing. His green eyes glittered from the helmet's opening for a few moments before he clanked the visor down, drawing himself to his full height.

"If you are to claim your destiny, Arthur Pendragon, you must unlock your voice," the Baroness told him from her chair by the window. "This fight cannot be won without words. You are a symbol. You must become the Once and Future King."

"I will." Arthur placed a metal fist in the palm of his other hand.

"Then it is time." The Baroness reached behind the curtain, and with every fiber of strength in her bony limbs, she lifted a longsword in a beaten leather sheath. This she held out to him on two hands.

"Behold," she said, "the sword that rose from the bosom of the lake." She laughed, a silent hag's chuckle. "Well, from the bosom of the attic, perhaps. This sword was forged in Venice in the 1600s, which makes it very special indeed, though not quite as magical as Excalibur. Still, I think, it will suffice."

The sword had a sloping, curved hilt, and a wide pommel, intricately carved with a leaf and vine motif that matched the armor. Arthur drew the blade out from the ruined sheath just enough to see how the metal glistened.

"It hasn't been sharpened in 100 years," she said, "but Mr. Marlin was kind enough to make it glow."

"Thank you, my lady." Arthur put his hand over his heart.

"Listen," said Mr. Marlin. They both paused and cocked their heads just so.

"I don't hear anything," Arthur said.

"Exactly," Mr. Marlin smiled. "It seems the ruckus has died down."

"I must admit I am a little disappointed," the Baroness remarked with a wry smile. "Ascending to Valhalla on a cloud of bomb-dust would have proved quite entertaining."

That night, Arthur slept, long and deep with the armor wrapped in a blanket under his cot. The flickering images behind his eyes were of swords and stallions and green men and ghosts, noble damsels, beautiful knights and wicked villains, and the glowing cup of Christ.

***

As he slumbered, so did James at his side, until James awoke to gentle hands on his arm. He stirred and turned on his back. He squinted in the dark. Mr. Marlin's face loomed above him with a finger over his lips. He beckoned, and James pushed the scratchy blankets aside. They tiptoed through the side door and into the dim kitchen. A single candle burned on the stove and shadows undulated in the corners.

"My lady needs something from you," Mr. Marlin said. "It may seem strange, but I ask you to humor her."

"Of course," James said. "Anything."

Mr. Marlin handed him a bundle of clothing, smelling strongly of bitter mothballs. James put the costume on over his pajamas, and Mr. Marlin helped him adjust the buttons, suspenders, and collar. Last came the old-fashioned cravat and aged cummerbund. They climbed the stairs in silence and stole down the corridors like thieves. James caught his reflection in a passing gilded mirror. He looked like a boy from a Charles Dickens novel, but a rich one, not Oliver Twist. And in a moment, he understood what he was to do.

Nim lay in her bed, eyes closed, her hands clasped over the heavy coverlet that dwarfed her gnarled body.

Mr. Marlin's guiding hands paused him for a moment near the vanity, where he took up a comb and parted James' auburn hair down the middle, combing it to either side. He patted the boy's shoulders and nodded.

James crept to Nim's side, and took her withered hand. She opened her eyes, and her expression melted into sheer joy, her dry lips crawled back from her teeth. "Matthew!" she whispered. "Sweet boy. Come to Mummy, darling."

Mr. Marlin helped her sit, and she wrapped her skeletal arms around James and kissed his forehead and his hair over and over.

"I'm sorry, darling, I'm so sorry," she said. "I should have protected you. I love you. We shall be together again soon."

"I love you too, Mother," James promised.

"I know who you are," she said after a time, releasing him and patting his hands. "Don't think me senile. But the illusion was enough. Thank you, James."

Chapter 14

The last week had been cold and damp, but summer struggled back for one last gasp, flooding the countryside with platinum light, every maple a bonfire. The schoolchildren wiggled in their seats, anxious for recreation time as Mrs. Balin droned on and on about maths. Many of the students had nearly nodded off when Mrs. Balin slapped her ruler down on Morgan's desk. "Mr. Dredde," she snapped, "perhaps you'd like to share what is so funny with everyone in the class?"

He sobered quickly. "No ma'am."

"Stand up, boy, and solve the equation on the board," she ordered.

Morgan dragged his steps to the blackboard like a man ascending the gallows. After a few half hearted squiggles, he came up with the number 39.

"Not even close," Mrs. Balin said, a frosty coating on her voice. "As you see, you need to be paying attention during maths to improve your skills, which are woefully inadequate, as we have all just witnessed." She paused, looking out over the room. "James. Come here and show Morgan how to do this properly."

"Yes ma'am." James took up the chalk and solved it in less than a minute, careful to show his work.

"Very good," Mrs. Balin complimented, clasping her hands over her skirts. "Morgan, you've got a thing or two to learn about maths from Mr. Wilde."

James passed Morgan on the way back to his seat, and shriveled as the hateful daggers that sprang from his rival's cold yellow eyes. A pit opened in his stomach.

His dread matured a few minutes later when Mrs. Balin let them outdoors for recreation time. Most of the students flung their jackets aside and raced out into the glorious weather, but James descended the back stairs with reluctant wariness.

Sure enough, they waited for him.

"Oy, queerie!" Morgan thundered, and sprung out from behind the hedge with Kenneth and Tommy. "Think you're so brilliant, do you?"

James tried to run, but Tommy darted forward and caught his wrist, yanking him back. Kenneth savagely kicked him in the knee and pushed him up against a tree. Morgan slammed him in the gut with a clenched fist.

"If any of you tattle, you'll be next." Morgan hollered at two girls as they snuck up the stairs to alert the adults of an attack twice as brutal as usual. They veered off and knelt next to the hedge.

Morgan pried up a sizable rock from the dirt. "Open your mouth," he snarled. "I'm going to smash out your bloody teeth!"

A whimper of fear escaped James' lips, though he had vowed not to give them the pleasure. Then, the side door to the mansion opened, and a knight came out into the sun.

James blinked rapidly and shook his head in disbelief. The metal-clad man clanked down the steps and charged for Morgan. The sword on his belt slapped against his hip. The sound of the armor alerted the bully, and he turned, tripped in surprise, but managed to keep his footing.

A hush fell over the crowd of schoolchildren. Making no sound, the classmates crept up to watch a legend unfold.

The knight drew breath into his lungs. "Let him go," he ordered, his baritone rumbling through the metal visor.

"It... it's Arthur!" one of the girls called, recognizing a red patch sewn over the elbow of his jacket. "It's Arthur in there."

"But... his voice," whispered another.

Morgan gaped for a moment, and then dragged back the shreds of his dignity. A cruel, blistering laugh spilled from his lips. "What the hell do you think you're doing dressed like that? Playing pretend like a little toddler?"

"Let him *go*," Arthur commanded, stepping closer. "I'll not warn you again."

"Shut up, you stupid git." Morgan heaved the rock in his hand at Arthur with all his might. It clanged harmlessly off of his chest plate.

"Yield," came the cool voice from beneath the visor. "Now."

Kenneth and Tommy shared a hurried glance, and then dropped James, who sank to his knees. Together, they rushed toward Arthur, fists raised.

Arthur let the blows fall. They could not hurt him. They tried to push him over, to rip the armor from his body, but he was as immobile as a mighty oak. Raising one hand, he clanged his gauntlet into Tommy's nose, bloodying it, and tripped Kenneth into the dirt. They slunk away without another word, abandoning their leader.

The knight turned to Morgan, and drew the sword at his side. It caught the afternoon sunlight, sending piercing beams into the eyes of his foe. Morgan squinted, and held up a hand, and then fell back onto the ground. He scrambled through the dirt to get away.

Arthur dropped the tip of the blade over Morgan's throat and let it hover there as a threat. Morgan froze, panting like a terrified rabbit.

"You will never hurt James again. Ever," Arthur said. "If you put a hand on him, you'll answer to me." He turned to the rest of the class. "That goes for all of you." He nudged Morgan with his shoe. "Now run away, coward."

Morgan rolled and got to his feet. With one last wrathful glance, he sprinted off into the old orchard.

Arthur nodded, and turned back to James, who stood by the tree. He clanked a few steps closer, and knelt, driving the end of the sword into the dirt so that it stood on its own accord.

James took a few tentative steps forward, reached out, and lifted the helmet from Arthur's head, spilling his black curls everywhere.

He fell to his knees, tucked the helmet under his arm, and kissed Arthur's forehead, and then, after a deep breath, his lips.

They grinned at one another and stood up. Arthur towered over his slight-framed friend. "Wherever did you get all of this?" James asked, running his hand over one of the gauntlets.

"The Baroness, Lady Barlow," Arthur said.

"Nim!" James cried. "I should have known. Come, we must go tell her what's happened." He took Arthur by his metal-clad hand, and they raced toward the mansion. As they clattered through the door into the classroom, Arthur swept James to the side just in time to miss Mrs. Balin, who stood there, arms laden with books, a look of stupid wonderment smashed across her pinched face.

"What in God's name?" She started. Then, as they neared the doors to the marble hall, "Get back here!"

They flashed past Miss Pelles near the stairs. "Is that a sword?" she squeaked. "Oh my."

Miss Ivaine met them in the hallway outside of the Baroness's bedchamber door. Her cheeks were wet, but in their haste, the boys did not notice as she ran in the opposite direction, back toward the stairwell.

"Nim!" James cried as they burst through the door. "Nim, did you see it? Arthur's become a warrior, and his voice! He showed those cowardly blighters."

Nim sat in her chair by the window, the curtains parted, looking down on the very tree where Arthur had drawn Excalibur. Her hands were clasped in her lap, and she leaned back on the cushions. Her head lolled to the side facing the sunlight.

"My lady?" Arthur tried. "My lady, did you see..."

Nim's eyes were closed, and her tired mouth affixed in a gentle smile. "Nim. Nim?"

James knelt at her side and patted her hand, and then lifted it to the arm of the chair; he squeezed her fingers. He reached out and stroked her cheek with his knuckle. "Wake up, Nim. Don't tell me you've napped through..."

The door opened behind them, and in came Mr. Marlin with Miss Ivaine at his side, sniffling into a handkerchief. Mr. Marlin carried a black case at his side—an army medic's kit. He set it on the bed and opened it to remove a stethoscope.

It was a dream, James thought. None of this was real. Perhaps Nim played a prank, pretended not to hear them.

"Let me help you," Miss Ivaine whispered as Mr. Marlin put the stethoscope in his ears. Her fast fingers unbuckled Arthur from his armor, which she returned to the dress dummy that stood watch over the vanity and the jewelry box.

Mr. Marlin knelt in front of Nim and placed the end of the stethoscope on her chest, listening. He tried several places on her emaciated body, drawing aside her soft white blanket to reveal her dressing gown. The brooch sparkled in the sunlight, dancing pin-pricks of shimmer over Mr. Marlin's face.

James watched, immobilized, as Mr. Marlin removed the stethoscope from his ears and placed it around his neck. He picked up Nim's other hand, and wrapped his fingers around her wrists, and then touched her neck in several places.

He stood, and put the stethoscope back in the bag, and shut it with a final, fatal snap.

"No," James said. Hot bile singed the back of his throat and molten tears erupted.

"Yes, James." Mr. Marlin clasped his hands behind his back and stared out the window at the children playing below.

James put his face on Nim's hand and wept. Arthur knelt and wrapped his strong arms around him and pressed his face against James' shoulder. After a time, Mr. Marlin brushed them gently aside and lifted Nim like she was no more than a bundle of sticks, setting her on the bed with tender care. Miss Ivaine was there with a white sheet, and they shrouded her.

Arthur held James while he cried, smoothed his hair, his touch gentle despite his powerful hands. The adults melted away.

Time passed. The light in the window changed. James raised his head and accepted the handkerchief from Arthur's back pocket. "Sorry, it's not so clean," he said.

"That's all right." James dabbed his nose and face. All of his tears had come out. All of them. For Nim, for the war, for his absent father, for his mother's disappointment, for Morgan's tortures, everything. He was empty. A calm stole over him, and his heart was comfortably languid.

Arthur bent down and kissed his cheek. "Are you going to be all right?" he rumbled.

James considered a moment before taking his knight's hand. "Yes," he said.

***

When James awakened Arthur a few nights later, he groaned and tossed his broad forearm up over his face.

"Ssh!" James warned. "You'll wake the others."

Arthur pulled on his jacket and trousers over his pajamas, as James had done, and together, they tiptoed into the delicious smell of the kitchen,

Mr. Marlin was at the door to greet them. "Welcome, Sir Arthur. Welcome, fair James. Your feast awaits."

"Have I got a treat for you boys," Mrs. Galhad grinned, stepping away from the stove to reveal the prize. "Wild turkey, shot just yesterday by Mr. Marlin!"

James could not help but let a lusty, "Ooh," slip from his lips. There were scones and jam, and all the turkey and potatoes they could eat, saved up from the rations and gifts sent for the Baroness by friends and family. There was even a small box of chocolates.

Mrs. Galhad, Mr. Marlin, Miss Ivaine, and the boys sat at the round servant's table and ate with relish. There was wine, and lively conversation.

"Has there been any more trouble with those rascals, James?" Mr. Marlin asked around a forkful of turkey.

"None," James grinned, wiping his lips. "They're terrified of Arthur now. Even without the sword and armor."

The chocolates were consumed with great relish. The adults laughed as the boys tried to lick the tiny crumbs from the inside of the box with eager tongues.

Mrs. Galhad and Miss Ivaine cleared the table and cleaned the kitchen. James and Arthur were warm and sleepy; they held hands under the table. Mr. Marlin appeared from upstairs with a box-like object covered in a cloth. He set this in front of the boys, and lay a cream-colored envelope atop it. Their names were printed on the outside.

"Go ahead," he prompted.

Arthur looked at James, who plucked up the envelope and opened it. Inside was a small piece of cream stationery. The writing was jagged, trembling, and barely legible. "For... when... I've gone to Avalon," James read.

Mr. Marlin whipped the cloth away, revealing Nim's mother-of-pearl and opal-studded jewelry box. James gasped, and gently slid open the first drawer. Arthur lifted the insect pin and held it to the light. It was all there, all but her wedding ring, which would rest on her finger until Judgement Day.

"She's left this..." James gulped. He glanced up at Mr. Marlin.

"To you, James," Mr. Marlin said. "And the antique armor and sword shall go to Arthur, along with a modest sum of money."

Miss Ivaine dabbed her eye with the corner of her apron. "She'd have left you boys the whole house if her family would have allowed it," she revealed. "Oh, you have no idea what joy you brought her in these last days, loves."

"Ah, I almost forgot. There is one more thing." Mr. Marlin reached into his coat pocket and withdrew a small leather-bound book. "This is a first edition," he said, "signed by Lord Tennyson himself."

The gilded letters on the cover read *Idylls of the King*.

"I shall lock everything up safely for you until you are able to return home," Mr. Marlin promised. "My lady has a lawyer in London who will contact your families upon your return to see about what you'd like to do with the pieces, whether to keep or sell, whatever serves you best."

"I'll never sell Excalibur," Arthur vowed.

Mr. Marlin smiled, a tired, knowing curve. "We shall see what the war brings," he said.

James hugged each of the adults in turn, as did Arthur. They yawned and stumbled with exhaustion as they were sent back to bed. In the dark, Arthur lifted his cot and moved it a few paces to the left. Now, in the night, should thoughts of his father trouble him, James' hand was well within reach.

They joined fingers in the midnight country quiet, broken only by the occasional snore as the other boys dreamed.

"I miss Nim."

"So do I," said Arthur.

A few moments of quiet. Then, "I love you, Arthur," James whispered.

Arthur said, his mighty voice now soft, "The old order changeth, yielding place to new, and God fulfills himself in many ways, lest one good custom should corrupt the world. Comfort thyself."

"Goodnight."

Chapter 15

Lance and James paused and listened at the room door a moment before Lance eased down the handle so they could slip inside. They shared a silent chuckle — it was funny, James supposed, trading one symphony of snores for another. Only this time, Arthur and Mrs. Wylit were able to make a layered harmony; his deep sawing breaths perfectly accompanied her nasal wheeze. Lance went first, and they tiptoed through the minefield of baggage to step carefully over Mrs. Wylit's skewed legs and her rough-bottomed bare feet. Lance settled down on his cushions on the floor, and James gingerly lowered himself onto his side of the bed. He moved to slide in next to Arthur when Lance caught his arm. Silently, he beckoned James with his hand, and patted the cushion on the floor next to him. James slid off the bed again and sat with his back against it. Lance leaned close, and James was again perfumed with his scent.

"I understand now." Lance's breath stirred the little curls next to James' ear in gentle puffs.

"What do you understand?"

"I know why Granddad told me about you and Arthur, and what happened at Willowind House." Lance inched nearer, and pressed his shoulder into James'. His closeness was suddenly overwhelming — James felt the same buzzing paralysis as when he'd stuck his finger onto the worn place on a lamp cord as a child. "I'd always thought it was because the whole thing was like a legend, a grand adventure. You know, a good old war story. I never understood why he told me about... well, why he didn't change it. Why he told me the truth, that Arthur was a boy and you were a boy. In his retelling, he could have changed one of you to a girl easily."

"Why?" James asked.

They both froze for a long moment as Arthur muttered something in his sleep and rolled over with a little moan.

When his rhythmic snores resumed, Lance took a breath. His Adam's apple bobbed up and down in the dim light of the street lamps outside. At last he turned, and put his hand over James', which rested on his knee. "He told me all of it because he knew. He knew that I'm like you. I'm like you and Arthur."

"Really?" James gasped, then put his free hand over his mouth. After a moment, he removed it and whispered, "You are?"

"I don't know how he knew. Nobody knows about me. No one ever threw rocks at me or called me a poof. I really didn't know myself until... well, until now. I always thought I was too busy for girls, that they were boring, that I had too much else to do, but... the truth is I never really fancied them at all." He pressed his face into the crook of his elbow for a moment, subduing laughter that threatened to break free. "I've never said it out loud before. But it's true. And somehow Granddad knew."

"He needed you to know that there were others like you in the world." Tears crept into James' eyes, and he dabbed them with the sleeve of his pajamas. If only Lance had chosen to make this confession while they were outside the room and didn't have to keep quiet. Lance looked as though he were about to burst, his cheeks flushed and his brow damp. "He needed you to see that it's possible to find someone to love."

Lance threw his arm around James' shoulders and pressed him close. "I want to shout it in the streets."

James hushed him gently. Mrs. Wylit snorted in her sleep, but did not move.

"I didn't know it would feel this... wonderful. To really know myself, to know who I am."

"Lance, I'm dreadfully happy for you," James said, "but as for yelling it in the streets... listen, take it from me. You do have to be careful, mate. Please be careful. Because they can do to us what they did to Alan Turing. We can go to jail, have our names blackened, all of it. A gang of those Teddy Boys could murder us in cold blood and nobody would care. Do you understand?"

"It's awful."

James hushed him again, but Lance went on. "Well, it is. There's nothing wrong with us. We were just born this way, weren't we? There shouldn't be any laws against love."

James patted his knee sagely. "It's not a fair world, Lance. More often than not, it's a cruel one. I... I would be devastated if anything happened to you. I know Arthur would, too," he added quickly. "So let's all agree to watch out for one another."

"Of course. I promise." Lance pulled away and grinned at him. "I'll never get to sleep," he muttered.

"Well, we have to try." James took Lance's hand again. "I *am* honored."

Lance cocked his head, raising a quizzical eyebrow.

"I'm honored to be the one you told first. That I was here when you realized it."

Lance smiled, and his dimples emerged to greet the rest of his face. "My pleasure, mate."

The next day, as they walked to the bus station, Lance distracted Mrs. Wylit with a few sensational headlines in the newspaper. That gave James a quick chance to tell Arthur in hushed whispers about the night before. Arthur's broad face lit up and his eyes sparkled at the news about Lance's realization. "Never thought we'd have a friend who was like us." Arthur watched Lance dance the newspaper in front of Mrs. Wylit, pointing to photos of American movie stars. "Suppose that's why he's so..."

"Understanding," James finished for him.

"What were you doing up having a chinwag so late?" Arthur asked as they waited for the light to cross a busy intersection.

"I saw him again." James told Arthur about the man under the streetlamp. "And what's this I hear about you chasing a man in a long coat in the village? And you never told me about it?"

"Sorry, luv." Arthur clammed up as a man in a business suit fell into step next to them. He and James unconsciously moved apart as they crossed the street to catch up with Lance and Mrs. Wylit. "Mrs. Wylit was being such a pain. And then we were off on the train, and..."

"You forgot?" James raised a sardonic eyebrow as they neared the station. Lance and Mrs. Wylit tasked themselves with finding the correct bus stand as Arthur and James trailed behind and bickered under their breath. "Really, Arthur?'

"Couldn't see him properly." Arthur hefted his suitcase. "I'm not sure it was him. It could have been anyone."

James set down his suitcase on the curb and crossed his arms.

"Don't be cross," Arthur whispered as travellers walked past them, unaware of the lovers' spat that unfolded inches away. "There's been a lot going on. You said you weren't sure yourself if it was anything at all."

"I would have liked to have been told is all." The flushed deepened under James' freckles. "And I know what I saw last night. I saw that same man in that same coat lingering around our neighborhood back in London. For pity's sake, he's probably here right now watching us."

"Why?" Arthur demanded out of the corner of his mouth. A young woman strolled past with a fine summer hat pinned over her carefully curled hair. She turned and gave him an inviting smile. He smiled and winked back before seamlessly returning to his quarrel with James. All part of the charade. "Why would someone be following us?"

"What if it's the police? On some kind of... fairy witch hunt? It's far from impossible, Arthur, and you know it."

"I'm sorry. I really am. But I think... well, you're a writer. You have a wonderful imagination."

James bristled at him a moment, and then picked up his suitcase and joined Lance and Mrs. Wylit on a bench to wait for the bus.

They drove through gentle hills dotted with sheep, toward a darkening sky that eventually opened up in a downpour. After a half-hour ride, the rain had decreased in ferocity but was still intent on soaking Welby through and through. They exited the conveyance and opened their umbrellas. Arthur, being taller, held his umbrella up for James, who, if he wanted to stay dry, was forced to walk shoulder-to-shoulder with him. Simply touching Arthur's arm leached away James' previous frustration, and he offered an "I'm sorry" smile that Arthur returned.

They trudged along the wet street, past charming cottages and low stone walls, the lush green lawns and brilliant flowers all glistening with rain. The address in Mr. Marlin's book led them to a small white house up the road from St. Bartholomew's church and graveyard.

Lance glanced at Arthur, who in turn nodded to James. James squared his shoulders and trotted up the small stone stairs to the door to knock. Within a few moments, a round, kindly-looking man with graying sandy hair answered. "Yes?" His eyes, small and brown, darted behind his perfectly circular wire-rimmed glasses from face to face.

"Good morning—" James began. As he did, a loud whistle trumpeted from within the house. It was a teakettle.

"I'll get it," called a voice, barely audible over Mrs. Wylit, who had dropped her bag and pressed her hands over her ears with a piteous moan.

"Make it stop," Vi begged as her face went crimson and her legs buckled. Lance dropped to his knees on the wet flagstones and took her around the waist. He hoisted her to her feet as the kettle in the house went silent.

"It's over, Mrs. Wylit." Lance attempted to pull her hands away from her ears. She resisted him a few moments, and then slowly moved her palms away.

"Christ," she swore, and shrugged Lance away to pick up her bag and dig for her flask.

"What's going on? What's the matter?" A tall, thin man in dark clothes and a priest's collar came to the door and stood behind the bloke with glasses.

"I haven't the foggiest."

"I'm so sorry." James stepped back from the door. "It's that... erm, she doesn't... she can't listen to a kettle whistle."

"She looks about to faint." The priest drew the sandy-haired man back by the shoulders and held the door open for them. "Please, bring her inside."

"Father Joseph—"

The priest ignored him and ushered James and the rest through the door, and then stepped out to help Mrs. Wylit up the stairs. Inside was a small, quaint sitting room upholstered entirely in faded floral prints, none of which matched one another. The priest helped Mrs. Wylit onto a couch and sat beside her. She fanned herself with her hand a few moments. "Don't mind me," she mumbled, "I'm just a little broken is all."

"I'm sorry your friend is poorly," the sandy-haired man said to the trio that lingered near the door. He removed his glasses and polished them on his shirtsleeve. "But I'm afraid I don't want whatever it is your selling. I hate to hurry you along, but it's not a good time — my aunt is ill."

Arthur looked pointedly at James, who said, "Your aunt wouldn't happen to be Mrs. Louise Galhad, would she?"

"Why yes, she is. Do you know her?"

"We do," Arthur said. "She was with us at Willowind House during Operation Pied Piper back in '42."

"Remarkable," the man exclaimed. "Father Joseph, did you hear that? These blokes were with that class of children that evacuated to Willowind House. That was back when Auntie used to cook for Lady Barlow!" He paused a moment. "And you are..." He raised a bushy eyebrow in Mrs. Wylit's direction.

"She's our..." Arthur looked at James and shrugged.

"Landlady." James wasn't much for the Bible, but it seemed wrong to lie to a priest.

"Father." Mrs. Wylit sagged against the young priest's shoulder. "Walk me over to the church. I want to give confession."

Father Joseph's boyish face glowed with sudden righteousness. "Of course, madam, of course. I can tell that you have burdens to unload."

"So many burdens." As Mrs. Wylit wobbled to her feet, she tossed a little wink in James' direction. Father Joseph led her out of the house, and held her under his umbrella. They disappeared down the lane before Lance shut the door behind them.

"Your aunt must be very ill," James said, "if the priest is here."

The man snorted. "Oh, it's nothing like that — just a cold. Father Joseph wanders over here because he knows I have butter biscuits from Sweden. Speaking of which, we were about to have a little nibble. Let me — please, sit, and I'll get the tray. Auntie is napping, but I can wake her in a bit."

"Thank you." They sank into the worn couches and chairs. James shifted uncomfortably as an errant spring poked into his arse.

"I'm called Milo, by the way," the man said as he returned with the tray.

"Pleased to meet you. I'm James Wilde. This is Arthur Pensinger and Lance Benwick."

"I'm sure Auntie will be thrilled to see you all grown up. Please, help yourselves. I'll go wake her." Milo disappeared up the narrow staircase, his pudgy hand gripping the white painted banister to keep his balance.

The Swedish butter biscuits were everything they could have hoped for. And so was Mrs. Galhad. A little rounder, her hair now snow-white, but she was still kind and jolly; her small dark eyes glimmered with the same good humor James and Arthur had known all those years before. With Milo's help, she descended the stairs wrapped in a cavernous flowered dressing gown, her feet stuffed into pink slippers.

"James and Arthur! My Lord, I never thought you'd come for a visit." She lurched into Arthur's arms, and then squished James against her motherly frame. "And I'm sorry dear, I don't remember your name — were you in James and Arthur's class as well?"

"No, ma'am. I'm Lance Benwick. Mr. Marlin's grandson."

"Harold's grandson? Oh, come here." She squashed him as well before practically falling into what was clearly her favorite armchair. It had an imprint of her body that she fit into like a key. "Oh, my dear, I'm so sorry I couldn't make it to your grandfather's funeral. I've been sick with this terrible cold for weeks now, and my doctor says I'm not to travel. I'm so terribly sorry to hear of his passing."

"Thank you." Lance leaned closer so she could take his hand in hers to pat it like it was a soft kitten. "I miss him very much."

"Mr. Marlin was butler in Lady Barlow's house, wasn't he?" Milo stirred milk into his tea.

"Yes indeed. Oh, he was a wonderful soul." She sighed and clucked. Milo handed her a cuppa, which she accepted and drank as they talked and dipped their biscuits. "And isn't it lovely that the three of you are friends." Her eyes flitted from James' face to Arthur's, and then to Lance's. Her unspoken question was obvious enough to

James — were he and Arthur still together? Yet, he couldn't answer — not with Milo, an unknown, in the room.

"Mrs. Galhad," said Lance, "I must admit we're here on a bit of an errand. Right before my granddad passed away, he said something about Lady Barlow's son, Matthew."

As soon as the 'thew' left his lips, Mrs. Galhad's pink cheeks washed white. She dropped her biscuit onto the front of her dressing gown.

"He said..." Lance glanced at James, who nodded. "He said that Matthew is still alive. And he asked me to find him. I took it as his dying wish."

"Who's Matthew?" Milo asked through the butter biscuit in his mouth.

"Milo, dear, will you go to the shops and get me another bottle of cough medicine? Mine's nearly gone." Mrs. Galhad gave a cough for effect that spread crumbs over her hand.

"I can go later... oh. Er — yes." Milo read the expectant faces in the room, and to his credit, dutifully put on his wellies and mac, and left the house.

"So." Mrs. Galhad sighed and sipped her tea. "So he told you."

"Yes." Lance leaned forward to put his elbows on his knees. "But that was all he said. Only that he was alive and he wanted us to find him. We found your address in his things, and my mates here thought that since you were at the house when Matthew lived there, you might know what happened."

She pressed her lips together a moment before speaking. "Boys, I want you to think very hard about this for a moment before I go on. First, if I tell you, you must promise to never tell another soul. I don't know if Mr. Marlin broke the law, but let me say that there were consequences for what was done. Second... sometimes it's best to let the dead stay dead, if you understand me. Matthew Barlow drowned himself in the river when he was fifteen. That can easily be the end of the story."

"Then why did my granddad want us to find out the truth?" Lance fired back with sudden impatience.

"That I don't know." Mrs. Galhad slowly shook her white head. The lines on the sides of her mouth deepened with her frown. "He made me promise to take the secret to my grave."

"Please," James begged, and leaned forward like Lance was. "Please, Mrs. Galhad. Tell us what you know."

She bit her lip and let loose another sigh. "All right. But remember — I never told you this. And what I'm going to tell you *never happened*."

The trio nodded.

"It was late one night. Lord and Lady Barlow had guests over, and I was up late with the kitchen maids putting things away and scrubbing down the pots. I sent the maids off to bed, but decided to stay up and... well, to sneak a bit of dessert. I was sort of, erm, hiding in the dark I suppose you'd say, having a bit of cake, and who comes into the kitchen but Mr. Marlin and Matthew. I was over in the corner on a stool near the stove, and they had nothing but a candle with them. Matthew held the candle while Mr. Marlin went into the pantry and filled a bag with things — sardines and biscuits and the like. I was silent, and they didn't notice me over in the corner.

"Matthew added the food to the rucksack on his back, and Mr. Marlin gave him instructions. He told Matthew to go to the river to leave tracks to follow, and then to put stones in his jacket pockets and toss it in the water. Then, Matthew was to follow a sheep trail through the hills to an old churchyard. There he said Mr. Blanchard would meet him. Matthew was crying, but he seemed... resolute. He and Mr. Marlin embraced, and that's when he noticed me, sitting there with a damn cake fork in my mouth.

"Harold said that I must keep quiet and do nothing until he returned. His eyes... well, you know, you've got the same eyes, lad." She motioned to Lance. "The way his eyes looked, I felt I had to listen. And comply. I knew Harold was a good man, and it seemed to me like Matthew was in some kind of trouble. About an hour later, Mr. Marlin returned through the kitchen door, and there I was, just as he left me, on the stool by the stove. He swore me to secrecy, said I was never to tell. He didn't say what would happen if I did — and I didn't ask. I respected him too much. I suppose he could have had me sacked. Doesn't matter — he asked me to keep the secret and I did.

"Well, the next morning the house was in an uproar. Lady Barlow found Matthew's suicide note under her bedchamber door. A footman found Matthew's jacket in the river. The authorities searched, but they never recovered his body. Of course they didn't." She gave a soft chuckle. "Matthew was alive. But he was gone. And Mr. Marlin had helped him fake his own death."

Mrs. Galhad shook her head. "I never understood why they did it. Of course, we all knew that Matthew and his father were at odds — but so many sons and fathers are the same way. Matthew was fifteen, hot headed, stubborn... I had no idea he was so miserable. Mr. Marlin must have thought it best, even though it nearly destroyed Lady Barlow. I think that's why he stayed with her to the very end, took such good care of her. He knew what he'd helped Matthew do to her. Why though, for God's sake, I can't imagine."

They sat in silence for several uncomfortable beats. "Mrs. Galhad." James broke the country quiet. "I think I know why Matthew felt he had to do what he did. He was... like Arthur and I. If you remember."

"I do. I know what the church says, but the two of you were..." she smiled, for the first time since she'd begun her tale, "perfect," she finished.

"We also found some papers in Mr. Marlin's things." Arthur put his arm around James now that he was free to do so. "They were drafts of Matthew's suicide note. It was clear. I think Mr. Marlin saved him."

"Saved him?" Lance sat up straighter and gave Arthur a quizzical look.

"I think," Arthur said as he squeezed James closer for a moment, "I think that if Mr. Marlin hadn't helped him fake his death, he really would have killed himself. Mr. Marlin gave him another way out."

Mrs. Galhad sat back in her chair with a deep sigh. "I understand now. Of course Harold wouldn't have wanted Lady Barlow to suffer more than she had to. If Matthew was set on ending his life, at least Mr. Marlin could spare her the pain of, say, finding his body, or seeing him dead. Matthew would simply disappear, and Mr. Marlin would be there to help his mother pick up the pieces." Mrs. Galhad shook her head sorrowfully, and ate another biscuit. "Well. " She dotted her lips with a small napkin. "Let's say you chaps find him alive somewhere. What then?"

James looked at Arthur, and then Lance. They turned back to Mrs. Galhad. "We don't know," James said.

Chapter 16

In a call box outside Nottingham Station, Arthur rang his mother, Matilda. As usual, she was ecstatic to hear from him, and rambled on for some minutes about his father's new plastic surgeon, and the artist who had helped create a partial facial prosthetic that looked so much like him before the war that in dim light you could hardly tell the difference. "I know you hated selling that suit of armor," she said after she'd paused to breathe. "But at least you were able to keep the sword. And you must know how much it meant to your father and me."

"'S all right, Mum." Arthur kept his voice low to prevent her hearing the nearly unconcealable disappointment threaded through it. "Didn't fit me anymore anyway. Medieval blokes were shrimps."

She laughed gaily. There was a pause, and a crumpling sound as she put the receiver against her ample bosom a moment. "George?" she called. There was no response. She put the phone back up to her ear. "How's our James?"

Arthur's mother knew. She knew everything about him, and he never had to open his mouth and say a single word. He supposed it came from all those years of stuttering — he'd rarely even tried to talk. She was a good mother, and she adapted, learning to read all of his nonverbal signals, sense his moods and needs with almost telepathic certainty. The first time she'd seen him with James, when they'd returned to London, she knew they were more than best friends.

But they'd never told his father. It was never a "good time" to tell his father. Implying that his father had suffered enough. Mum always said that Arthur's father, once they'd told him, would learn to accept it, but that his "heart was weak" or "he's in so much pain." Arthur had come to believe that his father would die not knowing who he really was.

"James is..." He gave an impatient sigh, and tried to find the right words. "We're traveling. I can't say more. But is there any money from the armor left?"

She exhaled in shock. "Well, yes. A little. Why?"

"I need you to wire it to Lloyd's Bank in Lincoln. Trip's lasting longer than we thought."

"Arthur." She said his name with suspicious slowness. "You aren't in any trouble, are you?"

"No, no." He knew what she was thinking. Because his identity, who he was, who he loved, it was all illegal, wasn't it? "Trying to get something done for a friend. It's important."

"All right. There should be a little over forty quid waiting for you, if you think it'll be enough."

"More than enough."

"When will you be home?" Matilda asked, no doubt threading the phone cord through her fingers as she always did, ever since he was a child. She was a knitter; her hands hated idleness.

"Dunno."

"Oh, Arthur."

He sighed and tried again. "Sorry, but I really don't know." What would James say? "The situation is... delicate. 'N a long story."

"Swear to me on Excalibur that you aren't in trouble."

"I swear."

"Please ring me as soon as you get back."

Arthur rang off and exhaled to make his chest as small as possible. This was necessary to fit out the door of the call box. He pushed to exit and looked up at the plump clock tower that adorned the red brick station. He'd meant to check the time, but found himself musing at the tower's charmingly pudgy shape. If James had been there at that moment, his first instinct would have been to laugh and share his observation. But James was in the station waiting with Lance and Mrs. Wylit. One of the most important things in his life,

Arthur thought, as he shoved his meaty fists into his pockets and hung his head, was that he had someone that he not only loved, but could share everything with, every thought and whim, without fear of judgment or reprisal. He only hoped that James felt the same, that there would never be any secrets between them. But ever since they'd begun this journey, James seemed somehow remote, far away. Arthur longed to be back at the flat, with Mrs. Wylit tucked downstairs, the two of them on the couch watching the new telly.

They had about an hour to wait for the train to Lincoln. Arthur fingered the coins in his pocket, and went to the newsstand for a paper. Then he returned to the bench where the rumpled crew lounged, baggage tucked between their feet.

"How's your mum?" Mrs. Wylit leaned forward toward the match flame that Lance offered her.

"She's well." Arthur tucked the paper under his arm. He locked eyes with James and jerked his head towards an empty bench about three meters away. James stood and followed him. They sat, and Arthur handed him the front page whilst he spread the sports on his lap.

"Something you want to talk about?" James asked after a few minutes of half-hearted flipping.

"Wanted you to myself for a few minutes."

James gave him a secretive, sideways smile and a chuckle. "Selfish, selfish."

"I should apologize properly." Arthur turned the page and pretended to examine the cricket scores. To the passerby, they were two young blokes reading the news. Maybe they didn't even know each other.

"For what?"

"The man in the brown coat." Arthur licked his finger to flip the page. The newsprint came up black on his thumb. "Should have told you right away about what I saw back in Meopham."

"There's loads of things on your mind right now. On all of our minds. I could see why you..." James trailed off.

"I didn't forget about it." Arthur put his elbows on his knees with a smart snap of his newspaper. "I chose not to say anything."

"Arthur." James dropped the news into his lap and turned sharply toward his boyfriend.

"Lower your voice."

James obliged him, and lifted the newspaper over his face again. Arthur stole a glance from the corner of his eye. James' cheeks were pink and his eye twitched, his jaw tight. "I'm sorry I didn't believe you. Thought you were... under stress. I was worried. Didn't want to play into it if it wasn't real." He paused, bit his lip. "But I did chase him for you. 'N now that you've seen him again, I believe it all."

"You mean now that Lance has seen him. Look, perhaps we shouldn't talk about this, all right?"

"I'm trying to apologize." Arthur's hands crumpled the sports page.

"No need." James said it breezily, but the color didn't leave his cheeks. He took a breath, and handed Arthur back the newspaper. "Let's forget about it."

"Don't you want to try and solve it?" Arthur hissed after him, but James had already walked away. Lance had Mr. Marlin's little black book, and was triple-checking the last known address of a Mr. William Blanchard.

***

The summer rain began again as their train pulled away from Nottingham Station, headed up to Lincoln. It was a short ride, and the little storm had worn itself out by then, a child throwing a temper tantrum. As the clouds cleared, James' tea called to him, and he left their cabin to find the loo. He was forced to pass three chaps in football scarves who loitered in the hallway, probably on their way to a match. James walked quickly, with his shoulders hunched, as images of Morgan and the gas mask flitted through his brain. They ignored him, God be praised, too busy shoving one another's shoulders and laughing.

"No, you're going to ask Rosie out, and that's final," one of them declared as James slunk down the hallway.

"I heard she's pretty fresh," another said, and they guffawed again. "You'll get a return on your investment like."

"What's taking you so long?" another berated his friend, an arm around his neck in a friendly choking gesture. "What are you, some kinda queerie?"

"If anyone's a damn queer, it's you," his friend fired back. More rough laughter.

At the toilets, a mother stood by the half-open door as her son combed his hair in the mirror. As James ducked into another toilet, she snarled at the boy, "Hurry up, will you? Acting like a sissy poof — what would your father say?"

James could cleary imagine the brokenhearted look in the boy's eyes as he gazed into the mirror. He knew, because he'd seen his own so many times. He put his hands on either side of the filthy metal train sink and pressed his head against the mirror, ragged breaths tearing into his chest as his face burned.

They were nearly to Lincoln station before James was able to compose himself and return to the cabin. As usual, Mrs. Wylit had drawn the curtains on the small windows leading into the hall. She was asleep on Lance's shoulder, and Lance himself nodded, his eyes half-closed. James slid into the seat next to Arthur, who looked at him quizzically as he pulled Arthur's hand off of his knee and clutched it in both of his own.

"What is it?" Arthur saw James' bloodshot eyes and the angry flush that blossomed on his cheeks.

James' mouth was pressed into a thin white line. Finally, he said, "How weary, stale, flat, and unprofitable seem to me all the uses of this world."

"What happened?" Arthur half-rose from his seat, and lifted his free hand as if to ask, *who needs to be punched?*

James kept hold of his other hand and pulled him back into the seat. "Nothing like that. Only things you can't protect me from."

"Tell me." Arthur's green eyes were earnest, angry, and expectant beneath his thick black brows.

James gifted him a sad smile, and reached up to brush an errant ebony curl from his forehead. "We should wake them. It's our stop."

Lance jerked awake at James' gentle touch, but Mrs. Wylit needed to be hauled to her feet. She'd had a "dry throat" on the journey. As Arthur lifted her by the arms to steady her, the seam in the armpit of her blouse gave way. "I can fix it," James promised. "Get her bag, Lance."

Together, they managed the baggage, including Mrs. Wylit. James sat with her sagged against him on a bench while Arthur and Lance looked at the bus schedule. Though he always took a moment, forced himself to admire anything beautiful that his eyes fell upon, James had no patience for the 1850s Tudor revival facade of the station, done in stately brick. He put his arm around Mrs. Wylit and hugged her close like an overboard sailor clutching a life preserver. A life preserver that stank of sweat and whiskey and perfume ten years old.

Mrs. Wylit knew. She had to know. And yet she'd come all this way in a pathetic attempt to take care of them, to see them through the journey, determined to try to help even though she was far more of a hindrance than an asset. But she knew who he was, who Arthur was, perhaps even who Lance was, and she stuck by them, left the cave-like cluttered flat she haunted to come with them. Passengers streamed out of the station, and swirled in eddys around their bench like the tide around a rock. There went the football hooligans, and the mother, dragging her son along behind her with an angry hand.

Mrs. Wylit sat up, burped, and turned to the side to vomit a brown stream flaked with what might have been a biscuit. "Maggie," she muttered — or, at least, that was what it sounded like — and heaved again. James pulled her wild hair back away from her face, and when she finished, mopped her mouth with her handkerchief.

"What's wrong with you, Vi?" He rocked her gently in his arms. "Tell me why you do this to yourself."

"Maggie," she whispered again.

At that moment, Lance and Arthur returned. "It's close enough to walk." Lance held up the black address book.

"I don't think Vi's up to walking," James said, then warned Arthur, "Mind the sick."

"Oof." Arthur stopped his huge foot in time and avoided the puddle.

"Let's go." Mrs. Wylit stood up, so fast that she pitched forward into Arthur's arms. He steadied her, and she opened her bleary eyes. Vi pushed her wild curls back again with an oddly dignified gesture and held out her hand. Lance gave her the bag, and she shouldered it. Then she crooked her arm out to him, and he took it. Leaning into Lance like a crumbling watchtower, she shuffled down the street. Arthur and James followed.

"She's a tough bird." James shook his head.

"Speaking of birds," Arthur said, "Always knew she ate like one. Never realized just how little it really was."

"She's sick, Arthur." James shifted his suitcase to the other hand. "Now that she's with us all the time I see it."

Arthur nodded, but did not speak. There was nothing more to say, James thought, at least not now. One thing they did know about Mrs. Wylit was that she had no relatives. "No kin to call my own. Not anymore," she had told them on more than one occasion, the liquor giving her declaration the maudlin flair of a radio drama. So, there was no one to tell, to send her to, to help her.

None but us, James thought, and winced as Mrs. Wylit stumbled over a crack in the pavement, though Lance was there to catch her.

Soon enough, they found themselves standing in front of the arched door of a small brick row house about a mile from the train station. The cardboard sign in the upper right window said ROOMS TO LET.

Arthur's stomach rumbled. James' echoed in solidarity. He hoped Mr. Blanchard would be as accommodating as Mrs. Galhad. It was nearly teatime anyway.

The person who stomped to the door after they'd had to ring the bell several times was, at first glance, definitely *not* William Blanchard. He was far too young, perhaps ten years older than Arthur and James, although the years had not been kind. They revealed themselves in his thinning mud brown hair and quivering tum. Mr. Conner had one as well, which he affectionately called his "pony keg." While the tummy lump was fatherly and endearing on a man of Mr. Conner's age, it seemed unhealthy when paired with this fellow's youthful arms and sallow skin. He wore a dirty undershirt and pajama trousers.

"Keep your knickers on," he snapped, and yanked the door open wider. "Lookin' for a room? It's fifteen quid a month, no private bathrooms." He fixed his watery brown eyes on Mrs. Wylit. The whites were threaded through with blood. "No women." He leaned against the doorframe with his arms crossed. "Christ, especially her. She looks pissed."

"We just had a very long train ride," James explained as Lance drew Mrs. Wylit back from the door out onto the sidewalk again.

The man at the door took a toothpick from behind his ear and made as if to say something rude. Arthur stepped forward to stand shoulder-to-shoulder with James, which let his height speak for itself.

"Don't need a room," Arthur rumbled in his deep bass. "We're looking for someone."

"Does a Mr. William Blanchard live here?" James asked.

The man stared at him, and gnawed the toothpick.

"He'd be in his seventies." James choked back a nervous cough. "Military man from the Great War."

"I know of him." The man used his large wet tongue to migrate the toothpick to the other side of his mouth. "What's it to you?"

"We're trying to find him." James shifted uncomfortably to his other foot.

"Well, that's bloody obvious, innit?" The man removed the toothpick from his mouth and stuck it behind his ear again. "You his relatives? Old codger owes me back rent."

"He was friends with my granddad," Lance tried as he adjusted Mrs. Wylit's weight against his hip. "They were in the war together."

The man spit at their feet. "Well, ain't that a sweet little story."

"Do you know where he is?" Arthur inched forward again.

"You may want to step back, boy." The man unfolded his arms and drew himself up to his unimpressive height. "The bigger they are, the harder they fall, innit what they say?"

"We're not looking for trouble."

"Could have fooled me." The man spat again. His body odor tingled in James' nose, and he winced at its bitter potency. "Say I do know where he is. What's it worth to you?"

"We have some... money." James nudged Arthur, who dug into his coat pocket for his wallet.

"Unless you want to pay me his three months back rent, don't bother." The toothpick went back into the man's snaggle-toothed mouth.

"Then, what can we offer you?" James guided Arthur back with one hand and inched forward himself, eyes open wide and innocent. "Please, there must be something you want. We desperately need to find Mr. Blanchard. It's a matter of a man's dying wish."

The man laughed, quietly at first, and then with a loud, shrill, mean openness. "Oh, I suppose, if you're that desperate, and it's a matter of the heart, well, wouldn't I be cruel if I didn't tell you." He broke to laugh again, a donkey yelp. "All right, if you want to know what happened to old Blanchard, I do have something you can do for me. Get me what I want, and I'll tell you everything."

"Yes," James agreed. They were getting somewhere.

The man laughed again, hard enough this time that he had to bend down and slap his knee.

"What d'you want?" Arthur pushed against James' warning elbow.

"I want my damned football cup, that's what I want." The man ripped the toothpick out of his mouth and threw it at their feet, next to his glob of spittle. "My mates and I won a tournament in upper school and I kept the cup. Well, times was hard, you know how it goes — and I had to hock it, didn't I? Well, the arsehole who bought it's Mr. King — his daughter's some slag I went with for a time — and he keeps it behind his bar to use as goddamned ashtray. That's right, down at the Hawk and Chick. He does it just to mock me, to mock my mates, y'see. Get the cup back from him. Bring it here and I'll tell you whatever you want to know."

"How are we supposed to do that?" James wondered.

"If I knew how to do it, I wouldn't be asking some Frankenstein and his pet poof for help, now would I?" He moved to slam the door.

Arthur's hand shot out and caught it, massive fingers splayed out over the weathered wood. "Promise," he growled. "If we get the cup, promise you'll tell us about Mr. Blanchard."

"You have my word, Frankenstein. Now get your damn hand off my door."

Arthur drew his limb back, and the door slammed.

"It's Frankenstein's monster, you twit," James grumbled under his breath as they turned to go.

Lance patted his shoulder reassuringly with the free hand that wasn't supporting Mrs. Wylit. "And Arthur's obviously your pet, not the other way round."

Chapter 17

After a bit of asking, they managed to find the Hawk and Chick, a tiny pub squeezed between a wireless repair shop and a closed-up bakery. It was a brick blight with filthy windows. Inside was cramped and strange — the nook of a bar stood off to the right, tucked against the far corner. It was sectioned off from the rest of the pub by a half-wall that ran almost to the doorway they had crowded into. The tables and chairs and darts board were crammed on the other side of the partition. There were only two stools at the bar itself, and one of them was broken, laying on its side like a wounded warrior.

The walls were lined with built-in shelves, which suggested the little space had been something else before, a shop perhaps — but instead of tearing them out, the owner had filled them with *things*. Objects lined every available space: books, taxidermy, dusty fake plants and flowers, and decorative plates and beer steins as well. However, fish and fishing dominated over all else; tacked to the wall were old lures, poles, baskets, nets, and hats, as well as some trophy bass and other species James couldn't identify. A shapeless, beige man and his equally drab female companion lounged at one of the tables staring silently at their pints.

Behind the bar, sitting on a stool, was an old man in a green wool sweater vest and a brown cap. He had a lush white beard kept trimmed close to his jaw. "Evenin'," he greeted, and thumbed up the bill of his brown cap. As they moved inside, he extinguished his cigar stub into a small golden trophy cup that sat among the whisky bottles on the shelf behind him.

"There it is," Lance mouthed at James, and jerked his head in the direction of the football cup. Aloud, he said, "Why don't you all get a table? Drinks are on me, mates." He winked.

James selected a table as far away from the dour-looking regulars as possible, in the back near the dartboard. Arthur lowered Mrs.

Wylit into a chair and propped her against the shelf behind her, which rattled the collection of dusty porcelain figurines of fishermen and fisher boys.

"Surprised he didn't call the place Fish and Tadpole or the like." Arthur sank himself into a chair in increments. James listened to the groans and pops of the old wood in hopes it would hold Arthur's weight.

"He didn't seem like a... well, he didn't seem grumpy." James rested his suitcase beneath his feet. "Lance is so charming. I'm sure he'll have the cup back in a heartbeat."

Mrs. Wylit's back stiffened, and her eyes shot open. "Charm isn't everything, young man," she scolded as she rubbed her temples and forehead. "They say Hitler was charming."

"Oh, for pity's sake, Vi," James hissed as the drab couple shot questioning glances their way. "Are you *really* comparing him to Hitler?"

"I'm only... saying," she grumbled, and shoved her hand into her bag to rifle through for her flask. "Don't say I didn't warn you," she snapped at Arthur.

"No, no, no." Arthur plucked the flask out of her fingers when she came up with it. "Can't believe there's anything still in there."

"You've got a pint coming." James pulled a sleeve of biscuits from his suitcase. "Please eat something."

Mrs. Wylit clawed one into her mouth. "I'm watching you." Crumbs tumbled from between her chapped lips.

"Hate it when she stops making sense," Arthur rumbled, as if Mrs. Wylit wasn't sitting right next to him. "She's nutters when she drinks."

James did not mention aloud the predictions she made, and how they often came true. It was easier, now, in this place, with the problem presented before them, to ignore it. But in his mind he ran through the catalogue of her strangely accurate rants. By the look on Arthur's face, James thought, he was thinking the same thing.

Lance emerged from the partition with a tray of pints. These he brought to the table and passed out to each of them. He sat down with a weary sigh.

"Oh dear," said James.

"I'll say." Mrs. Wylit dragged her pint to her mouth and gulped like an animal at a trough.

"He's not a bad chap, our Mr. King." Lance sipped his own bitters. "But I'll be damned, he does *not* want to give up that cup! I've explained everything to him, the whole predicament. Hates the landlord we spoke to – named Tom by the way – because of something that happened with his daughter. He told me he'll be putting out his cigars in that cup until the day he dies. He suggested that Arthur beat the information out of Tom, which would no doubt delight Mr. King as well." He sighed again. "I put it on thick, lads. I offered him money, too — nothing worked. He told me to wish you all a good night and best of luck. He's happy to serve us here in the pub, but that's the end of it."

"Charm isn't everything," Mrs. Wylit said down into her pint glass, and then punctuated it with a burp.

"I gave it my best go." Lance crossed his arms, a sour, disappointed pout to his full lips.

"'Spose it's my turn then." Arthur stood, nearly scraping his dark curls against a trophy swordfish's blade.

"Arthur, you're not going to—"

"Don't worry." Arthur went around the partition, and each step rattled the chotchkies on the walls.

However, it was only a few minutes before he returned, eyes wide and blinking in bewilderment. "Don't know what that Tom did to his daughter," he said, "but that cup..." He shook his head again.

Mrs. Wylit shoved back her chair and swayed to her feet. She lit a cigarette and blew the smoke to the ceiling. "Never send a man to do a woman's work." She turned and stumbled up to the bar, using the backs of chairs for support as she went.

"Oh no, no, no," James groaned, turning to his beer for support. "This is our worst idea yet. Vi, come back—"

It was too late. She disappeared around the partition and did not emerge for quite some time.

"Maybe she's getting somewhere," Lance suggested with a hopeful shrug.

"More like getting into trouble." As the last word left James' mouth, Mrs. Wylit rounded the corner. Her steps were steadier, and she had a cup of water in one hand and a mug of tea in the other, complete with a lemon slice. She sank into her squeaking chair and set the other beverages to the side, reaching first to drain her pint. "He said if I drank these, he'd consider it," she said, "but I don't think he will. Stubborn as a bull. I offered him anything and everything." She gulped the tea and winced. "And I mean *everything*. Apparently he's happily married, as if such a thing existed."

The drab couple had had enough and fled for the door after tossing a few coins on the table.

"Vi, you *didn't*," James squealed in a barely-concealed stage whisper. "You didn't, did you?"

"I'm only saying." She drained the tea and set the cup back on the table with a clang. "There it is. I'd do that if it means helping you ungrateful cabbages."

James put his head in his hands. Arthur, now that they were alone, was able to pat his knee under the table. It did little to reassure him. "The trail can't end here." Lance slammed his fist into his open hand. "All right. Here's the plan. Mrs. Wylit, you return the tea cup, and drop it on the floor — make a big scene, all of that, you're a natural, luv — and then Arthur, you grab the cup—"

"No, no, no." James stood and slid past Lance to exit the wobbly table. "No. All of this is awful. There has to be a reason that Mr. King wants the cup this badly. I have to make him understand that our cause is more important somehow."

"Look, mate, I've already tried talking to him, tried to get the sympathy vote," Lance shot back. "He's got a heart of stone."

James gazed into Arthur's eyes, green to green. "Let me try," he begged. Arthur reached out and squeezed his hand. "If I can't get the cup, we can try Lance's plan. But the last thing I want to do is rob some old man to help this horrible Tom person."

Arthur raised James' hand to his lips and kissed his knuckles. "All right. I know you can do it, James."

James nodded and rounded the wall to the bar. Mr. King had the radio on for the cricket scores. He leaned back on his stool and had his leg drawn up, calf resting on the bar. The appendage ended just before the ankle, and the old man rubbed the stump, and winced as if it ached. When James appeared, he dropped his leg down again with a graceless, embarrassed move.

"I'm sorry." James opened his hands, a mirror of the temperance card in a tarot deck. "I didn't mean to intrude."

"Think nothing of it." Mr. King motioned him forward. "Another round? Or, let me guess — you're here to plead with me about that chav Tom's football cup."

"May I sit?" James motioned to the remaining bar stool.

Mr. King cocked his head, and raised his fingers to his ear as if he hadn't heard. "Sit down?" He shrugged. "Go right ahead, sonny. You're a strange band to be sure, but I suppose you're paying customers."

"What kind of fish is that?" James motioned to a cheap painting that hung above the bar of a man reeling in a strange creature with whiskers.

"Catfish." Mr. King reclined on his stool to light a cigar. "We don't have them here."

"But they have them in America, yeah?" James put his elbows on the bar, eyes bright with interest. "I read about them. Mark Twain."

"Indeed they do. Caught some there meself. Me uncle took me to the states for a fishing trip when I were a young man." He nodded down to his leg. "That was long 'fore this. And before you ask, no, I didn't lose it in the war."

James knew better than to ask what had happened. "What else did you fish for in America?"

"All kinds. That bass up there. Largemouth. Caught him in Lake Superior."

"It's enormous." James showered the dusty trophy with an admiring gaze.

"Almost pulled me out of the boat." Mr. King laughed, and poured himself and James a pint. "Most lads fish with their fathers, but mine was always working. Me mother's brother, Harvey, he taught me to fish. Most of these things were his." He motioned the antique rods and reels and baskets. "He taught me to weave a fish basket out of reeds and vines and things if you're ever lost in the woods."

"Is that the trumpet-shaped thing?" James listened and sipped his pint, his whole body intent on absorbing what Mr. King spoke. The barkeep went on for some time about how fish baskets worked, how unsuspecting creatures swam in but couldn't get out, and what his uncle had taught him about weaving his own in the wild.

"Did you take your son fishing when he was a boy?" James asked as Mr. King reached up and lifted down one of the fish traps for him to hold.

Mr. King coughed, and ashed his cigar into the football cup. "The Good Lord gave us me daughter Elaine."

James let a long pause go so they could both drink their pints. "And so you taught her to fish," he said to break the silence.

Mr. King nodded, and reached back to take down a bottle of gin. He poured them each a small glass. James threw it back and smacked his lips in enjoyment. He'd never done a shot of gin before, and he rather liked it. He knew it made Arthur sick — he couldn't stomach anything but beer and maybe a glass of table wine.

Mr. King sipped his gin, and then stared into it as if waiting for portents or images to appear. "Aye, I did teach our Elaine," he said after a time as he swirled the liquor with one hand. "When she were a little sprout. She had a little rod in her hand before she could hold a spoon." He smiled at the memory, but his eyes were sad. "She were always an active gell — ran about the neighborhood playing with the boys. She was brilliant at footy. Her mother was always concerned she wasn't... well, that she wasn't inside playing with dolls or summat girly. But she was happy, truly happy. And she could fish. Better 'n me." He chuckled. "She could tie off a lure faster than you can say 'Bob's your uncle'. When she got older, I taught her how to ride the bus to the edge of town so she could go fishing whenever she wanted."

James polished off his pint, and Mr. King set out another with as much skilled speed as his daughter apparently tied fishing lures. "Do you still fish together?"

Mr. King took an exaggerated drag from his cigar. The smoke wafted free of his mouth and swirled around his beard as he stamped out the cigar into the golden cup. He looked at James, and his eyes were red. "No." He paused to draw another thin cigar from his shirt pocket and chew off the end. He spat it defiantly at the football trophy. "Not since she went with Tom for awhile."

The rawness of this wound was so obvious that James feared poking further. He waited, and his eyes strayed from time to time to the golden football trophy. Well, it probably wasn't made of real gold, he thought. Brass, probably, or something even cheaper. For something so cheap, practically worthless, even, it held an ironic amount of meaning for Mr. King, and Tom for that matter.

He thought about asking, *what did Tom do to her,* but instead led with, "I'm sorry, Mr. King. That must have been difficult for you. And for Elaine."

"She loved the water," he went on, without prompting. "Fishin' in it. Swimmin' in it. I told her she'd grow gills if she weren't careful. Shame, really, that she were a city girl. I think she were born for the countryside. But she liked city things, too. When she were toddlin' around, I'd take her on the streetcar and the buses. She always begged to ride on top."

James took a measured drink and attempted to steer Mr. King back in the direction he needed. "But when Tom came, that was a different story."

Mr. King nodded, mouth drawn down. His frown etched deep lines in his tired, kindly face. "She fell for him, probably five years ago. Used to come in here regular, more often when he wanted to see 'er. Now they both stay away." He sipped his pint, and swiped foam from his mustache. "I dunno what she saw in 'im, but she wanted to do everything right for 'im. I think she were worried, being in her late twenties and not having caught a husband yet. She learnt the names of all the players on his favorite football teams, memorized about twenty years of cricket history, all of it. She never wanted nothin' more than to please 'im. What did he do in return?"

Mr. King punched his mouth down into a thin white pucker. "All he did were tell my gell what was wrong with her. He only wanted a whore and a housemaid, someone to look after that flea-trap boarding house. Tommy told her fishin' and the like, all the things she loved, it were all... unfeminine. Unbecomin' of a woman. That she ought to take up sewin' so she could fix his socks, put on lipstick and look at movie star magazines. And God help her, she believed him. All of it."

"Oh, no," James whispered, and covered his mouth with one hand. "No, she didn't."

Mr. King nodded, and his head drooped like a horse about to die from heat and overwork. "I saw what it were doing to her, and o' course I missed her comin' to fish with me. I just *missed* her."

"Of course you did." James lent forward on his elbows again. It struck him, then, how odd this was — the barkeep in need of a sympathetic ear, instead of the other way round.

"I told her to break it off with him. At first, she told me I were nutters, that I should be happy for her. She was so sure they'd be married, children, everything. Thank God it didn't come to all that. After a few months, she started to see the things I saw, how worthless Tom was and how horrible he made her feel. So she left him."

"Hear hear," James affirmed, after a swig of bitters.

Mr. King lifted his shoulders as if they weighed a thousand pounds, and gave a miserable shrug. "She weren't ever the same. She still took up sewing and lipstick and movie stars and tea sandwiches and high heels. And she's been miserable ever since."

James ran the pads of his fingers over his lips. "And that's why you bought Tom's trophy when he was down on his luck, and use it as an ashtray."

"If there was a place in the loo, I'd put it there for blokes to piss in." Mr King tapped his cigar against the cup again with vehemence.

James waited a good while before speaking. His heart broke for Mr. King and Elaine. But he could not forget his purpose; could not forget Mr. Marlin and Matthew.

"Well?" Mr. King demanded, and threw back another shot of gin. "You got nothin' to say?"

James took a breath. This was thin ice, but he edged forward regardless. "Putting out your cigars in that cup isn't going to change

Elaine back to the way she used to be. Only you can do that. By talking to her. Showing her how much you love her, even if she never gets married."

Mr. King locked him in an infuriated, dead-eyed stare.

"It's society. It's this town, these times, these people," James barreled ahead, and hoped to reach his point before Mr. King tossed him out of the pub. "Society tells women they need to wear makeup and keep house, get excited about a new Frigidaire — most importantly, get married and have babies. For the longest time, Elaine didn't care about any of that on the outside. But inside she was bothered by, I don't know, seeing school friends marry perhaps. She likely spent a long time wondering what it was that was wrong with her, what made her a freak. And when Tom started paying her attention, telling her all of her so-called faults, she thought 'Yes! I've sorted it out. If I can fix these things, I can be normal.' But she'll never be normal. Because she's better than normal. She's vibrant and exceptional. Yet, she doesn't see that she is."

Mr. King's cigar ash was long, and it fell on the bar before he could flick it away, so intently was he staring at James. "How d'you know?"

"I know a thing or two about the world telling me I'm abnormal. Judge me if you like, but I'll tell you the truth, Mr. King. As I've said, that using that trophy as an ashtray isn't going to help Elaine. It doesn't even help you. Sure, it's jolly good to see Tom upset about it, but it hasn't given you Elaine back. It hasn't made you happy."

Mr. King stared at him, motionless.

"But it would make *me* happy," James said, "to trade it for the information we require to find out where Mr. Blanchard is. I need to do this to find the long lost son of a woman who was kinder to me than my own mother. It was the dying wish of a dear friend, and I need the information. If I give Tom the cup, he'll tell me. And if he won't, my tall friend will beat the tar out of him."

After a long silence, Mr. King said, "Now that, I'd like to see."

"But it won't fix Elaine," James reminded him. "And it won't fix Tom. Tom's going to be an arsehole for the rest of his life, and nothing you or I do is going to change that. But if I can complete my quest, good can come from it."

Mr. King stared down at his fishhook-scarred hands. He said, "Will you tell me what to say? To Elaine? How to start... how to begin..."

"Yes," James promised.

Mr. King stared deep into James' eyes, two pools of earnest emerald, and reached behind him. He lifted the football trophy, and handed it over the bar into James' waiting hands.

Chapter 18

Lincoln, past midnight, was well lit, though deserted and inhospitable. They'd hauled the suitcases and Mrs. Wylit for many blocks. The merriment of their victory, as well as the libations they'd consumed, had worn off. The troop was grim and exhausted. They had a path forward now, but no place to stay for the night. No buses or cabs to be found, and no hotels. They'd left the only boarding house they knew of, and, suffice to say, they weren't welcome there anymore.

It was James' turn to let Mrs. Wylit lean on his arm. She came out of her stupor in a foul mood. "If we're going to sleep in the bloody train station, let's stop off somewhere and get a bottle, why don't we?"

James was inclined to agree, though liquor did nasty things to his head in the morning. He could already feel the creeping clutch of a headache as a result of gin passing between his lips. Arthur put a hand on his shoulder and gave him a grim, apologetic smile that was likely meant to brighten his spirits. It didn't. Perhaps they shouldn't have enraged the owner of the only boarding house they knew of.

They followed the train tracks through a row of shops. It began to rain, and Lance shook his fist at the sky, cursing. As Arthur went to jiggle open their limp umbrella, Mrs. Wylit raised a shaking finger, its tip stained with flaking red polish. A brick and stone Saxon tower with a clock face barely visible in the soggy gloom rose up in the moonlight.

"A church." Lance huffed out a sigh of relief. "Well, we are weary travelers on a sacred mission, aren't we? Perhaps they'll grant us sanctuary."

"There's not going to be anyone inside," James muttered, but dragged Mrs. Wylit after the others anyway. As a train roared by on the tracks a mere block away, they shuffled, bedraggled and pathet-

ic, to the nave door of the ancient, crumbling house of worship —
St. Mary le Wigford. To James' total surprise, it opened when Lance
pushed on it.

Their ears were immediately assaulted by the roar of a vacuum.
Mrs. Wylit shoved the party inside to get herself out of the wet, and
suddenly they were standing in the nave of the 900-year-old church.
The sacred space swam in a mighty mechanical humming sound.
Over this soared a deep bass voice that belted out "Chattanooga
Choo Choo" as if to serenade the train that rattled past.

For all the antiquity of the exterior, the interior was strangely
modern. Tables and chairs were set up in the nave, for bingo or some
such. Bulletin boards sat along the walls, pinned with historical information about the church, as well as fliers for community events.
In the Lady Chapel on the far left hand side, next to the sanctuary, a
willowy man with thick Buddy Holly glasses rammed a groaning vacuum over the blue carpeting. As he worked, he sang his lungs out to
fill this ancient house of the Lord with the words of a Glenn Miller
song.

When the singing janitor saw them, he gave a violent start, and
dropped the handle of the vacuum. He gaped a moment, and then
scooped it up and flipped the switch off. "You're lucky I don't have a
heart condition," he called through the echoey chapel.

"Sorry to startle you." Lance wove through the tables and chairs
to stand at the edge of the chapel's blue carpet.

"It's too dark to get a proper picture of the dedication stone." The
willowy janitor shoved his thumb up under his short-billed hat and
scratched his forehead. "I suppose you can look around inside a few
minutes, but then I'm off."

Arthur lumbered up to Lance's side, and put a hand on his shoulder. "Sanctuary," he said.

The janitor froze, in mid-wind as he coiled up the vacuum cord.
"What's that?"

"We need sanctuary," Arthur repeated, and his deep rich voice reverberated through the church in a way that was instantly holy. "We're strangers here and we have no place to stay."

James shifted uncomfortably as Mrs. Wylit's rancid breath rolled over his neck. There was no way this was going to work.

"Sanctuary?" The man's voice gave an adolescent squeak. He cleared his throat. "Well. I mean, if you ask for sanctuary, I suppose — well, I'm not the priest, but I know what Father Dale would say."

They waited a long beat.

"And he would say..." James began.

"Oh. Yes, that you could stay. Mmm. Yes." Speedily, he wrapped up the cord and strapped it to the side of the bulbous machine.

"T-thank you," Arthur stuttered. He shook his head, the way he always did when the childhood impediment returned, as if he could buck it off of his mouth like a horse throwing a rider. "You're very kind."

"Please don't leave it a mess." the janitor called over his shoulder as he lugged the vacuum into a nearby closet. "We have a christening in the morning."

"You'll never know we were here." Lance held up one hand while placing the other over his heart.

"In the storage room you'll find some cots and blankets and things. We were a shelter during the war." The janitor removed a handkerchief from his back pocket and wiped his nose on it. "Allergic to dust. Imagine that. Now I can't swear to the condition of said cots and blankets. Might be motheaten or some such."

"Please, don't trouble yourself."

"Here." The willowy man hurried across the nave to a small table that also held a bingo cage full of multicolored balls. He lifted up a huge metal lunch pail and set it next to the cage with a definitive clank. "Sandwiches, and an apple. I brought it in, but went to Mum's for tea this afternoon and she stuffed me." He rubbed what James thought was no more than a microscopic bit of pudding tum.

Arthur tried gallantly to refuse taking the man's supper, but the janitor insisted. "I had a feeling I'd be doing the Lord's work tonight," he said, stepping into his wellies and pulled on his mackintosh. "Sometimes when I'm here cleaning the church I get a tingle, just right here." He quivered his fingers at the base of his neck. "That's our Father telling me it's time to do his work. I thought, 'God, how can I do your work so late at night when I'm going to go home and go right to bed? I'm too knackered to do your work, Lord.' And behold, here you all are. And I still get to go home to bed!"

With that, he opened the nave door. "Please clean up before seven. Father and Mrs. Dale will be in to set up for the christening. Goodnight." He sprang out the door into the rain, and clanked it shut behind him with a wooden thump.

They were left in the 11th century haven then, as the rain pattered on the roof and lashed against the stained glass windows. The wind sighed through the organ pipes, a sweet, sad sound. The men looked at one another in disbelief and Mrs. Wylit belched. Without warning, a train rattled by on the nearby tracks and shattered the surreal moment.

"Holy pilgrims we," Lance laughed, and set down his bag. "I can't believe..."

"Let's not think too hard on it," James advised, "because my arm's about to go numb." He tried to shift Mrs. Wylit to the other side. She stood for a moment on shaking legs before Arthur swooped in and eased her into a chair.

They regrouped. Lance and Arthur went to the storage cupboard to find the cots while James eased her out of the chair and took Mrs. Wylit to the loo. While he patiently washed her hands and face, she seemed to shake back to full consciousness, and stared at him very seriously with her bloodshot eyes.

"What is it, Vi?" He wrung out his handkerchief and draped it over the faucet to dry in the night.

"Don't do it," she said, low and slow. It gave him a shiver when she talked like that, in her voice of prophecy. "You'll want to, but don't. You'll hate yourself."

"I still don't understand what you're talking about." James hauled her to her feet and picked up her jacket from where it had dropped on the floor in a sad heap. "All your cryptic little messages aren't helping anything."

"You heard it on the wireless," she warned, and kicked off her shoes. She tried to bend down and pick them up, but nearly plunged into the wall. James steadied her then picked her shoes up himself.

"I heard what on the wireless?" he asked in an exhausted sigh.

"What's going to happen. And you thought, why, that will never happen to me, couldn't happen to me."

He shoved her shoes in her hands, and steered her out the door into the nave again. Lance and Arthur had found the old metal cots, stretched with aging canvas, and some army blankets that were indeed pocked with moth bites. They'd set up their accommodations in the sanctuary, which seemed blasphemous, but was farthest away from the door and the draft. The kindly janitor had turned off the lights except for a few electric sconces that protruded from the columns that held up the buttressed ceiling. The gold of the candlesticks and chandeliers glinted dully in the soft light. Somehow, the echoey stone chamber was drowsy and cosy.

James tucked in Mrs. Wylit, who stared at him with her silent, accusing eyes, until her head lolled back and she began to snore. He tucked the blanket around her limp body and turned her head to the side so her snores weren't quite so violent. Lance had set up two more cots in front of the altar and prepped them with blankets, and Arthur was busy creating a pile of blankets for himself to lay on. He was far too long for the little cots, and with the decade that had passed since their use, they were of dubious strength.

There were five ham sandwiches in the lunch pail. "Where does he put it all?" James wondered, surveying the food that seemed to spring magically from the bottomless metal box.

"Where do *you* put it all?" Arthur reached out to pat James' flat abdomen affectionately.

"I've got to enjoy it now." Lance took up a sandwich and un-wrapped the wax paper. "You've seen my father. That pot belly is what I have to look forward to. He looks like a tea kettle with spindly little legs."

The image lightened the mood as they sat on the floor with their backs to the communion benches to eat, and did their best to mind the crumbs that fell into the aging carpet. "My dad looks like me," Arthur said around the ham in his mouth.

"Shaped like a capital T," James said. "Isn't he?"

Lance laughed and agreed with a flash of his white teeth. "How about you, mate? Do you have a belly to look forward to, or has your father aged well? Don't tell me you'll go bald."

Though it was logical for Lance to ask, the question hooked into James and tugged with a painful, disorienting jerk. His mind swam backward to the singular vague memory of his father he could conjure up — a man with smeary spectacles, fuzzy hair, and always wearing clothes that seemed too big. The memory-father was faceless, a blank bank of pale flesh with glasses over where the eyes ought to go. James thought too of beige and dark brown, of pipe smoke, and the joyless void left in his father's wake. *I suppose that means I must have loved him,* he thought. Now the vague sensation of being carried in those skinny arms, being lifted into the air, laughing, grabbing at his father's glasses.

"James?"

"He didn't know his father," Arthur shifted closer to James on the floor as if to shield him from something. "Left when he was young."

"Sorry, mate, I didn't mean —" Lance coughed and looked away. "Look, do you want to paste me?" He held out his square chin and pointed a finger at it that was marred with a smear of mayonnaise. "Go head, I won't flinch."

"Don't be an idiot — you didn't know." James tried to air it out with a cheerless little laugh. "Really, it was so long ago, it doesn't matter." He forced his features into a smile. "I hope he isn't bald or podgy."

They ate in silence for a while, staring at the darkened stained glass windows. One of the panes depicted a young girl praying on a pillow, her saintly face raised to Heaven. Something about it struck James as particularly sorrowful, but he wasn't sure if it was the glass girl, or the sudden memories of his father.

It was very late. James and Lance stretched out on their creaky canvas cots, and Arthur bedded down on his pile of blankets.

"I still can't believe you threw the sodding thing at him," Lance said after a stretch of silence. "Did you hear the clang as it ricocheted off of his head?"

"It was more of a toss." Arthur's words floated up from the darkened floor.

Images of the golden cup clanging off of Tom's shoulder in a cloud of cigar ash replaced the father shadows in James' mind, and he clamped his hand over his mouth to keep from roaring with laughter. "It didn't hit him on the head. At least not the first blow. I think it sort of cartwheeled up and bopped him, though."

"He was just so smug about it." Arthur laced his fingers over his broad chest, eyes on the ceiling. "The way he talked about Mr. King. Called his daughter a slag. Couldn't help myself."

"Do you think he was telling the truth?" Lance asked the question that was on all of their minds. "That Mr. Blanchard is really in the loony bin at St. John's?"

"There's only one way to find out." James turned on his side and propped himself up with an elbow. "We'll have to go there and ask to see him."

"But if he's a loony, how is he going to tell us anything about Matthew Barlow?" Lance reached into his coat pocket and shook out a cigarette, but did not light it. Instead, he tapped it incessantly, pensively on the back of his hand, eyes distant. "This could be where the trail ends, lads."

This settled them all into discomforted silence. However, after a time, this dissolved into Arthur and Mrs. Wylit snoring in tandem.

James had never been a sound sleeper, as his mother was always quick to point out. Strange places, strange beds — well, what could be stranger than a cot in a church with a dedication stone dating back to the Roman era? He'd always envied Arthur's ability to quite literally fall asleep standing up in a phone box (it *had* happened once before). It was lonely, being the only one awake. Even after they'd reckoned with Morgan and his gang, James remembered, Arthur was able to slumber away in the repurposed parlor of Willowind House.

But now he wasn't alone. After a quarter of an hour, he watched Lance get up and stroll to the chapel side of the church. He paced awhile with his eyes on the stained glass windows, and finally lit the cigarette he'd been playing with. The smoke went up around his head, a misty halo crowning his silhouette in the dim light.

James turned and looked at Arthur's placid slumbering face. He looked twice as young when he slept, an errant black curl resting against his eyebrow.

James stood, and trod softly over the ancient stones of the nave. Lance turned, and his devastating smile crept up the corners of his mouth. "My partner in insomnia," he said softly, and opened one arm. James slid beneath it and let Lance fold him into a half-embrace.

Chapter 19

James forced himself to pull away. The heady scent of Lance's cologne, mixed with the sweet tendrils of tobacco smoke (somehow so much less acrid than whatever Mrs. Wylit inhaled) was too much. He felt himself sliding into the scent, the moment, and Lance's touch with an abandon he found distinctly alarming. They stood shoulder to shoulder and gazed on the stained glass, despite how dull it was in the dark of night. Occasionally, the colors popped in the headlights of a passing car.

"When I get home, I'm going to sleep for a week," James groaned softly, just to say something, something to help this feeling slide. "In my own bed."

Lance raised the cigarette to his mouth. The white paper of the stick was temporarily stained red as a car drifted past and cast light through the rosy glass before them. "Back home with Arthur." Smoke curled in tendrils from the corners of his full lips. "To your own flat, your own life, your own bed." He smiled and showed half of his two rows of straight white teeth. The curve of his cheek was devastating in the dim light, but it was more of a half-grimace than a smile, more sad than consoling.

"Yes." James didn't know what else to say.

"I suppose you're eager to have this over with. So the two of you can get back to your lives."

"I'm happy to do whatever it takes to fulfil Mr. Marlin's last wishes." James crossed his arms over his wrinkled beige shirt; a sudden, protective gesture.

"Oh, no, that's not what I meant." Lance turned and faced him, and took a small step closer to put a reassuring hand briefly on James' shoulder. "That must have sounded like... no, that's not — cocked this one up, haven't I? I meant, well — what I'm trying to say is..." He filled the silence with a drag from his cigarette. "I'm jealous," he finished.

"Jealous?"

Lance nodded, and scratched the back of his golden head with one thumb. "Yes, if I'm going to be honest. The two of you will go back to your lives, go back to the home you share. And... well, I hate to whinge and feel sorry for myself, but I can't imagine, after all of this, after what I've understood about myself, discovered, if you will — I can't imagine going back to my parents' house, back to my job at the law office, back to Meopham."

"Then don't go back." James followed Lance as he began to absently pace the bank of windows along the side of the chapel. "Nothing says you have to stay. Now that Mr. Marlin's gone. You could move to London, too."

"I think I shall have to." Lance raised a foot and put out the cigarette against the bottom his shoe. He crossed his arms and sighed at the stained glass. "Can you believe it? It's daft." He gave a gentle chuckle that rubbed James' ears as sardonic. "Three fairies and a madwoman sheltering in a *church*. Claiming sanctuary."

"We're on a quest, like so many pilgrims before us." James flicked invisible dirt from his shirt sleeve to avoid Lance's gaze.

"I find it funny." Lance reached out and tapped the multicolored window with one finger. "You know, my mother's a real Bible-beater. Don't know where she got it from — Granddad wasn't really. Perhaps it was what he saw in the war, I don't know, but he always had an excuse not to go with us to church."

James nodded. "When I knew Mr. Marlin, he seemed rather secular, I suppose. Lady Barlow as well. Though there was something about her that was," he paused, "mystical. I can't explain it." He smiled at the memory. "I wish you could have met her."

"Me, too. I know it was difficult for you, leaving home and being trapped there with those bullies, but I almost wish I'd gotten to go off on Pied Piper. But Meopham, well — our little village wasn't much of a target for the Germans." Lance strolled over to the altar of the Lady Chapel and rested his fingertips lightly on the cloth. Then, he reached out and grabbed the silver cross that adorned it. James sucked breath in through his teeth at the sacrilegious nature of it, but stifled it with a little laugh.

Lance laughed as well, and turned to waggle the cross gently toward James before putting it back. "Whew." He pretended to drag a palm over his perspiring forehead. "I thought maybe my hand would burst into flames."

"Are you a vampire?" James smirked as he took a few steps closer and crossed his arms an eyebrow raised.

"I vant to suck your blood..." Lance put his fingers on either side of his mouth and hissed like a cornered cat. James guffawed, and it echoed through the empty church.

"Hush! Sleeping!" Lance lunged forward and grabbed James' shoulder with one hand, and pushed his other over James' mouth. They froze that way for a moment, their foreheads inches apart, before James gently stepped back. Lance kept the hold on his arm a fraction of a second too long, and a flush of blood pooled in James' cheeks again.

"Right, a vampire that lives with his mum," Lance laughed.

"From personal experience, I can tell you that we monsters prefer to move out as soon as possible," James said as he played with his hands, not sure where to put them. Lance's quizzically-arched eyebrows urged him to continue. "My mother knows — she's always known. And she tried to make a go of it, to be fair, but..." He shrugged. "She was embarrassed of me. At twelve I could see the relief on her face when she packed me onto that train with Arthur and the rest of the children. Though, now that time has passed, I think she realizes this is who I am, who I'll always be. Now, she's terrified for me, that I'll be arrested or beaten or worse."

"God, if Mother ever found out." Lance rubbed his lower lip with a grimace at the thought. "Well, I told you how damned churchy she is. That's why the cross ought to have burned my flesh at the touch. Because, well, you and I." He flung his arms out and gave one dramatic spin. "All of this — this building is dedicated to a faith that casts us out. I remember sitting in the pew as a child and listening to the preacher belittle the 'sinful sodomites.' No one said 'amen' louder than I." He leaned against the altar and rubbed his forehead first, and then his cheek, as he shook his head. "That night in Grantham when I confessed to you, I felt invincible. I felt so free and joyous. Only, over the last few days the glow's worn off, and I'm worried. I'm worried about what it means to be who we are in this world. Terrified. Like your mum."

"We have to protect each other." James sensed some kind of thick force around his legs resisting his forward motion toward Lance. But he was able to push through and put a hand on Lance's shoulder.

"Thank God—" Lance stopped himself with a curve of his full lips that twisted with irony. "Thank *someone* I found you."

And somehow it happened, then, what shouldn't have, what James never dreamed would occur — Lance embraced him. No, if the truth was to be told, they embraced each other. And kissed, hip to hip, against the altar dedicated to the Mother of God.

It was a rushing sweetness. That was all James was aware of in those moments when Lance's mouth was on his, as they crushed together. After the initial tide of euphoria subsided, it was strange — he swore for a moment he heard lute music, and pulled away. No, some kind of auditory illusion, because the only sounds in the church were Lance's panting breaths, and the innocent snoring from the opposite side of the room.

Lance put a hand in James' hair and drew him forward again.

Chapter 20

James woke to the gentle pressure of a soft, paw-like hand as it caressed the small of his back. He knew instantly it was Arthur: how many times had those hands touched him? The number was unfathomable now, after ten years of the deepest companionship either of them had ever known. A love and kinship that felt blessed, legendary.

And now, perhaps, ultimately doomed.

James' eyes flew open and his breath died in his lungs for a few long moments as the events of the previous evening flashed through the camera in his mind. *You feckless idiot,* his mind shrieked, *what have you done, what have you done?*

It was only a kiss. Another thought clawed desperately at the first one in an attempt to drag it back down. *Between mates. It was his first time. He ought to have that experience with someone he trusts, someone safe.*

Someone with a partner. Who happens to be another best mate.

Just a kiss — nothing more!

It was more than one. And you let him do it.

Arthur's meaty hand shook him gently. Each imprint of his fingers burned James' flesh through the musty blanket and the fabric of his shirt. He jolted and took a breath, and did the best he could to reset his face. James allowed the hand to guide his shoulders around so he was on his side, facing Arthur, who sat on the floor next to his cot.

"Should get moving before long." Arthur rubbed circles with his thumb on James' shoulder. It scraped over his flesh like sandpaper. "Sun's up."

James glanced over at the stained glass windows of the Lady Chapel, the only witnesses to his infidelity. They blazed now with technicolor glory. Mrs. Wylit slept with her mouth open in a pool of kaleidoscope light, haloed by her tangled hair. With her face slackened and bathed in the churchly glow, she looked equal parts saintly and otherworldly, a pagan figure turned Christian for the purposes of converting the wild peoples of this isle.

Lance snored nearby as well, but James could not see his face. He had the entire blanket wrapped around himself like a cocoon. Or a funeral shroud.

"G-good m-morning." James sat up and pulled away from Arthur's reach. He bought himself time by checking his wristwatch.

"You sound like I used to back in primary school." Arthur offered a half-smile over his broad, even-featured face and regal brow.

"I s-suppose I do." James swallowed, or attempted to, with a desert throat.

Arthur cocked his head slightly. His curls shifted to compensate for the movement. "Is... something wrong? James?"

His own name pierced his heart with a shard of guilty ice. It melted and bubbled up inside him then, like vomit, threatening to erupt. As he stared into Arthur's emerald eyes, their ring of thick lashes, the circle of gold that crowned his pupil, the truth welled up in him, beat through his blood, and pounded at the door of his lips. The urge to confess was so strong inside him, he felt physical pain from the hairs on his head to the middle of his bones.

He took a breath, and swallowed it all back, locking up his mouth in a grimace that was supposed to be a smile. "No, nothing's wrong." His throat tightened. "I didn't sleep well," he added, and it sounded authentic, to his ears at least.

Arthur's face fell. If asked to do so, even to save his soul inside the church, James couldn't have described the look Arthur kept smiling, but something drained out of his eyes at that moment. He patted James' knee and stood up to stretch. Dozens of pops echoed up his spine.

James' chest relaxed in increments with the sudden euphoric rush brought on by his lie's success. This was immediately followed by a thick nausea that looped through his midsection as bile burned up his throat. For the next few hours, he would exist from moment to moment, riding a pendulum that swung back and forth between relief and guilt, pelted by constant mental questions. Would Lance tell? Could they really keep this secret? Would he ever tell Arthur? Should he take it to his grave? Or in a few months, when this was all over, could he tell Arthur in such a way that it wouldn't hurt, would seem like a joke? *Oh, Arthur, you wouldn't believe what Lance did, of course I felt bad for him—*

Arthur went to wake up Lance as James roused Mrs. Wylit, who was in a particularly terrible and combative mood. In the washroom, she slapped him as he tried to help her dress. His reflection in the water-spotted mirror sported a shadow of her hand on his cheek, inflamed in red. "Stupid boy." She shrugged on her wrinkled and smelly jacket and brushed her hair into a lopsided bun with sober, businesslike strokes. He realized in a terrible moment she was stone sober, though her skin was as sallow and her eyes as bloodshot as usual.

Had she seen? Did she know?

"Why did you do that?" He demanded. If she knew, he wanted her to be out with it.

"I can prepare myself. I'm not a child. I could dress a squirming two-year-old in three minutes flat." She adjusted her wilted collar. "That's a feat. You couldn't do that." She turned to him, and tears stood out in her eyes. In a sudden torrent, they spilled over her cheeks in two long rivers.

"I've had plenty of practice, what with trying to keep you presentable." James stuffed his shirt into his pants and yanked up his suspenders. He turned to his own reflection in the mirror and tried not to look at his face as he dampened and combed down his hair. "What are you blubbering about, Vi?"

"I think the golden era is over." She opened up her pocketbook and withdrew the silver flask. Mrs. Wylit raised it to him in a solemn toast, and emptied it down her throat. Then she turned to the mirror and splashed water on her face. She patted it dry with uncharacteristic dignity, then whipped out a tube of red lipstick and applied it, though the rest of her face was bleak and bare. "War paint." She capped the tube and dropped it into her purse.

"What the hell does that even mean?" James shouted after her as she hauled up her bag and left him in the washroom alone. "Can't you make *sense* for once?"

When James had gathered himself enough to face the others again, he returned to the church proper to find the blankets and cots returned to the store room. Lance was waiting for him near the door. The luggage, Arthur, and Mrs. Wylit were nowhere in sight, presumably outside already.

"Lance." He rushed to him. "I—"

Lance offered his movie-star smile, and put both hands on James' shaking shoulders. "Listen, we don't have time to talk it over now. I want you to know two things. First, I won't say anything to Arthur. Second, I don't regret a single thing." He dropped his hands down to James' and gave them a gentle, loving squeeze.

"Oh God," James murmured as he lost himself in Lance's ocean-blue gaze. It was all he could say. It was a prayer for help.

"Come on. Stiff upper lip." Lance opened the church door, and they joined the others.

Since they'd saved money on their accommodations the previous night, it was agreed that they should walk back to the train station, have breakfast somewhere nearby, and hail a cab to take them to St. John's Hospital, the lunatic asylum.

They managed to find tea and toast and jam in a small teahouse next to the train station. James tried to eat, but it stuck in his throat. Arthur ate his, but without the usual relish with which he generally

consumed foodstuffs. Mrs. Wylit filled her tea with whiskey purchased on the way to breakfast, and then daintily added sugar and a
lemon slice.

Lance broke the silence by dropping his half-eaten toast back
onto his plate with a desolate sigh. "I know the feeling, mates." He
raised his napkin to his lips. "This leg of the journey's got me scared.
This really could be the end of our leads. If we can't find Mr. Blanchard, well, then where shall we look for Matthew Barlow?"

"He might not remember Mr. Marlin." Arthur swallowed the
rest of his tea with a grimace. "He might not remember anything at
all."

"Poor man," James piped up. It was a relief to have something else
to think about, another problem to try and solve besides his own.
"To think he fought with Mr. Marlin in the Great War only to be
carted off to an asylum. He must not have any family to care for him."

"Terrible to be alone like that." Arthur turned to James and
caught this gaze for a moment longer than was comfortable. After
insuring the employees were busy with the morning train rush, he
reached up and brushed a crumb from the lapel of James' jacket. The
act was as intimate as it ever was, but struck James as doubly so. The
guilty ice refroze and pricked his heart again and he had to look away
to stare down at his bread and jam.

The first cabbie they hailed recoiled and drove away when they
asked to be taken to the asylum. The second raised his bushy eyebrows high over his wrinkled face, but leapt free of his vehicle to
load their luggage without a moment's hesitation. It would be a good
fare — the hospital sat on a hill about two miles from Lincoln proper. The black automobile wound up a long lane before it pulled to a
stop outside a massive, imposing building which housed the primary
wards of the hospital.

As they exited the car, James turned a full spin to take in the vast-
ness of the hospital complex. The lawns seemed to stretch for miles,

peppered with other buildings, a water tower, and scored with winding paths and well-trimmed hedges. A man in beige work coveralls stood a few yards down the cul-de-sac, using a rake to spread mulch beneath a line of bushes. He was tall, stretched-looking, and his hair blew in the cool wind that was sure to precede a summer rainstorm.

A rainstorm was all they needed, James thought with a shiver. The hospital was gothic enough on its own, a giant structure of stone, something constructed to look stately and refined that only resembled an Italianate military fort. Or a prison. It, and many of the outbuildings, were in need of refreshment and repair, peppered with cracks and stained with years of rain and mold. Gently lilting on the summer air came a distant yelping shout, followed by a sobbing cry. James shivered and instinctively stepped closer to Arthur, who bent next to the car to pay the cab fare.

With his money clenched in his fist, the cab driver was anxious to leave this place, and sped over the crushed gravel of the cul-de-sac to race back towards town. The sudden roaring of the car startled the man tending the bushes, and he yelped. He took up the rake in a defensive stance and crouched behind the bushes. "Get away!" He brandished his weapon at the diminishing form of the automobile.

It was only then James realized that the groundskeeper was also likely a patient of this hospital. Still clutching the rake, he turned to the visitors, who stood there stupidly with their baggage. Arthur stepped in front of James, and Lance put his hand on Mrs. Wylit's arm. Mrs. Wylit shook him off with impatient violence, and dropped her baggage at her feet.

"Vi, what—"

Mrs. Wylit stepped toward the patient. There was a long moment where they all feared the worst, that he would raise the rake and rush at her. James and Lance both darted forward to grab her arm, but Lance was faster and James stepped back out of the way. The sudden movement startled the man with the rake again, and he crumpled to the ground, whimpering.

"Let me go. Let me go to him."

"Vi, please!" Lance begged.

"I'll paste you, don't think I won't."

Lance threw a helpless glance over his shoulder at James and Arthur. Mrs. Wylit wiggled her arm free and closed the distance between herself and the patient. She wobbled in her heels over the gravel, unsteadiness aided by the whiskey tea.

"There there, now." She knelt down next to the patient. Mrs. Wylit plucked the rake from his hands and set it on the ground, and to everyone's surprise, he let her do it. "What a lovely job you've done on these bushes, luv. Why don't you stand up and show me?"

The man rose to his feet. "I'm sorry." He dragged his sleeve over his nose to clear his face. The patient gave her a short bow. "I get upset sometimes." He extended a sudden formal hand. "I'm Silas Barkley, pleased to meet you." The totally normal tone of his voice and his mannerisms stunned James.

"Viola Wylit." She shook his hand.

The man twitched a moment, and wrinkled his nose. "You smell like whiskey, Miss Viola Wylit."

"That is because I am a drunk, Mr. Barkley," she replied with a bob of her head. "I'm quite damaged, actually."

"So am I." Silas flashed her a sunny grin. "Of course, that's why I'm here on holiday."

"Room for one more?" Mrs. Wylit said, and they laughed. Rather flirtatiously, if James was being honest. "Kettles," she went on, "mine's kettles. I can't stand the whistling, you know. It sounds like..." She trailed off, her mouth working uselessly.

"The Blitz?"

She pressed her lips together and nodded, and they stared a long moment into each other's haunted eyes.

One of the vast front double doors swung open, and a man in an attendant's whites came out, his steps quick, his homely face concerned. A ring of keys jingled at his waist. "Silas!" He jogged up to Mrs. Wylit and the patient, ignoring the rest of them completely. "I told you to rake the leaves along the east path. You shouldn't have come over here by yourself."

"I finished," Silas explained with a shrug. He picked up his rake and leaned on it. "I know it's near the road, but nobody ever comes up here this early."

"I heard you cry out. Was it the taxi?"

Mrs. Wylit and Silas both nodded.

"My mother was hit by a car," Silas explained politely to Mrs. Wylit, who nodded in understanding. "And now I have an..." he thought for a moment, then parroted what sounded like an academic, doctorly voice. "Adverse reaction."

"Can I..." the attendant flubbed as he suddenly noticed James, Lance, Arthur, and their baggage. "Help you? Are you..." He nodded toward Mrs. Wylit. "Erm, checking in?"

"No, no." Lance held up both hands in a nonthreatening display. "We're here to inquire after a patient that may be here. And visit him, if possible."

"Oh, you didn't come to visit me?" Silas pretended to pout. "That's a shame."

"Maybe next time." James was thrown by how genuine Mrs. Wylit's smiles were as she spoke with this Silas, a total stranger. Perhaps there was some kind of instant bond between them, as Vi had suggested — the bond of damage.

"Why don't you step in," the attendant said, "and I'll go find someone."

As they gathered their things and climbed the stone steps, Mrs. Wylit turned back to Silas and dropped a wink. He gave her a salute, and disappeared around the corner of the building, back, perhaps, to a place where he would not hear automobiles pass.

The foyer of the hospital was as large as the Lady Chapel, and saturated with echoes. Two monumental stone staircases, one leading to each wing of the building, converged in the middle of the back wall and spilled down to the floor. Everything was hard, made of huge slabs of stone. It was cool and shadowy as the day's light diminished to make way for the rain. The walls were painted a soothing blue that did nothing to placate James' racing heart.

"I'll be back in two shakes." The attendant jogged up the staircase, bearing left, and disappeared down a hallway.

"This place is something out of Lovecraft," James whispered to Arthur, who bumped his shoulder reassuringly. The aging foyer had the trimmings of a library, perhaps, or a fine hotel's main lobby — an alcove at the point where the staircases converged, decorative carvings, and the like — but it carried a profound weight, a haunted quality that could not be ignored. James wasn't sure if it was the cracks he saw here and there, the worn look of the stair banisters, or the dull floor tiles. Perhaps it had more to do with the intermittent cries and other strange sounds that came faintly from down the hallways on either side of the stairs.

They listened anxiously until another sound came to their ears — footsteps, clipped and brisk, easily identified as the heel of a woman's shoe. Moments later, a nurse appeared, and marched down the stairs in her uniform — a blue dress with white sleeves and collar, covered with a white apron. The white cap pinned over her severely parted, perfectly curled black hair bobbed as she walked.

"Good morning. I am Mrs. Hartley, ward matron." She said no more, but stared at them with annoyed expectancy.

"Good morning." Lance gave her his most charming smile. "I'm Lance Benwick. This is Viola Wylit, James Wilde, and Arthur Pensinger. We came here today to find a Mr. William Blanchard, who was a friend of my late grandfather Harold Marlin. They fought in the Great War together, and we have some important questions to ask him regarding my grandfather's... well, the last thing my grandfather said to me. It's a very important matter, if you understand my meaning."

Matron Hartley's expression did not change. Her stony face made it impossible to judge her mood, or her age. She was emotionless, as stony and empty as the foyer of the hospital. "I'm sorry to inform you," she said, in an equally unremarkable tone, "that Mr. William Blanchard died over a month ago. No relatives came to claim his remains, so he has been buried in our cemetery. I can show you his resting place, if you wish."

Chapter 21

"She could have at least let us wait inside." Mrs. Wylit huddled under Arthur's umbrella and shivered. "Nasty, nasty witch. I think she likes giving injections. Lots of injections and electroshock treatments. I bet she's got a gold star on her wall for every lobotomy she's done."

Arthur said nothing, his face still red from the argument they'd had with Matron Hartley, who had refused to tell them anything at all about Mr. Blanchard. "You're not family," she repeated, over and over again, with the same measured, condescending calm. "I cannot release any details to anyone but the family." Nor would she tell them if she had contact information for Mr. Blanchard's relatives. No matter how they explained, begged, pleaded, it did not matter — and when Matron Hartley had had enough, she'd marched into a nearby office and called them a taxi. And told them they were to remove themselves or she would call the attendants to escort them.

Mrs. Wylit shifted her weight, and stumbled a bit on the wet gravel. Arthur caught her and kept his arm tightly around her shoulders to keep her upright and out of the rain.

James gazed longingly at their backs from where he stood with his own umbrella next to Lance in front of the stairs. If all was right with the world, James would be under Arthur's arm right now. Not that he deserved to be there.

"What are we going to do?" Lance wondered in a defeated, mumbling voice as he kicked a stone at his feet. "I can't let my grand-dad down, not after all of this."

"We'll think of something. Perhaps... Tom?"

"You don't think that bridge is burnt?" Lance reached into his jacket pocket and shook free a cigarette. He lit it with a frustrated sigh. "I don't see a path forward, lads. I think we're finished. If we're lucky, there'll be a train home today. Wouldn't you say, Arthur?"

Arthur glanced over his shoulder at Lance, and fixed him with his green gaze for an uncomfortably long time. Then he looked at James before turning around without a word.

Oh God. James bit his lip against the tears rising in his throat. *How weary, stale, flat, and unprofitable seem to me the uses of this world.*

Behind them, the door opened.

"Here to chase us with your broom, witch?" Mrs. Wylit sneered around the mouth of her flask. But as they turned, they saw the attendant who had been in charge of Silas and the other grounds crew, who undoubtedly must be inside now with the rain increasing its soggy insistence.

He opened an umbrella of his own and stood with them. "I'm sorry you didn't find what you came for. It *is* sad, Mr. Blanchard, you know." The attendant reached into the pocket of his white trousers and handed Mrs. Wylit a piece of folded paper. She took it between her quivering fingers. "That's Silas's address. He wanted me to give it to you in hopes that you'll write, Mrs... Wylit, wasn't it?"

She nodded with a knitted brow, her mouth dropping open. James knew something was about to come out, and physically winced in advance.

"I like him." A raindrop settled on her red-smeared lips. "I really do, and I'd love to write him. I'll write him every day. If you do something for me. For us."

The attendant scratched the back of his balding head. "What, exactly?"

"Tell us about Mr. Blanchard. Tell us everything you know."

He held up the hand that wasn't being used to hold the umbrella. "Now, you know I can't do that — you're not—"

"The family, we know," James groaned.

"But there isn't any family, is there?" Mrs. Wylit took a step forward, unmindful of the rain. It spattered in heavy droplets on the piece of paper between her fingers. "That's the tragedy of it all. Nobody came to claim him. Nobody ever will. No one cares what happens to people in places like this. People like Silas." She shuddered, and dragged her hand over her mouth, smearing her lipstick. "People like *me*."

"But we care." Lance picked up where Mrs. Wylit was silenced, too full of something inside of her to speak. "He was apparently one of my grandfather's close friends. We're probably the closest thing he has to a family now."

The attendant scratched his head again and sucked air between his teeth. "You *promise* you'll write?"

"On my baby's grave." She held out her fingers for the cigarette in Lance's hand. Thunderstruck, he gave it to her. She put her smeary red lips around it and inhaled. When the smoke curled from her nose and mouth, she was from another world, a thing with a bloody mouth and shimmering eyes. "Tell us."

The attendant eked some half-words from his numb lips before he began to make sense. "Mr. Blanchard was brought here by his landlord — said he'd lost his mind and couldn't pay the rent anymore, couldn't locate any relatives. The old man had no place to go, and he was deteriorating. Quickly, mind you. Dementia, and, er..." He motioned clumsily to Mrs. Wylit. "Like you were saying to Silas..."

"Trauma." The cherry of the cigarette glowed in her vast, bloodshot eyes as Mrs. Wylit took another lungful.

"He was pretty far gone when he came. Very confused. He'd wake up one day and think he was back in hospital after being wounded at the Somme. We'd all try to set him straight, and it'd turn into an argy-bargy every time. He was with us for about half a year, and then one night he faded away. It was peaceful-like, if that eases you any. Say, mind if I..." He put up two fingers and brought them briefly to his lips.

Lance gave him a cigarette and lit it for him. "Got to hurry before they miss me." The attendant coughed and his smoke mingled with Mrs. Wylit's. "Right. What'd you say your granddad's name was?"

"Harold Marlin," said Lance.

"Aye, he called me Harold or Harry a few times." The attendant gave a series of sad shakes of his head.

James perked up with a sudden thought that blazed across his brain like lightning. "Did he ever talk about someone called Matthew?"

"Matthew? Aye, not often, but sometimes."

"What did he say?" Arthur took an eager step forward.

The attendant coughed on his cigarette again as Arthur and his umbrella blotted out the outline of the gray sun. "It never really made sense, but he would say things like, oh, Matthew's in Scotland and he's all alone, he'll never come out of that house now, he's never coming home."

"Scotland!" James cried, with such a start he nearly fumbled his umbrella. "Scotland! Matthew's in Scotland!"

"Scotland's a big place, mate," Lance tempered as he squeezed James' shoulder. "Did he mention where in Scotland Matthew was? Any city names, counties, anything?"

The attendant shook his head no, and stole a glance at his watch. "I've really got to run, or Nurse Hartley'll have my head like John the Baptist's on a dinner platter."

"Belongings." There was a sudden spark in Arthur's eyes. "Items, a suitcase — did Mr. Blanchard come to you with luggage?"

"The landlord sold off anything of value, if that's what you're getting at."

"Haven't you been listening?" James snapped, unable to help his tone. The tension inside him was as taut as a violin string. "Are you daft, man? We aren't interested in money or valuables, we need to know where to find Matthew."

"All right, the landlord did bring a suitcase. It had pictures, papers, clothes — things he couldn't get a farthing for to pay the back rent, you know."

"Where is the suitcase?" Without realizing what he was doing, James dropped the umbrella and put his hands on the attendants shoulders, and hooked his fingers into the fabric of the man's uniform. "Please tell me it wasn't tossed out or burnt—"

"No, no, it's in storage." The attendant tried to step back, but James had him fast. "There's a shed round back beneath the water tower. It's where we put everything that isn't... claimed, you know."

"We need his suitcase." Arthur drew up, it seemed, even a few inches taller.

"Let me go, mate, people could be watching." The attendant pushed James' hands away, and then stuck the cigarette back in his mouth. "Look, I can't do that — I really shouldn't have told you what I did."

"It's our only chance." Lance's knuckles were white on the umbrella handle. "C'mon, mate, you've been such a friend so far. You want Vi to write, she'll write — a hundred letters, two hundred —"

The attendant backed up, and slowly climbed the steps without turning his body away from them. "I've done all I can." He flicked his spent smoke into a puddle. "You know where it is, and you know what happened to him. Any of the rest of it's on you." He turned to Mrs. Wylit. "I'm sorry I can't do better than that, luv. I pray, for Silas's sake, that what I've given you is worth a note or two. He seems to think you'll have plenty to talk about." With that, he disappeared inside the vast, echoing halls of the hospital.

Moments later, the taxi arrived, and they rode in stony silence back down toward Lincoln. The driver, a kindly sort, it seemed, took them to his cousin's home not far from the cathedral. The woman appeared shrew-like, but was willing to let them stay in the furnished apartment above her tea shop for the night, though she usually required a monthly lease. They must look quite the pathetic and bedraggled crew, James thought, as they ascended the stairs in a cloud of sweet smells from the shop below.

In truth, they were tired, they were hungry, they were defeated, and each of them could sincerely use a bath. Lance yanked open one of the front windows to let in the sultry after-rain mist, and smoked with angsty movements, vacant eyes fixed on the street below. Mrs. Wylit collapsed into an armchair and gave her mud-splattered heels a dismissive kick before she lit a cigarette of her own. James went to Arthur, and they sat on the plaid sofa without touching.

"*Now is the winter of our discontent.*" Mrs. Wylit quoted, breaking the silence before blowing a very acceptable smoke ring. They watched it float up to the ceiling before being chopped to bits by the fan blades.

"Vi," James all but whispered. He put his hand on Arthur's knee for support — he couldn't get the words out on his own. Arthur paused a long moment before putting his hand over James', obscuring it completely. "Vi, what... what baby—"

"What are you looking for out there?" Mrs. Wylit asked Lance. "That geezer with the old rotting Al Capone coat?"

It was the first that Mrs. Wylit had acknowledged their shadow figure, and Lance jerked his head back in their direction. The shock was momentary, however, and he soon turned his pouting, morose face back to the window. "He's not there, if that's what you're wondering."

Arthur tried this time. "Mrs. Wylit, what were you talking about a baby—"

Mrs. Wylit sucked in a drag. "I suppose it won't be long. We're really not far from that le Wigford place, especially if one takes the bus. He'll make his way. Like a cat, really." She put the stick to her mouth again, and then shoved her hand into her bag to rummage for the flask. "Drive off into the middle of nowhere and toss pussy out, and low and behold she's back the next day."

"Vi," James began slowly. "Are you saying you saw the man in the brown coat, the one that you and Arthur chased in the market? Here? Outside of St. Mary le Wigford's?"

"Outside, no." She ashed right on the carpet, and Arthur slid the heavy glass ashtray in her direction while James used his foot to rub it into the fibers so it would disappear. *If only it were so easy to get every stain out,* he thought. *Out, damned spot.*

"Try inside," said Mrs. Wylit.

"Inside!"

"It's not like the dear janitor *locked* us in." She stabbed out her cigarette. "It was right before dawn. I woke up for a wee and there he was, over by the nave door. He must have seen me moving, because out he darted, a rabbit back into his hole."

"Why didn't you wake us?" James demanded.

"What, after you finally fell asleep? We all know the insomniac you are." She poured fire down her throat again. "Besides, we'd never have caught him. He's a quick one."

"I don't understand. I can't think who it could be." James pushed up from the sofa and paced behind it. He alternated between wringing his hands and rubbing his chin. "Why is he following us?" James froze, and looked at Arthur. "You don't think it's the police, do you?"

"I think if we were going to be arrested, it would have happened already." Lance stood to put a reassuring hand on James' arm. James pulled away and went to the small galley kitchen to draw a glass of water from the tap.

"I agree it's strange," Lance went on, as he lent over to put out his cigarette, "but we have bigger problems. Wouldn't you agree, mate?" He bumped Arthur's shoulder with his fist. Arthur nodded without looking up. "I mean, are we finished? Is this really the end of our little endeavor? It certainly seems that way to me, I don't know about the three of you." He shook his blonde head. "I never thought I'd disappoint Granddad like this."

"Isn't only about you," Arthur rumbled from where he sat on the couch, elbows rested on his broad knees. He cradled his head in his hands and his black curls tumbled forward over the tips of his fingers. "James and I…" A strange twist agitated his mouth for a moment. "Mr. Marlin was… if it wasn't for him…"

"He was directly responsible for our relationship," James picked up for him, as he often did when words didn't come easily. He knew how much it embarrassed Arthur to stutter, and he tended to relapse during moments of high emotion. He often would cross his arms and say to James, *Well, you're a writer, you find a way to say it.* James went on. "Mr. Marlin and Nim helped us understand who we are, and that we deserve to be happy, despite what the rest of the world would say. And if Mr. Marlin wanted us to find Matthew, well, then we must find him. That's it — we haven't any other recourse."

"I wasn't trying to make it seem like it was for me to do, my problem." Lance leaned defensively against the doorframe leading to the front hall of the little flat. "He was my flesh and blood, but before he was in my life, he was in yours." He raked his hand through his hair, and it stood up, waving like wheat.

"Then what the bloody hell are you all arguing about then?" Mrs. Wylit shrilled suddenly, and launched her empty flask at the wall. It clanged, ringing like a bell, clearer and sweeter than James would have thought. "Find it. Find a damn way to do it, then." She marched on unsteady feet into the kitchen where she set about rifling through the drawers. They watched her in awe as she finally came up with a pad of paper and a pencil. She threw herself back down into the chair and perched the paper on her thigh to begin writing.

"Dear… Silas," she began, and then crossed it out. "My dear friend Silas… how have you been since I last saw you, which was this morning? I have been... very... bad." She licked the end of the pencil. "That's not a very descriptive word," she said. "James, what should I write instead? Disappointed? Devastated?"

"How about 'drunk?'" Lance snapped.

"She's right." Arthur rose to his feet on tree trunk legs.

"Well, of course she needs another word besides 'bad,'" James agreed. "What is this, a primary school composition?"

"He means about doing something." Lance uncrossed his arms and stood close to Arthur, who had wandered to the window to stare out into the sunset. "What should we do? Arthur, if you've got an idea, share it, mate."

"Said he gave us everything he could. Really, it was everything we needed," Arthur rumbled into the sinking light of day that bathed the panes of wavy, water stained glass. "We know where the suitcase is. All we have to do is go and get it."

"What, from the asylum?" James' eyes shot wide, green ringed in white.

Lance and Arthur nodded in sync, looking at one another with their determined jaws clenched.

"They'll have night watchmen, for sure," Lance reasoned, still looking at Arthur and gauging his approval. "But we can get past them. Especially if there's something else happening in the hospital that might require their attention."

"A distraction." The hint of a smile chased over Arthur's features. "Mrs. Wylit," he asked, "how'd you like to see that Silas fellow again?"

Chapter 22

"Well, gentlemen. Mrs. Wylit." Lance gave a mockingly formal bow, one hand still on the rim of the cab's door. "Perhaps we'll see you in the clink later as we all await the King's pleasure. Sorry. The *Queen's* pleasure"

"Be careful." James tapped on the glass of his window and rolled it down. Arthur bent, and blocked the sliver of moon from his vision. James reached through the door and grabbed his jacket sleeve. "Whatever's — look, do be careful, Arthur."

Arthur held his gaze, green to green, for a long moment, before breaking it away. His features were sullen and immobile; he was anxious, assuredly, about the task before them, but James could sense something else running beneath, as though he held dowsing rods and had discovered an underground aquifer. Arthur looked at Lance and said, "I will."

The cab left Arthur and Lance at the bottom of the lane that led up to the asylum, and continued on to the front door to dispose of James and Mrs. Wylit. The hospital grounds were bordered by hedges and a row of trees that provided cover and a chance to sneak in unseen.. The night was, as luck would have it, especially dark, with a slivered moon and intermittent clouds that blocked the stars. Of course, there were floodlights attached to sections of the building, but their light wash was by no means comprehensive. St. John's was old, and its time was running out, now that the war was over and wards such as these were closing all over the country in lieu of more modern facilities. There was a chance, with a distraction, that Lance and Arthur would be able to sneak to the shed that the orderly had revealed to them.

Back at the flat, there had been much discussion about who would be best for each job. James had pushed to accompany Arthur — even with the strange way Arthur had been acting, he couldn't imagine one of them going to jail without the other. James wasn't strong, but he could be fast on quiet feet. These were skills that aided him in the past when he'd needed to escape Morgan and his gang.

Arthur, however, wouldn't hear of it. Lance himself agreed when James brought up how often Lance used charisma to get himself out of trouble, and wouldn't that mean he'd be better running interference for Mrs. Wylit? This logic fell on deaf ears. Arthur wanted Lance to help him break into the shed, and to play lookout, and that was that.

It was so rare when Arthur insisted on something that James was unsure how to react. In the end, he'd thrown up his hands and the discussion (if you could call it that) had ended there. Lance seemed to have no issue deferring to Arthur, though James wished he'd shown more backbone. Perhaps he was feeling guilty for what they'd done, which James supposed he rightly should. Why should he hold all the guilt for what had happened in St. Mary le Wigford?

Mrs. Wylit lolled next to him on the seat. She fumbled open her bag and withdrew the mostly-empty bottle of pear brandy they'd found abandoned in the kitchen cabinet in the rental flat. As she raised it to her lips, James snatched it from her grasp. Mrs. Wylit cursed and stared him down with a bloodshot, iron gaze.

James looked at the bottle, and smelt it. He recoiled, but nevertheless brought it to his mouth and took a long pull. Though he managed to swallow it, he fell into a coughing fit that brought tears to his eyes. Mrs. Wylit guffawed and slapped the back of the seat. The cabbie glanced in the rearview mirror and chuckled as well.

"Ugh, good God." James caught his breath and shoved the bottle back into Mrs. Wylit's hands. "I thought you drank that garbage to feel *better.*"

Mrs. Wylit toasted him, and took a slug herself. "It's the initial burn, lad. It goes away."

"Yes, I suppose you're quite numb to it," James snapped as the cab pulled up to the front steps of the hospital.

"Quick, do my face." Mrs. Wylit reached into her bag again and handed James her lipstick. "I'm so excited I've gone trembly."

"Ah, young love." James took the lipstick and cupped Mrs. Wylit's face in one hand. With the other, he smeared the cheap lipstick over her mouth.

"Beautiful," the cab driver chortled.

"Bugger off," she said, the second word encased in an unladylike burp. "C'mon, James. Fate awaits us."

After he had received his quid, the cab driver was more than happy to speed off into the darkness, away from the bughouse, as he called it. And equally happy to get away from whatever his four passengers were planning.

They pounded on the doors until a wary janitor made the mistake of letting them in, only to watch them race up the staircase to follow the signs for the men's ward. There, James learnt a few things that he had not previously known.

First, apparently James's understanding of how the insane were treated was based more on novels and radio dramas than reality. One of the first rooms they'd passed was a large, open space with a circle of chairs in the center. A man in a lab coat sat next to a patient, who stood in front of his chair to address the audience. "Some days I'm happy, frighteningly happy. Others, I want to hurt…" In the few moments he'd watched, James had been entirely taken aback by what he'd seen. He'd expected drooling patients in straight jackets. These men sat and listened to one another, some smoking, looking like a group of blokes meeting for a quiet cuppa.

The other thing that James learnt, as Mrs. Wylit rushed in to Silas, who sat in the circle on a folding chair, was exactly how strong Matron Hartley was. As it happened, she displayed a great deal of physical prowess. She snatched his arm from behind and bent it up to his shoulder blades before she slammed his chest into the wall. James hollered, but her grip was pure iron.

"Don't struggle — you'll make it worse." Her voice was cool poison in his ear. "Now, what on earth are you doing back here?"

"Viola!" Silas rose from his chair. She stumbled to him and put her arms around his neck in a quick, messy embrace. "What—"

"I say, who are you? What is this?" The doctor stood as well, and the patients turned to one another. The room bubbled with questions. One patient started laughing, long and loud, perhaps a little too long and too loud.

"Oh, Silas, what a bird you've caught there."

"I met her this afternoon," he said. "She and her friends came 'round asking about poor old Mr. Blanchard, the war vet. Hartley had to tell them he'd passed away."

"This is a private therapy session, and it's well past visiting hours." Matron Hartley slackened her grip on James, confident that her show of force was enough. It was. Though having a dust up with a matron would provide a sufficient distraction, James wasn't entirely sure he could win. "You need to leave. Immediately."

"I want to tell my story." Mrs. Wylit clung to Silas. "That's what you're doing, isn't it? That's why you're here? Telling your stories, and the doctor can tell you what's the matter with you, yeah?"

"Madam, it's quite a bit more complicated than that," the doctor sniffed. "This is a new method called group therapy. And yes, we ask each member of the group periodically to share, but—"

"Out of the question." Matron Hartley took James by the elbow. "Come on." She beckoned impatiently to Mrs. Wylit. "I will call the attendants if I have to."

"Let her speak." Silas turned to his fellow patients. "Don't you all want to hear her story? Maybe Dr. Brown can help her. They do this nonsense over in the women's ward, right?" He turned to Mrs.

Wylit and put his hands on her shoulders as a toothy grin spread up his thin features. "I can't believe you came back to see me."

"I want to hear it," the loud laugher insisted. "C'mon doc, let her speak. You've always said we need to tell our stories, share our pain. You can't expect her to keep it bottled up if it needs to come out."

"Look at her," said another. "She's distressed. Sit down, luv, have a smoke, tell us all about it."

The doctor refused, but a chorus of indignation swept over him. At last, he held up his hands. "All right, all right. You're right. I'd be a hypocrite if I didn't at least try to offer my assistance for a few minutes. Besides, for some of you who don't like to share your thoughts and feelings, let this be an example for you. Our guest wishes to freely share what's on her mind."

"You can't be serious." Matron Hartley dropped James' elbow and flounced around the circle to the doctor's side. "Random people bursting into our facility, interrupting treatment, bothering the patients—"

"It's no bother," one called. "C'mon, Matron Heartless."

There was a quiet but significant, "Oooohhhh" between the patients. James guessed that calling Matron Hartley her less-than-flattering nickname had been an accident, or a very well-played card.

"Find her a chair," the doctor said firmly.

"But, doctor—"

"Find her. A chair."

A few of the patients clapped as Silas dragged another folding chair away from the wall, and shoved it into the circle next to his. James, forgotten in the doorway, slunk to the side as Matron Hartley stormed out. Her shoes spoke her echoing disdain as she stomped away down the tiled hallway.

"Thank you." Mrs. Wylit arranged herself primly on the metal chair with her handbag in her lap, and accepted the cigarette that someone sent round the circle. She took a drag and looked at the doctor. She should have looked silly, James thought. This was all a distraction so that

Arthur and Lance could get the suitcase. But she appeared stoic to him then, quietly sad and beautiful, weathered and strong but ultimately vulnerable. She opened her purse and withdrew a handkerchief, which she used to gently dab her lipstick and fix a smudge at the corner of her mouth. "How do I begin?" Her words were met with hallowed, expectant silence. Every eye in the room was fixed on her.

"You may begin wherever you wish." The doctor bowed slightly to her in a kind, gentle gesture. The others in the therapy circle were reverentially quiet.

Silas put his hand on hers, and she squeezed it. "Tell them about the kettles. Y'know, like me and the car engines."

"All right." Mrs. Wylit took a breath, and squared her shoulders. James was riveted against the back wall, his elbows on the bubbling paint. "Tea kettles. Any loud whistling noise. Sometimes a train, if I'm right next to it. I hear them, and it's like I can't breathe. I can't move. Sweat breaks out all over my body. I want to be sick, but I can't."

Silas nodded his head as if he completely understood, though everyone else remained frozen, afraid perhaps, that if they moved they would startle this gentle sparrow into flying away. "I didn't realize it — I mean, I knew, but I couldn't make the words come — until I met Silas." She glanced at him and gave his hand another squeeze. "A five minute conversation. But it was like he knew. And he knew... that I knew... and I ... I know why it is, now. The whistles."

Fat tears dropped from her eyes in a sudden flood, a rush down the mountain like unexpected snow melt. But her face remained perfectly placid and pale.

"Tell them, Viola," Silas prompted after a long minute. "Go on. Doc says this is a safe place."

"Yes." The doctor seemed to suddenly remember that he was supposed to be in charge of this therapy. "Yes, indeed. Nothing leaves this room."

"When the bombs fell," she began, her voice barely above a whisper, "they always whistled first."

"You were in London during the Blitz?" the doctor asked softly.

Mrs. Wylit nodded. She lifted the handkerchief dreamily up to her face and dabbed her eyes.

"Did you lose someone, Viola," Silas said, "like I lost my mother?"

James heard a little rustle behind him. He jumped and looked back at the door. Several attendants and a few sisters were clustered in the dark hallway beyond, listening. Well, perhaps this distraction had worked after all. Though the nature of this visit to the hospital, he knew in that moment, had entirely changed.

Mrs. Wylit inhaled, and the tears stopped. Her body and face went rigid, and James thought for a moment she was going to have a stroke. At last, her voice eked out, "My baby. Maggie."

"Oh, God," James breathed, the words barely audible.

"She was two years old with golden curls." Mrs. Wylit's voice was unsettlingly robotic, unnatural. "Crushed by a chimney." She turned to Silas and her voice became warm and conversational. "Well, of course I wished it had been my husband instead of her. His being crushed, well, I could have lived with that. All wives expect to outlive their husbands, it's a fact of life. And one night I told him as much, and he left me, so there's that." She put the cigarette in her mouth and pulled on it. "I got his mother's house in the divorce, if you can believe it. And so I live there and I rent the upstairs to two f—" James winced, thinking she was about to say *fairies*. "Friends," she said. "And if it weren't for them, nobody would give a damn if I was alive or dead." She paused. "Including me."

James jerked when something wet dropped onto his wrist. He re-alized it was a tear from his own eye. He scrubbed his sleeve over his face. Many of the men who listened did the same, and it seemed as though even the doctor was sniffling a bit. They were so transfixed at that moment, that they did not hear the muffled banging sounds that floated in from outside through the open (though barred) windows. James' melancholy heart dived deep into the cavern of his chest at the sound. Arthur and Lance. Had to be. Breaking into the shed.

Under the shadow-scorched moonlight, Arthur gave the old shed door a final kick. The padlock snapped and the door rocketed open with a groaning shutter. He and Lance froze, and listened for shouts or steps rustling through the lawn's manicured grass. After a few moments, they heard nothing but the whisper of a few cars along the street and a lonely dog in the distance.

Arthur and Lance tiptoed inside. Something brushed Lance's face and he slapped a hand against it in case it was a spider. It was not, and was in fact the pull-chain of a bare bulb that hung from the small wooden room's roof. He yanked it, and the space was illumi-nated with weak light. The shed contained a few rusted snow shov-els, some unused hedge trimmers, and a wall piled with suitcases and trunks. Each was labelled with a brown paper luggage tag affixed to a handle or a hinge with string.

"Each of these belonged to someone. This many people were for-gotten about." Lance shook his head with a cluck of his tongue.

"Hurry." Arthur began on one side of the pile and Lance on the other.

"It has to be on top," Lance reasoned, "since he died a short time ago." He picked up another tag and squinted at it in the low light. "I think..." Lance drew his matchbook from his pocket and struck a flame. In the flickering glow, the name on the tag came to life. "This is it. This one." He shook out the match and lifted down the suitcase, a battered brown thing marred with scuff marks. "I've got it."

"Let's go." Arthur went for the door, and Lance followed, pulling the cord and turning off the light. Soon, they were back out on the cool grass.

"I don't think anyone's spotted—" Lance began, when Arthur turned and drove his fist hard into Lance's gut. Lance's breath burst from his mouth in a shocked *woosh* and he doubled over. The suitcase thumped to his feet as he wrapped his hands around his stomach.

Arthur stood there, towered over him, silent and pale-faced in the moonlight. He watched as Lance groaned, went down on one knee, and then slowly unfolded himself to stand. Arthur expected him to cry out, to protest, to question. *Why'd you do that? What was that for, mate?*

Instead, Lance looked at him, and then bent down and picked up the suitcase. "All I can say is that I'm sorry. I could give you all of my reasons and excuses, but something tells me you'd rather not hear them. Besides, we'd best get a move on before someone notices us." He winced, and massaged his ribs. "Unless you need another go."

Arthur felt the rancor that had erupted in him and filled his fist ebb away as Lance hefted the suitcase and limped away. All that was left was the misery. He'd expected that hitting Lance would make him feel better. Help straighten things out. But somehow, the black pit in his chest only widened.

Chapter 23

Dr. Brown put his car in park and turned around in his seat. His worried eyes shimmered earnestly in the low light of the streetlamps. He watched Mrs. Wylit as she put the flask to her lips. She offered it to him, and he waved it away. "You've been drinking," he said, "Because of the pain?"

"I ought to stop, I suppose."

"Not immediately." Dr. Brown looked at James, who was nestled in the small back seat of the little tan auto as well, close enough to smell Mrs. Wylit's sweat mixed with the remains of her perfume and her alcohol-saturated breath. "If you've been like this for some time, cutting off the supply cold turkey could be very dangerous. Fevers, seizures, the like. It depends on how long you've been like this."

"As long as I've known her," James said taking responsibility for Mrs. Wylit's side of the conversation. "But that's only been about a year."

"That's long enough." Dr. Brown frowned and shook his gray head. "I recommend cutting back, of course, but until she's ready to be put under a doctor's care, it's dangerous for her to dry out all at once."

"Besides," Mrs. Wylit took another dram of liquor, speaking on her own behalf to remind the two men she was with them in the car, "if I'm not drunk, I don't see the future, do I?" She elbowed James in the ribs with a gentle poke. "Then how am I supposed to be of use to anyone?"

Dr. Brown's eyes bulged a moment and he shared a meaningful glance with James. "Are you sure you don't want to check in to my hospital? You'll receive the best of care. We can treat your alcoholism as well."

Mrs. Wylit shook her head. "We're on a journey, and the lads need me to see it through. How are the knights of the round table supposed to complete their quests without a witch or a wizard or a green man or some such?"

"Mr. Wilde..."

James sighed. "I won't force her. Besides, how can I? I have no legal right to do so. I told you she doesn't have any family that I've been able to locate."

Dr. Brown lifted his hands from the steering wheel with a helpless flap. "All right, then. Well, goodnight. I hope to see you both again soon. And Silas asks you to please write."

"I will," Mrs. Wylit promised.

"Again, sorry about the... dramatic entrance." James opened his door and went to the other side to retrieve Mrs. Wylit.

"Thank you, Doctor."

Dr. Brown waved, shook his head again in pensive disbelief, and drove away. The street was quiet in the dark hours of the night, and the rental flat was dark.

"Oh God, they've been arrested," James lamented after a quick search of the flat did not reveal Lance or Arthur.

Mrs. Wylit emptied the pear brandy bottle and tossed it in the kitchen sink. "No, they're not," she wavered after a watery burp. "They're out at the pub."

"At the pub? That's—"

"Your oracle has spoken." Mrs. Wylit wove her way down the hall to one of the bedrooms, decorated simply in wood, red, and white. She flailed her feet out of her shoes and collapsed on the lacy white coverlet, leaving a smear of lipstick on the pillow case.

James went to the window and threw back the curtain. His eyes scanned the street for Arthur and Lance, but the shops and the sidewalks were deserted. He paced for several minutes before he gave up and trotted down to Mrs. Wylit's room.

He expected her to be passed out, but she lay on the bed as a corpse in a coffin, hands threaded together by her fingers over her midsection, blank eyes fixed on the ceiling. James had to check twice to be sure she was breathing.

"Come on, Vi. You've got a decent bed to sleep in tonight, you might as well be comfortable for once." He took her elbow. She eased up, a pliable doll, but lapsed back into an eerie frozen position, deflated, her arms laying in her lap like an unused marionette.

"Get undressed. Come on, now. Look, if they're at the pub like you said, there's nothing to worry about."

She was silent. She did not blink.

"Vi, you're scaring me. Stop it this instant." Shaking her shoulders gave no result. With a heavy sigh, James took off her jacket and unbuttoned her blouse. "My arm's on fire after that awful matron threw me into the wall," he complained, "but all right, let me take care of you, my fussy baby." He winced as he said it, even as it came out of his mouth. Baby. Baby Maggie. Crushed by the chimney.

In recompense, he patiently undressed her down to her slip, and eased off her stockings. He hung up her jacket in the closet, and rinsed out her blouse and nylons in soapy water. These he hung on the shower rod and opened the bathroom window to let in the cool night air. They'd be dry by morning. When he returned from the loo, she'd collapsed back on the pillows, but still fixed her eyes on nothing, her face entirely vacant. He scolded her again and took a wet handkerchief to the smear of lipstick on her face, and then climbed onto the bed to sit beside her and brush her hair.

She clung to him suddenly, her arms locked around his ribs, as if the world was spinning and she didn't want to be thrown off of it. He wheezed as she squeezed, but he put his arms around her when he realized the silent, bloated tears had erupted from her eyes again.

Not knowing what else to do, James hushed her, patted her like a scared dog. "Listen, Vi, you scare me when you're like this. Totally numb and... I think you ought to..."

She made no indication that she heard him.

"Let go," he said, and lay back with her cradled against him on the cool pillows. "Let go. Let go, Vi. Stop holding it in."

"Holding what in?" The preternaturally flat voice was back, the one he'd heard in the meeting, so hollow and empty. It made his scalp creep to hear it. "I said it all at Silas's meeting. Well, no I didn't. I suppose there's plenty of misery left. It was my fault, you know."

"Maggie... was your fault?" He scoffed. "Vi, it was the bloody Nazis who—"

"We'd all taken to sleeping in the same bed," Mrs. Wylit continued as if he'd never spoken at all. Her tears flowed over her lips and spattered when she spoke. "But it was a small bed, and I was so tired. Sean sprawled out like a starfish, and that left Maggie and I a little sliver to lie on. She was asleep on my arm, and it was getting all pins and needles. I only wanted a good night's sleep. I was so tired." She drew a deep, shuddering breath. "So I picked up my baby and I lay her down in her room, on her little mattress, covered her up with her pink blanket. And then I went back to my bed and I went to sleep, deep sleep. I only woke up when I heard the whistle. And the chimney, well, the chimney fell through Maggie's room, on a bed that should — have — been — empty." Mrs. Wylit heaved as if struck with a convulsion. James clung to her. Was this one of the seizures the doctor spoke of?

The dam broke, and Mrs. Wylit pitched her face into his chest. Her sobs shook her uncontrollably as her loose fist beat the pillow and James' stomach. James let her strike him for a few moments before he anchored her arm under his. Her tears and spit soaked his shirt. He lay in silence and held her.

"Sean — never — forgave — me," she hiccuped after several long minutes.

"You never forgave yourself."

She bucked in his arms again and renewed her wails, though they were muffled against his shirt and suspenders. They went on for what felt like hours. James lay with her until he felt his muscles would give out from applying the constant pressure it took to keep her still. At last, he had to relax his grip. She was a stone woman in his arms. James eased himself away and settled her down on the pillows. Vi was fast asleep, her face that of a plaster saint.

He stepped away from the bed on trembling legs, folded the coverlet up to her chin, and shut the bedroom door.

It had been some time since they'd slept in any relative comfort or privacy. The flat had two bedrooms and a recently updated loo that James knew he ought to take advantage of— have a real shave and a shower, air out his clothes, wash a few items in the sink. Yet, he found himself on the sofa near the window with a random novel he'd found on a shelf. He pretended to read it in the low lamplight, and checked out the window every few moments for Arthur and Lance.

Despite what Mrs. Wylit had said, he became convinced, as the hours passed, that Lance and Arthur had been caught and arrested. Of course Arthur could defend himself in lock-up, and he would protect Lance. But if there was any notion, any inkling by prisoner or bobby as to their sexuality, they would be in real danger. There were criminal charges for that, too, layered on top of the trespassing and burglary.

James had just made up his mind to pick up the flat's telephone and ask the operator to connect him to the local police station when elated laughter floated through the open window. He leapt out of his seat to look. There was Arthur, with Lance at his side, the two of them chuckling like a couple of school mates. Arthur carried a battered leather suitcase at his side. James' breath whooshed from his lungs and his muscles relaxed, so much so that he had to flop back down onto the sofa to avoid falling to the floor.

He rose to his watery legs as their heavy-footed steps stomped up the stairs. James managed to stand as Arthur opened the door with a hollow thud as it swung into the wall. "So then, so then I said," Lance giggled from behind Arthur's hulking shape, "so then I said, 'who invited Buddy Holly?'"

Arthur's shoulders shook as he tried to stifle the laughter and shove it back down his throat. "Ssshh."

"Come in and shut the door," James ordered, and Lance complied. "Where have you been? I was worried to death. Hush, now, Vi's asleep."

"She could sleep through Gabriel's trumpet." Lance kicked off his shoes and stumbled a bit to the side. He caught himself on the wall and grinned at James from beneath a sheaf of his wheat-blonde hair. Then he winced, righted himself, and gently rubbed his midsection and ribs.

"Are you drunk?" James looked from one to the other. Instead of answering, Arthur clomped over to the small oval table in the kitchen. James managed to move the candle holder and the doily beneath it out of the way before Arthur slammed down the suitcase.

"You're both pissed, aren't you?" *Impressive*, James thought. It took a solid ten pints for Arthur to really feel the effects. No wonder they'd been gone for hours.

"Well, we had to celebrate a... theft well-burgled." Lance punched Arthur's meaty shoulder. "And have a good long chat, right Artie?"

James gaped at them. Arthur had *never* let anyone call him Artie. James hadn't ever wanted to, but even Arthur's parents never called him Artie.

Lance winced and pulled his shirt free of his pants. He hiked it up to display his flat, hairless stomach. "Not bruised up yet," he slurred, "but I'm sure it'll be purple in the morning, eh?"

"What happened?" James demanded.

"Scuffle at the pub." Arthur drove his elbow into Lance's shoulder for a quick jab. "Got the suitcase, all right? Are we going to open it, then?" Arthur spun the case around to face James' side of the little table.

James set down the candle holder and doily on the kitchen counter, and unbuckled the leather strips that held the case closed. The hinges were rusty, and the suitcase opened with a resistant moan.

It was sad, really, how little Mr. Blanchard possessed at the end of his life. Inside the case was a military dress uniform littered with moth holes. There were a few books, a stereoscope with a set of stereographs depicting images of the French Riviera, and a pile of old photographs.

"Look at this one." James lifted a weathered image of a pack of Tommies lounging in front of a white tent. Some were seated on crates with their legs balanced on gunny sacks. They wore their uniforms, complete with forage caps, but were clearly at ease, arms around one another. "Lance, this has to be the young Mr. Marlin. He looks exactly like you. Look, there."

The soldier farthest to the right sported a dark, swooping mustache, but otherwise seemed an exact copy of Lance's face.

Lance smiled, and held the photo closer to the light. "That's Granddad, all right. And one of these others must have been Mr. Blanchard."

James set aside the crumbling photos with careful fingers, and moved a worn pair of shoes out of the way. There was a small box that contained a dried boutineer and woman's wrist corsage, a couple of buttons, and a few foreign coins. The suitcase was empty now, except for a yellowed manila envelope. James lifted it and used two fingers to gently coax it open. He turned it over, and a packet of papers slid out onto the table.

"D'you think there's anything to eat in here?" Lance groaned as he sank into one of the kitchen chairs.

"Really, Lance, now?" James sifted through the pile of papers. There were some old love letters, addressed to someone named Ellie, and Mr. Blanchard's birth certificate. There were also two death certificates for a Mrs. Clara Blanchard and a Mr. Maximilian Blanchard. "Based on the dates," James mused, as he squinted at the spindly handwriting of the county coroner, "these must be his parents."

"Where did it say they're from?" Lance asked as he opened and shut cupboard doors.

"Bath."

Lance shrugged. "Well, I suppose we could go there and ask everyone in town if they knew the Blanchards."

"We have their former address," James said. "We could start there."

"Seems like a long shot." Arthur crossed his arms over his barrel chest.

"I hope we find something—" James' breath caught in his throat as he unfolded the final piece of paper from the bundle. His eyes shot over the page like a train cutting through the countryside. "Gentlemen, I think I've found what we're looking for." He turned the paper to face them. It was curled on the edges and covered with professional-looking calligraphy and smeared typeface. "If I'm reading this correctly, this is the deed to a cottage in Portree on the Isle of Skye. And look here."

James' finger indicated where someone, probably Mr. Blanchard himself, had penciled one word in the margin of the legal document. The word was *MATTHEW.*

They stayed up a few hours more speculating. Of course, after Matthew Barlow pretended to commit suicide, he'd need a place to live that was off the beaten path, a place no one would recognize him. Mr. Marlin or Mr. Blanchard had purchased the cottage in the far northwestern region of the Scottish Highlands. They couldn't be sure he was still there, by any means, but it was a clue, a direction so desperately needed.

At last, exhausted, they turned in to sleep as the dawn pinkened the horizon. Lance curled up on the sofa in the living room. James checked on Mrs. Wylit. She hadn't moved since he'd left her. He returned to the other bedroom to find Arthur undressing. James closed the curtains and turned out all the lights except the small lamp next to their bed.

Arthur closed the door behind them.

It had been an endless span of days, it seemed, since they'd had a bedroom to themselves, and any semblance of privacy. Still, they had to be silent, but they were used to it — the walls of Mrs. Wylit's house were thin enough to warrant caution.

They made love. After, James dozed in his partner's arms as tiny fingers of dawn crept through the lacy curtains.

Arthur shifted, and James turned to him. They lay forehead to forehead. Arthur stared into James' face with the intensity of someone trying to, perhaps, memorize something they wouldn't see again for quite some time. James was sleepy, but the sad wistfulness of Arthur's expression needled him. He opened his mouth to speak. "What's—"

"There's—" Arthur said at the same moment.

James paused. "You first," he prompted after a time.

"Nothing," Arthur said. "You were saying..."

James swallowed. "N-nothing. I forget what I was going to say." He rolled onto his back and rubbed his eyes. "I'm so exhausted."

When he turned back, Arthur was still staring at him.

"Aren't you tired?" James asked.

"Yes."

"We should get some rest." James kissed Arthur's lower lip, a brief peck, and closed his eyes.

"Suppose so." Arthur turned away from him and pulled up the blankets.

James stared at the back of Arthur's head, dread gnawing at his guts, until he had no choice but to fall asleep.

Chapter 24

James closed his fingers, still pink and wrinkled from his morning bath, around the cool porcelain door knob and turned it. Mrs. Wylit's room was dark, and the air was stale and close. A scent lingered, but he was unable to place it — the smell was a bitter mix of old cigarettes, perfume, dust, and human body, but something else, too. Something salty. A scent of sorrow.

Mrs. Wylit lay in the exact same position he'd left her the previous night. Her hair was slick with sweat, and stuck in clumps on her pale face. Shadows hung beneath her eyelashes.

James reached out to shake her shoulder, but his fingers froze in mid air. He couldn't bring himself to touch her. A horrid thought clawed its way through his mind — what if she was dead? He could imagine the terrible stiff coldness of her flesh were he to touch her skin.

Instead, he went to the window and pushed the curtains aside. With some effort, he drew up the window sash. Mellow summer morning light barged in, along with the sounds of cars and tourists on the street, but she did not move, even as the light fell over her bed.

He waited a few moments more, and then opened Mrs. Wylit's shapeless bag to gather her belongings. He laid out her blouse, which had dried overnight, the wrinkles pressed away with a warm cooking pan. As he straightened the doilies and china nicknacks on the dresser, he paused a moment to click on the wireless. With luck, it would rouse Mrs. Wylit.

It was the serial drama "Legends of Camelot." James laughed aloud. It felt like years ago when he'd last tuned in. God, was that the day of the coronation? It seemed an unfathomable distance. A lifetime ago.

"*-broken, Merlin,*" the actor playing Arthur lamented over the airwaves. "*My beloved Guinevere, the beautiful queen of Camelot, the apple of my eye, has been unfaithful to me.*"

"*It was as I foresaw in my crystal ball,*" Merlin reminded His Majesty, a rather rotten dig at an already broken man, James thought.

"*And if that was not painful enough,*" the king went on, "*my most valiant knight, a man I called my brother...*" his voice caught in a crackle of static, "*...Lancelot.*"

"*What is to be done with them, Arthur?*" the creaky-voiced wizard asked.

"*Some are—*" The king's voice hitched once more. "*Some are calling for the queen's execution. By fire. The same death suffered by witches for time immemorial.*"

"*It would fulfill your subjects' thirst for justice.*"

"*Lancelot will be banished forevermore,*" Arthur proclaimed, "*though it pains me greatly to think I will never see my friend again. And I cannot— I cannot see how I could harm Guinevere. The Abbess of Carfax came to visit, and she offered Guinevere a place in the nunnery. She would spend the rest of her days in prayer, and ministering to the sick.*"

"*Perhaps you should accept her offer, my king.*"

"*What is your wisdom, great Merlin? Please, old friend — I am in desperate need of your council.*"

The old man sighed. "*I am afraid the decision is yours, Majesty. But I can tell you that the age of our great kingdom — the Age of Camelot — is drawing to a close. The sun sets upon us, Arthur.*"

The king groaned in sorrow. "*What am I to do?*"

The radio announcer broke in. "*Tune in next week for the stunning conclusion of 'Legends of Camelot.'*"

An advert for dish soap came on, and James blinked. He realized he'd been rooted to the spot, staring at the wireless, locked onto the actors' words. He shook his head and turned.

Mrs. Wylit's vast, watery eyes stared at him beneath her matted brown curls. "Whatever *will* King Arthur do? It's too bad, really. Merlin warned him something like this would happen."

James' cheeks flooded with blood. "It's an asinine program. It's hardly based on the old legends or even the source material. De Troyes and Tennyson must be rolling in their graves."

She said nothing. Her eyes were those of an old animal, a dog perhaps, sick or injured, aware in some instinctive way that it was dying.

"They brought back the suitcase of Mr. Blanchard's things last night." He pointed to her clothes, laid out carefully on a nearby chair. "We found the deed to a cottage in Scotland. He'd written 'Matthew' right on it in pencil, if you can believe it. So, you might want to get ready. I went to the market for breakfast things. After we eat, Lance is going to the train station for tickets. We'll leave this afternoon."

Mrs. Wylit sat up in bed and attempted to smooth down her hair. Her hands quivered violently, the quaking white claws tipped with chipping red.

James went to Mrs. Wylit's bag and removed the liquor bottle he'd managed to buy from a man mopping up last night's pub mess. He uncapped it and tried to hand it to her.

She pushed it away.

"Doctor's orders, remember?"

She nodded and took a swig, her eyes averted. "I can dress myself," she said after a time. "I'm not the queen."

"All right." He left, and closed the door.

Hours later, they'd returned the flat keys to the owner by way of a trusted bookstore owner, and boarded an overnight train to Inverness. Mrs. Wylit was ill. She shook and clung to James, even when he pleaded with her for release after several hours. People in the observation car stared at them openly as he helped her back and forth to the loo. He managed to convince her to take a few sips here and there. After what seemed like ages, Arthur seemed to have sensed James' discomfort and took over. It wasn't like him, James thought, to be so unobservant, so downright *unresponsive* to James' needs.

James excused himself to one of their two sleeper cabins to lie down and marinate in his knowledge that everything was terrible. It had been, ever since they'd stayed the night in the church. *Come now,* he scolded himself as he put his arms behind his head on the stiff train mattress. *We're almost there. Matthew's got to be on Skye somewhere. Or someone who knows what became of him. You're doing right by Mr. Marlin. The end is near — it has to be.*

But these thoughts did not soothe him, and neither did the rocking of the train. Because when it was all over, of course he would be relieved, pleased even, to have fulfilled the quest given to them by a dear friend on his deathbed, but what about after? After they returned to London, to the flat. Would things between him and Arthur still feel so... strained? Strange? And what about Lance? Would he make good on his promise and move to the city, or would he return to his old life? Part of James hoped the latter was the case. In one way it was awful to think of, but if Lance was out of their lives, perhaps there would never be a need to tell their secret.

He groaned and rolled onto his side. After a time, his sulk bored him, and he returned to the observation car. Mrs. Wylit, apparently, had hobbled to the smoking car on her own, and left Lance and Arthur to discuss Matthew, Mr. Marlin, their adventures over the last several days, and eventually, the cricket scores. There was something exclusive and chummy about how they spoke to one another now. Bonded, James thought, over their burglary of the suitcase. Either way, he felt sulky and excluded again, and decided to check on Mrs. Wylit.

He found her clinging to a cigarette, hunched up on the window, a ragged doll crammed against the seat. She eyed him as he sank down next to her on the cushioned bench.

"How are you feeling?"

She shrugged, eyes on the window and the deep evening countryside. "Rotten. Sick. But it's odd. Also a bit... light."

It was times like these (rare times, but they did happen) that James wished he smoked. It would give him something to do with his hands. "You never—I mean, well, Arthur and I..." He fumbled for a few long moments. "You never mentioned."

"My daughter?" She exhaled fumes.

He nodded.

She tapped ash into the tray built into the arm of the seat. "My mum used to think our house in Whitechapel was haunted. It wasn't far from one of the places where Jack did his business."

She put the stick in her mouth and inhaled. He watched her arm shake.

"But she wouldn't let us *talk* about it. When something strange would happen, she'd make some big show about it being 'the ghost' but if we asked questions, she'd shake us and say, 'the more you speak of it, the more power it has.'"

She gently extinguished her smoke.

James cleared his throat and tapped his fingers against his trousers awkwardly.

"If I thought about it hard enough, I could make the past swim away." She ran her gray tongue over her cracked lower lip. "I could pretend, like an actress in a play. Pretend I was just some old rag whose husband had run off. A childless—" She stopped, and her hands clenched the arms of the chair with sudden white-knuckled force. After a long moment, she relaxed, and lit another cigarette. "Well, I'm not pretending, then, am I?" She gave a mirthless little chuckle. "I am an old rag with no husband and no..." She sighed out smoke, and turned to him. "Well, now, the play's over, and the costume's off, isn't it? The lights have gone down. Curtain's pulled."

"But you said it felt light. To have spoken of it."

"It does." She nodded. "I didn't think it would, but it does."

"Does that mean," he coughed a moment as her smoke swirled around him, "does that mean you'd like to go to a place like St. John's?"

She lifted one shoulder. "I don't know. Perhaps."

"Are you going to write to Silas?"

"Yes. I think that he's what I really need. Someone to talk to who knows." She made a gesture with her hand which, to James, meant, "everything."

They shared a silence, which Mrs. Wylit broke as the windows filled with orange sunset. "Do you think we'll see him in Portree?"

James woke from his uneasy reverie. "Who? Matthew? Well, we all certainly hope so. Though what we're going to say to him, I don't know. Of course, we'll have to tell him that Mr. Marlin passed away, and Mr. Blanchard as well. I'd assume he knows about his mother — Mr. Marlin must have written back in '42. But perhaps Mr. Marlin felt it was truly important for him to see Nim's grave and know how much she missed him. He must need our help in some way, otherwise we'd never have been sent on this wild goose chase."

"It's only a wild goose chase if we don't find our prize." Mrs. Wylit rolled the ash into a point in the tray, then raised her cigarette to her lips and flared the cherry. "Besides, I wasn't talking about Matthew Barlow."

"Then who— oh." He leaned forward and put his elbows on his knees to bury his head in his hands.

"The man in the brown coat," Mrs. Wylit mused unnecessarily.

"Yes, I know who you mean."

"Touchy. I was only asking."

James exhaled a violent sigh and sat up. "I don't know. I don't want to think about that now, Vi."

She blew a smoke ring. "Suit yourself."

They had supper in the dining car, and retired to the cabins. They'd be at Inverness station by morning to make their way to the bus that would bear them through the moors and across the lochs to the Isle of Skye.

"Mercy, please." Lance pulled his handkerchief from his trousers pocket and waved it as a white flag. "Damn your luck, Arthur."

Arthur grinned as he gathered up the cards from the floor. With James on the top bunk and Lance sitting on the lower one, Arthur could wedge himself against the door and sit for a card game.

Lance stood up and took the pack of cards to secure in his shirt pocket. Arthur squeezed partially onto the bottom bunk so that Lance could open the door. "Well, gents." Lance saluted them in farewell. "Goodnight. Tomorrow we'll be in Scotland, land of windswept cliffs and foaming seas, moors and heather, and, if we're lucky, perhaps a fine supper of haggis. The perfect place for an adventure, eh?"

"Haven't had enough adventure?" Arthur leaned over to sock Lance on the knee. Lance moved aside deftly to dodge it. "You want to try haggis?"

"Try it? I've had it. I love it." Lance rubbed his belly longingly.

James made gagging sounds from his perch on the top bunk with his unread book. "You can't be serious."

"Dead serious. It's going to happen. And you two are going to have some with me."

"Beat me tomorrow at whist, and I'll eat it," Arthur said. "Swear on my mother's good name."

"You're on. And you have to hold James down and make him try some." They laughed again, James a trifle uneasily. "Good night, then." Lance disappeared and the door closed, off to bed down above

Mrs. Wylit. James supposed Lance would be up again late tonight, but vowed not to find out, even if he himself was unable to sleep. Besides, the gentle rocking of the train and the repetitious sounds of the track passing beneath them were soothing. Perhaps he'd be able to sleep well. If the thing gnawing in his guts would let him.

Arthur took down the pathetic pillow from the lower bunk and added it to his bundled jacket. He curled up on the floor. There was no way he would fit in the train bed without his legs hanging over the side, which would inevitably lead to pins and needles.

"Are you ready for lights out?" James put his finger on the switch.

Arthur nodded, and James flipped off the bulb.

"Goodnight."

"Goodnight, James."

Pause. Whisper. "I love you."

"I love you, too."

James closed his eyes and tried to sleep, but the guilt in him still sat, a hot stone in his stomach, so deep it nearly touched his spine. At last, he couldn't contain it; he could harbor it no longer. He rolled to the edge of the bunk, and whispered over the side, "Arthur?"

Nothing, but there was no snoring, either. "Arthur," James tried again. "Arthur. Wake up. Are you asleep? Arthur, I have... I have something I need to tell you."

A long silence, and then the ruffling snort of a snore.

James lay back and closed his eyes, hands pressed into his midsection as if he could will the stone out of himself.

Chapter 25

As he gazed on the Scottish countryside in summer, it was astonishing to James that feasting the eyes on natural beauty — so beautiful it was unnatural, really — was enough to wash away one's strife, however temporarily. As he watched the rivers snake their way through the green and dun-colored terra, the constant prickle of guilt and anxiety in his stomach receded until it was no more bothersome than a particularly lazy fly buzzing about in search of a place to land.

James had a feeling of wellbeing, bordering on being giddy. Somehow, in some way, it would be all right. All of it. It had to be all right, his feverish brain reasoned, as his eyes drank in the glistening shadow of the sea ahead. They were going to find the long lost Matthew Barlow, son of their beloved Nim, and they were going to find some way to help him. That was what Mr. Marlin wanted them to do, may he rest. It gave James a golden, comforting sense of purpose.

He glanced over at Mrs. Wylit on seat next to him. Lance and Arthur claimed benches of their own on the opposite side. Both were asleep, heads lolled back on their shoulders. It had been a long, long bus ride.

Mrs. Wylit was awake, though, and gazed out the window with beaming affection on her face. James could see the landscape reflected in her eyes. "My husband always wanted to take a holiday to some place like this," she said. "I refused. Thought it was a waste of money. If one's miserable in life, why would a change of scenery do anything to solve it?" She sighed, and a strange expression — a soft, genuine, closed-mouth little smile — crossed her pale face. "He was an arsehole, but he might have been right."

Lodging was troublesome. Summer holidays had the hotels and guest houses full. The only place with an opening was an inn right on the scenic harbor, and the only reason the suite was free was because it was so outrageously expensive. They all pooled what they had, and came up with enough for two nights. That didn't leave much to eat, but they had no choice.

"This is the last stop," Lance mused as they hauled their luggage into the admittedly spacious room that, while plainly furnished, had a double bed and two singles — enough for everyone for once.

Famished, they wandered the quaint streets until they found a man selling fish and chips from a cart. They ate like animals, seated on the curb. Even Mrs. Wylit managed most of hers, though when she'd finished, James thought she looked a bit green. It stayed put, however, and they were refreshed, though still weary in their bones from the overnight journey.

Mrs. Wylit wandered into a shop for cigarettes, and James stood up to follow. Arthur put a hand on his shoulder. It was gentle, but the sheer weight of it was enough to keep James in his seat. "I'll go." Arthur climbed to his full, towering height to follow.

Lance and James watched them disappear into the shop in silence. The quiet continued in the mellow afternoon, the sounds of children laughing in boats on the harbor and the cry of the gulls weaving a symphony for them. After a time, Mrs. Wylit emerged with a cigarette between her lips. Arthur took a matchbook, dwarfed by his fingers, and lit it for her.

Lance smiled and used his shoulder to bump James'. "He's a good lad, isn't he?"

James nodded, though something icy and made of wire clenched at his heart. "Yes. Of course he is."

"The best." Lance trapped James in his pools of blue for a long but subtle moment. His expression was good-humored, but his smile twisted at the sides in a way that seemed longing or sad. "The very best, James."

James swallowed. "I-I know that," he stuttered as they stood.

"I'm sure you do." Lance turned and gave a comical little bow as Arthur and Mrs. Wylit approached. "Now that we have provisions of the tobacco variety, my liege, where are we headed next?"

"Shopkeeper suggested we talk to the postmaster," Arthur said as they neared. He herded Mrs. Wylit along as she gazed distractedly out over the port and the gaily colored shops and guesthouses surrounding it. "He might know where the cottage is."

***

The small post office was one of many storefronts in a white row building, and the inside was cramped with all of them in it. The pipe-smoking postmaster nudged his flat woolen hat and greeted them. Arthur stepped forward to explain their plight and handed him the deed to the cottage.

The postmaster squinted at the small print before lifting the glasses hanging around his neck to his face. "Can't be sure, but that looks like the wee place out quite a jaunt past the Cuillin Hills hotel."

"Do you know who lives there?"

The postmaster thought a minute. "I only took this job a fortnight ago," he admitted, "so I canna say fer sure. I know that old Campbell used to pay one o' his grandsons to deliver the post there. I've heard the children talk about a hermit, but I've never met him. Such is the nature o' hermits." He held out his callused hands apologetically.

"Would the boy be able to show us there?" Arthur asked.

"Aye, I'd think so." He nodded, and tapped his lower lip. "Might I ask... do *you* know the man who lives there?"

James and Lance shared a wide-eyed glance, but Arthur did not waver for even a particle of a second. "We knew his mother."

"I see." The postmaster opened his mouth and closed it, trapping his lips in a firm line that seemed to say, *"Quiet, it's none of your business."*

"Weel," the postmaster said after a swollen pause. "Let me ring the boy's father en see if he cain make yon trip." He disappeared behind the counter past the honeycomb of sorting bins and post boxes, and picked up the pea-green telephone. He dropped his voice and talked for several minutes, no doubt eager to gossip about the strangers who showed up to see the local hermit. He returned at last, and said, "Randy's spending the day and night at his Nan's. Sunday last he nicked from the collection plate – money for sweets, I'd wager. So he's over there working it off, painting fences and all. Won't be back 'till morn." He scratched under his chin with one yellow thumbnail. "Take ye mesel', but I'm on duty. Best to wait for the lad — he knows the way better'n I do. Have a bunk, do ye?"

Arthur confirmed this as Lance rolled his eyes and set his jaw in frustration. They agreed to meet the boy at the post office in the morning if it could be arranged. This was agreed upon.

With little money and nothing to do, they went back to the room at the inn to rest. This didn't last long, as anticipation seemed to gnaw at each of them. After a bit, they rose again, did some sink laundry, and went out to the harbor.

They sat on the stone edge of the harbor and watched in anxious, but somehow companionable silence as Mrs. Wylit flirted with the man who rented small boats to tourists. After a time of working her magic, she called out to Arthur, who sprang up with remarkable grace for someone his size. They got into a rowboat together, and Arthur's powerful arms soon had them bobbing out amongst the sailboats in the bonny sunshine. After a time, Arthur pulled the oars in and they sat in the boat together, talking, about what, James had no way of knowing.

Lance tossed pebbles into the water with lazy little flicks of his hand. There was a sort of dejected turn to his mouth, so James said, "I really think we're close. All we have to do is get out to that cottage, and we'll have fulfilled your granddad's wish."

Lance smiled at him, teeth brilliant white in the harbor sun, which streamed on them now though clouds loomed in the west. "I think you're right. Though I'll admit that in the past few days I've hardly thought of Granddad." He gave a mirthless chuckle. "Selfish of me, I suppose." He paused, and set the handful of pebbles down on the cobblestones next to him. "That's not the only selfish thing I've done on this trip, though, I'm afraid."

Arthur and Mrs. Wylit were black silhouettes surrounded by the golden flashes of sun off of the waves. Still they talked, passionately it seemed, both of them animated; Mrs. Wylit punched home her points into the air with the tip of her lit cigarette. They didn't seem to be arguing, but it still brought James wonderment — Mrs. Wylit hadn't spoken so much or at such length in his history of knowing her. James squinted, and tried to force his eyes to adjust as the boat bobbed in the wake of a larger craft. "Selfish?" he said to Lance, though his voice was airy and distracted.

"Yes, selfish." Lance flicked one of his stones into the water. "What I did in the church in Lincoln was selfish. James. James." He said the name twice until his companion tore his eyes off of the water and looked at him. "I'm sorry for that. I shouldn't have."

James opened his mouth to speak.

"Don't say it's all right," Lance interrupted before he could get a syllable out. James thought he saw tears mounting in those Hollywood-blue eyes. "Don't say it. I know you will say you forgive me for what I did, but you shouldn't. I knew full well in that moment what... well, I mean, for God's sake, me n' Arthur are mates, aren't we?"

"And so are you and I." James paused. "Right?"

Lance nodded, and looked away. It might have been the sun, but James could see his face pinken.

"But I didn't treat either of you like friends. Would a real friend have done that? I mean, think about it, think about the story you told me about the two of you back at Willowind House. Your story is legendary. It's a *legend*. Who was I to come in and muck it up?"

"Lance, legends aren't *real* people." James pulled up his legs to sit crosswise on the edge of the harbor walk. "Mythical people, heroes, gods, what-have-you, they exist in worlds of black and white, good and evil. They have destinies to fulfill. Our lives are a lot more complicated than that."

"I don't see it." Lance leant back to skip a rock over the gentle waves. "Think about it. King Arthur was a Christian ruler, yet his guide and mentor was a wizard. Many of the Knights of the Round Table possessed magical powers. The sorcery of the Old Religion mixed directly into that of the new order somehow. Tell me that isn't complicated, some shade of gray."

"But this is real life," James shot back.

"When are you going to realize what you have?" Lance wondered, chin in his hand and his elbow on his bent knee. "Y'know, I was content to keep my secret forever, even from myself. But because I saw how happy the two of you are together, how meant for one another you are — fated, even though apparently you aren't fond of that term — I couldn't keep it inside any longer." He punched one hand into the other. "If you asked me why I kissed you that night, I couldn't tell you. I knew it was wrong. But I think what I wanted was... to be a part of it all, somehow. To be legendary, too. To feel, even for a second, the way Arthur must feel, the way you..." He dropped his hands in a sigh. "Selfish. That's what it was."

"I know you don't want to hear it," James hugged his arms protectively over his midsection, eyes fixed on his shoes as they floated over the water, "but I do forgive you. I'm the one who ruined everything. I didn't say no. I didn't say anything. And now—" He swallowed, and spoke no more.

Arthur and Mrs. Wylit had ceased their conversation. She watched him, blank-faced, grim almost, as he brought the boat back. Lance whistled "Michael, Row Your Boat Ashore."

"Does he know?" James whispered, voice nearly obliterated by the chatter of gulls.

Lance smiled a sad little half-curve and went down to meet the boat.

James thought about that expression on his friend's face long into the night, after everyone else had managed to fall asleep on their growling bellies.

Tomorrow. Tomorrow they would find Matthew, and put an end to this quest. He tried to focus on this mantra, but every few seconds that expression on Lance's face would burn over the insides of his eyelids. With each flash, heat radiated through James' body and brought forth a cold sweat that stank of fear. The fear of losing everything, of the narrative spiraling out of control.

Your story is legendary.

A quiet sigh hissed through his teeth. James moved in increments in an attempt not to disturb Arthur as he climbed free of the inn's comfortable bed. A quick glance to his right showed Lance to be fast asleep in his own bed against the other wall. As he moved toward the washroom, two glistening eyes popped out at him through the dark, shining wetly in the moonlight that filtered in through the gauzy curtains. James gasped inaudibly and a shudder wracked his body before he realized that it was Mrs. Wylit, lying awake in her bed. She stared at him with silent eeriness.

"You frightened me." He sucked in a breath.

Mrs. Wylit said nothing, but raised her corpse-white hand and pointed to the window that overlooked the harbor.

James went to it and pushed the curtains aside. This time he could not contain the strangled noise of surprise that ejected from his throat.

The harbor was deserted, the boats having been moored for the night . The water lapped serenely against the stones and the pebble beach, illuminated by the swollen moon. The village was peppered here and there with warm, welcoming lights for travelers in the dark, but there was no sound or movement save the lapping of the waves and the far-off clanging of a ship's bell.

There, on the cobblestone walk, with his back to the water, and facing James' window, was the man in the old brown coat. He was backlit by the moon and James could not make out his features. He sucked in another breath to yell for Arthur and Lance, but stopped. The man lifted up one hand and waved to him. After a long moment, he waved again.

"Good God he waved at me." James clutched the window sill for support.

"I think he's ready for a chat," Mrs. Wylit suggested as she wiggled herself out of bed, joining James at the window with a cigarette waiting to be lit in her hand.

"What if he — what if—"

"I'll watch from the window," she promised through a breath of smoke. "Go on, then."

James stuttered out a few more incoherent syllables.

"Shh!" She put her finger to her lips. "Do you want to wake the whole building?"

James looked down at the figure once more, and then snagged Mrs. Wylit's liquor bottle from its place sticking half-out of her purse. He gave himself a good dose of liquid courage, put on his trousers and stretched his suspenders over his striped pajama shirt.

In a blink, he was out on the front stoop of the inn, and then closed the space to stand a few feet away from the man in the brown coat. As he neared, features made themselves more apparent — a slender man, in his middle age, with graying auburn hair and shiny round spectacles. His eyes were green, his eyes were—

Just like mine?!

He swallowed back down the nasty taste of bile, and Mrs. Wylit's liquor. "Who are you? W-what do you want?"

The man trembled a moment, his mouth gaping, fish-like. Tears came to his eyes and he wiggled out a handkerchief from one of the coat's old pockets. He raised his glasses to wipe his eyes. "James. You're James Wilde?"

"Yes," James shot back. "And who are you? And why have you been following us?"

"You don't recognize me," he said, a melancholy cast to his voice. "Not at all?"

"No," said James. Then, he squinted a moment. Something about — "I've... I've seen that coat before," he admitted. "A long time ago."

The man sniffed and let out a little relieved chuckle through his tears. "It's the last thing you saw me wearing — when I — when I *abandoned...*"

"Oh God," James prayed, to the deity he was not certain existed.

The man took a shuddering breath. "I'm John Wilde, James. You're my son."

Chapter 26

As dawn stained the horizon, James sat with his father, a man he hadn't seen since he was a little child, and they watched the sunrise over the Isle of Skye.

It took several minutes for John Wilde to convince James he was who he said he was, but after a time, it set in with a strange, otherworldly numbness. They sat down on the edge of the harbor, and his father asked him all kinds of questions. How had he done in school? Where was he working? What had happened to him during the war? How was his mother? James' mouth was dry from the responses, as well as the shock of it all.

"So, do you think you'll apprentice under this tailor, or stay in the bookkeeping business?" His father unbuttoned the old coat at last and took it off. It revealed a checkered shirt and a tweed jacket that had seen better days.

"I'm not sure." James fixated on his father's (how odd it was to think those words) worn shoes as they dangled over the water. "What I really want to do is write." He paused, and then straightened his back in the growing light of day to look his father in the face. "Why on earth am I letting you ask all of these questions? Don't you think I've got some bloody questions for *you*?"

James' father looked at his hands, then out over the water. "I suppose you do."

"Where have you been? Let's start with that."

John shifted so he could sit facing his son, one leg still dangling over the bank. "I live in Leeds, and I teach literature at the university. During the war I was an intelligence analyst for the RAF and got my education after." He swallowed audibly and broke their gaze a moment to look at the water. "I never remarried, and I never had any other children."

"Is that supposed to *mean* something?" James had not been aware until that moment of the cesspool of rage that bubbled within him. It sat beneath the shock of sitting here, hours away from finding Matthew Barlow, talking to his father, who had been nothing but a shadow in his mind for the last decade. "You left us. You said it yourself. Abandoned."

"I have no intention of defending myself." John's mouth curled into a pitiful little frown, and for a moment James had the eerie feeling of looking in a mirror through time. "What I did was unforgivable. But that's part of the reason why I'm here — to explain to you what happened all those years ago."

"Why now?" James flung a pebble into the harbor. The town slowly awoke around them; gulls came in from the ocean, and humans opened up doors as they called to neighbors and cooked breakfast. The smell of bacon over the wind made James' stomach yowl. "Why now after all these years?"

"I'm not sure if you'll believe me if I tell you." John shook his head with a sigh, and then caught James' green gaze in his own. "But I'm going to try." He pressed his lips together for a moment, then went on. "A few months ago, I was down in London for an educator's conference. I happened to be walking near Mr. Conner's tailor shop, and it was the strangest thing. I saw myself, a young me, come out of the shop. I couldn't believe it, but there I was, as if I was looking through a window back in time. And then I realized it — I wasn't looking at myself, I was looking at my son."

He sniffled again and put the handkerchief to his lips.

"And?" James prompted, his impatience not dampened by John's struggle.

"And so I followed you down to the corner, and there you met this bear of a man. The two of you walked together a few blocks to a brick row house, and went inside. I could see, as night fell, through the sliver of the curtains, the two of you... living. Together. Talking and laughing. And I knew right then and there."

Panic put James' heart in a vice. "What?" he barked.

"I knew you and your... flatmate, if you want to call him that, were... in love."

"What?" James resisted the strong urge to get on his feet and run. "How dare you, we aren't—"

"James, please. Please, stop. I know." His father put tentative hand on James' shoulder. James flinched away. "And when I realized, I knew I had to see you again to explain. To talk to you about all of this, because I know you'll... you might have some inkling..."

A sudden flashbulb exploded in James' head. "You're the one who called Mother!" he shouted. A man feeding the gulls on a nearby boat turned his head sharply in their direction. "You were calling her and hanging up, weren't you?"

His father went scarlet, but no utterance of denial slipped from between his lips. "I tried so many times," he whispered, "but every time I heard her voice, I froze. I wanted to apologize to her, and to ask her how to get in touch with you. Proper channels and all. But." He swallowed hard again, and his jaw quivered. "I'm a coward, I suppose. I hurt her as much as I hurt you, if not more so, and I'm still ashamed of what happened between us. My voice just froze."

"And so," James said, watching the blossom-colors seep away from the clouds as the golden sun rays fully encroached on them, "you decided to come and talk to me yourself. Except you've been too afraid to do that, and lurked about like some kind of creeper instead of getting up the courage to approach me."

"You've hit the nail on the head, son."

The word reverberated through James like a gunshot. "N-no," he stammered, "no, you don't get to call me that. I was still in *nappies* when you ran out on us."

"I know." His father turned away and dropped his leg. Together, they watched the fishing boats leave the harbor and head for fruitful waters. "After I tell you why I left, I'll leave. I understand if you never want to see me again. All I want to do is tell you my story, and ask you one question. Then I'll go. Forever."

"Why should I listen to your reasons?" James pelted the water with another pebble.

"Because I don't want you to make the same mistake," John replied. "I doubt you will, but just in case it all becomes... too much. And you decide hiding is easier."

Something in James' heart ruffled and awoke, a bird rustling the nest. "Hiding?"

"Yes, James." John sniffed, used his worn handkerchief again, and then tucked it out of sight. "You see, I — I suppose the plainest terms are best. No reason for euphemism. I tell my students their writing ought not to be so flowery and get straight to the point." He pinched a smile, perhaps at the irony of taking his own advice. "I'm a homosexual," he said.

James had often read stories where it was said that characters' mouths dropped and hung suspended in the air. He'd always found that description tiresome, but now, it actually happened to him.

"I've known this about myself since I was a lad." His father dropped his voice as an old man with a cane hobbled past behind them on his morning walk around the harbor. "I had a friend growing up, and so was he. We were best mates. And we were more." He choked on the last word. "Our families found out, and it was a nightmare. We were forbidden from seeing one another, and I was told that I must change or be thrown out of the house." He rubbed his chin and withdrew his handkerchief again, only to ball it up in frustration. "And so I did. I thought I could change. I started chasing after girls, pretending as though I liked them the way I'd loved... him. I pretended for so long I thought I was cured. Cured enough to—"

"Marry my mother." James' voice was just above a whisper as tears slipped between his eyelashes.

"And have you." John put out his hand as if to touch James' shoulder, but drew it away before making contact. "She was naive and I was in denial. For a year or so, I honestly thought it would work. But in the end I couldn't." He coughed. "So I did the most dishonorable, abhorrent, and cowardly thing a man could possibly do in that situation. I left you and your mother without an explanation. Once I fully understood what I'd done, how unfair I'd been, it had been too long." He put his hand to his eyes for a moment, and then let it fall. "If I hadn't seen you that day on the street with Arthur I might have never had the strength to find you. But once I realized you were..." He let the silence say *gay*. "I thought perhaps you could, someday, maybe years from now, find a way to forgive me."

James said nothing.

"When I made up my mind to approach you; when I finally found my courage, you and Arthur decided to take the strangest holiday," John said through a forced but hopeful smile. "I had to follow you and your companions all over this sceptered isle. Correct me if I'm wrong, but isn't that drunk woman your landlady?"

"She is," James said through a sigh that preempted what was likely to be a very long explanation. He took a minute to condense it in his brain.

"And Arthur. When did you meet him?"

"When the Jerrys started the bombing campaign, Mother thought it best if I left London." James started to retell re-vaporize the story.

"You were part of Pied Piper?" John Wilde interrupted.

James nodded. "Arthur was in my class, and together we went to a country manor with the rest of the children and our teacher, and a lady from the government. Things were awful at first. It's always been very hard for me to hide. People seem to know."

"Children can be so cruel." John's hand twitched again, as if he wanted to touch James in comfort, but he resisted the urge.

"Exactly," James said with a tone that denied any need for this man — his father — to empathize with him. "And they were cruel to Arthur, too, because he was enormous and tall then, as well. And he used to have a stutter. But Mr. Marlin, the head-of-household was a very kind man with an incredible heart. He and the lady of the house supported and encouraged Arthur and me. The Baroness's son was like us, and committed suicide when he was fifteen. Recently, Mr. Marlin, passed away. The blond lad with us is his grandson. Mr. Marlin's dying wish was that we find the Baroness's son, because we suspect he faked his death all those years ago."

During this explanation, John gave several involuntary jerks and blinked his eyes furiously. "What did you say the bloke's name was? Marlin?"

"Yes," James said, "why?"

"It sounds, eh, familiar, I suppose." His father shook his head as if to rattle out a pebble from between his ears. "Maybe someone I knew many years ago. I can't remember. You say the son only *pretended* to off himself?"

"Yes, and Mr. Marlin, by all indications, helped him. And I think he wanted us to go and help in some way. So we had to follow the clues. Mr. Marlin didn't leave us with much, but eventually, we found this." James reached into his pocket and withdrew the rumpled deed to the cottage. "This morning, well, in a few hours, a boy is going to show us how to reach this cottage. And then we'll see if anyone's home."

"An admirable quest." John's eyes were far away over the water. "I'm proud of you for coming so far to do right by your old friend."

James didn't know what to say, so he said nothing, and put the deed away in his pocket again, and adjusted his suspenders. It dawned on him that he was still wearing his pajama shirt and it was nearly broad daylight.

"I'm sorry if I frightened you with my," he paused, "creeping." John picked at his uneven fingernails. "I know you saw me on several occasions. Almost caught me a few times."

"Why did you run?"

"Nervous, I suppose. I wasn't as ready to talk to you as I thought."

"You have a lot of apologies to make." James stood and stretched his back. "Well, come on, then. It's time you met the others. And I need to get changed." His stomach howled with sudden ferocity.

"Hungry?"

James nodded. "We're a little short on funds at the moment."

"Let me take you all to breakfast." John eagerly pulled his wallet from his pants as if to show James he was good for it. "The inn has a restaurant, I'm sure?"

James shrugged, but did not respond, and instead went back into the hotel. Mrs. Wylit, having watched them from the window, had anticipated their arrival at the room, and opened the door before James could knock. She was dressed for the day and in mid-swig from the liquor bottle. "My morning medicine," she explained, and then stood aside so they could enter. The door to the loo was shut, and Lance sat on his bed in the midst of tying his shoes. "Oh, I'm sorry," Mrs. Wylit apologized as John gaped at her. "Be my guest." She offered him the bottle.

"No, thank you," John mumbled as he shifted from one foot to the other.

"James, where have you been?" Lance leapt up, and then froze as his eyes travelled from one face to the other. "Who — but you look—"

"Lance, this is my father, John Wilde." James crossed his arms and only gestured to his father with a jerk of his thumb. "Otherwise known as the creep in the brown coat."

John gave an awkward smile and hefted the coat that he held folded over one arm.

"Blimey." Lance blinked as if his eyes weren't functioning properly. "I thought the two of you were, ah, estranged, is that the word?"

"We were," John admitted.

"We *are*," James said at the same time.

John's face crumpled in hurt, but James pretended not to notice. "He saw me on the street a few weeks back and recognized me, and now he wants to make amends." James went to his suitcase to retrieve a mostly-clean shirt.

"So you followed us the whole way?" Lance stared, wide-eyed, at them, first one, then the other.

"It wasn't easy. That night you slept in a church, I slept under a hedge across the way."

James gave an unsympathetic little grunt. At that moment, Arthur came out of the washroom, showered, shaved, and dressed, with his pajamas balled up in one hand. He took one look at John and strode up to him on his tree-trunk legs, and extended a gigantic hand. "Mr. Wilde," he growled. "Interesting coat," he added.

"It's a pleasure to finally meet you, Arthur." John gave him his hand, and winced as Arthur squeezed it with what was likely intentional power before he stepped over to stand close to James.

James slipped his hand into Arthur's and pressed against his side. Arthur shot down a questioning frown in his direction. "He knows," James explained with a dismissive wave of his hand toward John. "He's... also. *Apparently*." His lip gave a malicious curl.

Arthur's emerald eyes widened in sudden understanding beneath the halo of his black curls. "*That's* why."

"It doesn't excuse what happened." James pulled his hand free of Arthur's grasp.

"I never said it did," John murmured softly, eyes on his shoes.

James sank onto the bed to put his head in his hands. Mrs. Wylit went to him to pat his back and offer him the bottle. He refused. "This is too much," he mumbled into his palms.

Mrs. Wylit gave a cheerless, wry little chuckle. "Oh, the Lord never gives us more than we can handle."

"That's a load of bollocks."

Arthur turned to Lance and John. "Could you leave us? You too, Vi."

When James felt Arthur's weight rock the bed, he lowered his hands to reveal his blotchy face. "Why now? In the middle of all this? He shouldn't be here. I don't need him to be here now with all his insipid little apologies."

Arthur took his hand and placed their entwined fingers on his own knee. "Loads to think about right now. Plenty of trouble and strife. What's one more thing?"

James had to allow an ironic giggle to puff out.

"We've come so far," Arthur said. "Let's find Matthew. The rest can wait until then. Unless," he paused, "you wanted to..."

James let Arthur's response hang in the air for a long time. "Wanted to what?" he finally finished.

Arthur let out a little grunt of frustration.

"Wanted to what, Arthur?"

Arthur looked at his watch. "We ought to go."

"Especially if *John* insists on paying for breakfast," James sneered. "As if that makes up for all those years of Mum and me , all alone."

Arthur put an arm around him for a moment and dropped his head as if in prayer. "It could be a start," he whispered.

Chapter 27

They'd been walking for over an hour when the boy, a sprightly mop-handle-skinny thing with curly hair that completed the mop comparison, pointed to the gray peak of a roof and a small chimney that had appeared behind a hill. "Tha's the place. Though ye willna see 'im. I put the post on his doorstep and he leaves me a coin a'times, or an apple."

"He never comes into town at all?" James asked as they slowed their steps on the dusty trail. To their right was a glorious expanse of rolling hills, then craggy cliffs over the Sound of Raasay. The day had clouded over and the sky threatened rain. This did nothing to diminish the beauty of it all.

"Nae sir, but betimes when I come there be letters to post, or a list of things set under a rock at the doorstep with some money. Then I go buy things and bring 'em to 'im. Food, or nails, or paint and such. He sends away for different seeds to plant." He thought a minute, putting a dirty fingernail against his chin a moment. "Haven't done that in some time. He must be eatin' badgers and coneys and the like."

"Who are the letters to?" John puffed, red-faced from the exertion.

"A Mr. Marlin, or a Mr. Blanchard. Every time."

"The letters he received," Lance wondered as he turned to the boy, "did they have money inside?"

"I woulna ken, sir." The boy lifted his button nose and pointed chin. "I'm no thief and I dinna read other people's letters."

"No thief?" James scoffed. "What about the collection plate?"

The boy's eyes bloomed large. "You ken abou' that?"

Lance put a reassuring hand on the boy's bony shoulder. "I only wondered how he made his living, how he afforded the groceries he'd send you for."

The boy shrugged. "I've barely even seen him. Just through the window. When someone comes up the lane his dogs bark. That's how he knows to go inside and draw the curtains." He rubbed his hands together. "I canna wait to see 'im. Wonder if he's got a scarred-up face."

"No." James firmly pointed back down the way they'd come. "We're very grateful for your help, but this is a private matter."

"At least tell me his name," the boy begged.

"Off with you," Lance ordered, and gestured to Arthur. "Or my friend Arthur the Giant will sit on you and smoosh you to jelly."

The boy turned and marched back down the path. He kicked innocent stones into the heather, hands shoved in his pockets, and swore up a storm that floated back to them on the breeze.

"Well then." Arthur let down Mrs. Wylit, who had been riding on his back for the last fifteen minutes. Dark rings of sweat damped his armpits and his hair was moist. "This is it."

"If he isn't here," Lance said, as he lit a cigarette, "God knows what we'll do next."

"He's here." John went off down the trail toward the bend. As they followed, the peak of the house and the chimney disappeared behind the small hill again. "I can feel it. He's *here*." The dogged emphasis of his face and words caused Arthur and James to share a glance, brows upturned.

As they rounded the bend in the path, they saw two canines of mottled heritage lazing beneath a small tree planted near the prim white cottage. One was small and terrier-shaped, its coat splotched with white and black. The other was bigger, with labrador ears and a tall, sleek body and bristly tan coat. As the boy promised, they bolted over and barked at the visitors in tandem, but pranced about in excitement rather than malice. And, as was predicted, the little cottage's curtains were drawn and its door tightly shut.

Lance held his hand out to the dogs, and they both submitted to a quick pat before they raced away behind the house, only to return with a stick and a length of thick knotted rope each.

Arthur studied the cottage, with James doing the same at his side, the two of them close enough that their elbows touched. It was tiny, to be sure, but well cared-for and recently painted. The dirt path they'd been following led up to the front door, and was flanked on either side by two expanses of tilled garden soil, which was fenced in with wire, sticks, bits of old furniture, and bundles of tightly-bound grass. Mounds of vegetables flourished in haphazard beauty — beets erupted from the soil, beans dangled like beads from a necklace, and tomatoes hung heavy and ripe from their vines. Two roughly-made but brightly painted flower boxes sat on either side of the cottage door, and spilled a beautiful curtain of color. At the base of these beds lay several cats of various ages and colors, sprawled out for their mid-morning naps, or sitting with their legs tucked up under them in such a way as they appeared to sit like loaves of bread in the grass. Bees visited the flowers, then cycled back to the heather-coated hills that rose up on either side of the place.

The cats regarded them with thinly-veiled annoyance as they approached the door. Arthur took a breath, and looked at James, then Lance. "I'll stand back."

"Right, probably for the best." Lance turned to James. "Well. Go on, then."

"Me?"

Lance and Arthur nodded, as did Mrs. Wylit. John stood in Arthur's shadow as the sun broke through the clouds, a stretched, pained expression on his face, his own green eyes wide and ringed with white.

James set his shoulders, took the last few steps to the rough wooden door, and knocked sharply.

They waited, scarcely breathing. There was no sound inside, and no one answered. James knocked again. And then again. "Hello?" he called. "Is anyone home? We... mean you no harm."

"And we're not selling anything!" Lance added with a helpful nod.

James knocked some more. "Please, sir. We... we know who you are. Mr. Harold Marlin sent us. We have his grandson, Lance, here with us. We need to speak with you. He wanted us to find you." He paused. "We have some bad news for you, and I'd really rather not shout it through a door."

With that, a small panel in the door slid open, and revealed two blue eyes narrowed in suspicion. James almost laughed — it was like something out of one of the gangster movies he loved and Arthur hated, as though this were the entrance to some kind of New York speakeasy. The eyes stared holes into James' face, then Lance's. "Harold Marlin?" a soft voice inquired. "He... he sent you?"

James nodded in relief. "Yes, he's asked us to find you."

The eyes stared at him for a solid half-minute. Then, the voice muttered, "No, no, it can't be, your eyes are playing tricks, playing tricks on you."

"What's that, sir?"

"Did something... happen?" The voice was barely audible above the sudden stiff sea breeze that whipped their clothing against them. "I haven't... eh, the money...?"

"If you'd let us inside, we could tell you," Lance suggested. Then he made the mistake of moving toward the door.

The panel slid shut with a terrified snap.

Mrs. Wylit left Arthur's side and sat down on the edge of one of the flower boxes. She put her cigarette in her mouth to free up her hands to pet the cats. They submitted, and one of the tuxedos rolled onto his back to have his tummy scratched. "Do you want me to have a go?" she asked after a time.

"No," they all chorused.

"Suit yourselves." She shook cat hair from her hand.

"Easy now." James drew Lance back by the elbow. He knocked gently again. "Sir? I'm sorry for my friend's... Please. Mr. Marlin tasked us with finding you, and we've come a very long way to do so. It's hot in the sun and we're terribly thirsty."

Millimeter by millimeter, the slat slid open again. "Do you have *proof*?" The voice that belonged to the wide blue eyes was taut and grating like a violin's E string.

James withdrew the cottage's deed from his jacket pocket and offered to slide it through the hole. "That came from the personal effects of Mr. Blanchard." The man took the document with weathered fingers, though the nails were clean.

Nothing but darkness from the slat in the door, and the crinkling of paper. "This could have come from anywhere," the voice said after a long pause. "Mr. Marlin never mentioned any of you save the grandson, and how should I know if that's really who you are?"

"Why are you afraid of us?" Lance kept his hands out in the open as not to spook anyone. "We came here to try and help you. My grandfather... look, please, open the door and we'll explain everything."

"You can explain through here," came the sharp reply. Then, "Why have you brought that big lug? Is he your bodyguard? Or will you use him to break down my door if I refuse to open it? I live up here in solitude for a reason. I never did harm to anyone, never came to your town. I'm not hurting anyone. It's your Christian duty to leave me be."

"I know you're not hurting anyone," James echoed, and nudged Lance back again. He flapped his hand at Arthur, who must have read the message and backed off several more steps. "We're only here to tell you some news that will change your way of life here."

"Maybe you *are* selling something. Does it look like I have a lot of money?"

"Please, sir, I'm begging you—" James' words hushed as he felt hands on his shoulders that guided him slowly to one side. At first he thought it was Arthur, but the hands were too small. It was his father, John, who moved him to the side and stepped up to the small stoop.

"Matthew Barlow," John said, his face white, his breath short, eyes wet with sudden tears. "Matty."

"No," the voice on the other side of the door whispered. "J-Johnny? Is it... no, it can't be, it can't, you're — you were — my eyes — I saw you as a young lad again and I thought—"

"Matty, it's me." John smiled as tears dripped from the corners of his eyes and fell on the rumpled collar of his shirt.

With a grinding squeak, the knob's handle churned, and the door swung open.

Before them stood a man in his middle forties. James immediately saw the resemblance between him and Lady Barlow, even in her advanced age. They had the same long, regal, rounded nose and oval chin. Matthew must have inherited his father's long arched brows and large mouth, with lips that seemed like they should smile easily but were now pressed into an anxious pucker. He wore a clean white shirt and linen trousers held up by suspenders, and a pair of worn slippers protected his feet from the cottage's stone floor.

"It... it's impossible," Matthew Barlow whispered, hallowed, as if he spoke in a cathedral.

"I know." John rubbed his eyes on his sleeve in a jerky, embarrassed gesture. "I thought it was you, but I couldn't believe that my son came all this way to find you, of all people."

The shocked paleness of Matthew's pallor shifted suddenly, filling his sun-marked skin with a deep pink flush. "I never thought I'd see you again." He stepped out of his house and leaned into a mutual embrace withe John's arms.

James stepped back and bumped into Arthur, who looked down at him with a face twisted in puzzlement, mirroring his own expression. "What in God's name..." James shook his head and looked at Lance, who threw up his hands.

"You've lost me, mate," he said. "But, this is the man, isn't it?"

"It's him." Arthur put an arm around James for a brief squeeze. "It's Matthew Barlow. Finally."

"But — how?" James sputtered.

After a long embrace, John and Matthew pulled back. "I must be dreaming," Matthew murmured. His gaze shifted wildly between James' face and his father's. "He's your spitting image."

"No, it's really me." John smiled, and it broke the worry from his face. "I know. I can't believe it either. It's like something out of an old story. A legend." He turned to the rest of the party, who gaped with open-eyed wonder — all but Mrs. Wylit, who had found a small white and tan cat and had coaxed it into her lap. "Shall we go inside? I think we all have much to say to one another. Much to explain."

"Of course." Matthew dabbed his eyes with a handkerchief that he'd found in his trouser pocket. "Please, come in, come in. Forgive my chilly welcome, I— I don't get visitors. By choice."

He led them into the cottage, which had been built long ago indeed. The centuries-old stone flooring and wooden beams told the tale of its age, but the walls were freshly painted the faintest shade of periwinkle and the glass in the small window panes was new. The front door opened into a long rectangular room that housed kitchen, sitting area, and a small library of books next to a heavy antique desk. Handmade shelves lined the walls next to a large wash basin and the ancient black kitchen stove. The furniture was old, but had been recovered with rustic fabrics, none of which matched, but seemed to be friends with one another. The decor consisted of small watercolor paintings and fresh flowers from the boxes outside, which perfumed the air with their fragrance, mixed with that of woodsmoke.

As they filed in, James heard a tiny mewing sound near the wash basin. He glanced down at an old apple crate turned on its side. Within was a folded blanket, and upon it lay a gray mother cat nursing a litter of kittens. All of them were black, except the one that was ginger-colored.

Matthew offered them seats. There was a loveseat, a well-loved armchair, and the desk chair. Mrs. Wylit perched on the small ottoman, and Lance said he was more than content to sit on the rug. Next, their host, clumsy with emotion, tried to find enough glasses to fill with water from his jug. They ended up with a few glass jelly jars and mismatched tea cups, but everyone was grateful to slake their thirst.

At last, they all sat, facing one another, Matthew and John on the loveseat, now and then looking at one another, seeking reassurance, perhaps, that the events unfolding weren't a dream. Silence.

Then, "What's her name?" asked Mrs. Wylit.

Matthew blinked. "Sorry, erm," he coughed into his handkerchief a moment. "Excuse me?"

"Her name." Mrs. Wylit pointed over her shoulder at the box.

"Oh." Matthew smiled and dropped his head in a sheepish nod. "Er, it's, ehm — Hippolyta."

"Your Majesty," Mrs. Wylit greeted the cat as she bobbed her head toward the crate. "I'm Viola Wylit."

Matthew let a strange laugh escape. It was not used to having an audience; especially a human audience. "A pleasure to meet you, Mrs. Wylit. I have a feeling you know who I am." He smiled with unabashed joy at Lance. "And you're Mr. Marlin's grandson. Lord, do I feel old now."

Lance laughed and apologized for doing so. "And these are my friends, James Wilde and Arthur Pensinger."

Matthew turned to James. "He... must be yours."

John nodded, and was quiet for a moment, his green eyes fixed on his hands. "Yes. My son. I married."

"And then left." James hadn't meant it to slip out, and was sorry, but resentment stripped that away in a burning instant.

John lowered his head a few degrees, then reached up to touch his handkerchief to his nose. "Yes. I'm not proud of what I did, but I couldn't stay."

Matthew put his hand over John's. The tenderness between them struck James in the gut, and the guilt came creeping back.

"James and I were sent to Willowind House as part of Operation Pied Piper," Arthur leant forward and put his elbows on the massive shelf of his knees. "That's where we met Mr. Marlin, and," he cleared his throat, "your mother, sir. Lady Barlow. Lady Barlow told us that you had died. But later, when Mr. Marlin was ill, he asked us, James and Lance and I, to find you. We set out to know if you were alive or dead, and to fulfill his wish."

Matthew put his fingers to his breastbone for a moment, and it was John's turn to squeeze his other hand. "Ah," he said, "so that's the connection between you all." He breathed to settle himself, and took a shaking sip of his water. "Harold Marlin is..." He glanced from face to face. "He's gone, isn't he?"

They nodded. "I'm so sorry," Arthur offered Matthew the strong but sympathetic bow of his head. "Loved him dearly."

"We've lost Mr. Blanchard as well," Mrs. Wylit piped up from the crate, where she was stroking one of the little kittens.

"Yes," James confirmed. "He died last year."

"Mr. Marlin told me that he'd been committed, but I didn't know he'd passed." Matthew gave a watery sigh. Still, his hand stayed locked in John's.

"I'm their landlady, by the way," Mrs. Wylit muttered, but no one was paying attention.

"Did... Did Mr. Marlin tell you why I came here?" Matthew dotted at his forehead with his sleeve to absorb perspiration. It was dark and cool inside the cottage, but still he flushed and his brow and neck were damp.

James looked at Arthur, then at Lance. They each gave slight nods. "Mr. Marlin sent us because... we're all like you. So you have nothing to fear from us."

Matthew raised a finger slightly above his knee and pointed at Mrs. Wylit with a raised eyebrow.

"Oh, no, well, I don't suppose I've ever asked," James replied with a little smile. "But she had a husband at one point. And she might have a boyfriend now, I'm not sure."

"I do." She replaced the kitten next to its mother and rejoined the circle. They watched as she withdrew the liquor bottle from her bag and took a swig. "It's medicinal. Ask James."

"The doctor said she wasn't allowed to suddenly stop. It has to be gradual." James grimaced as his father accepted a dram from the bottle when Mrs. Wylit offered. John shuddered at the taste.

"Trying to say," Arthur rumbled, "that we understand why you ran. Why you live here alone. And we've come to help."

Matthew stood suddenly and went to the small window over the wash basin. They watched as he looked through the clear glass, watched his shoulders as they shook, and eventually settle into a straight line again. He turned to them, and wiped his cheeks again. His face was tear-streaked, but beaming. "I've been here alone for decades," he said, "ready to live out my days without seeing another human being. To... insulate myself from a society that hated me for what I am. But I..." He swallowed and took a composing breath. "I'm so glad you've come. And you thought to... you found John."

"John found us." Arthur leaned back and spread his large palms over his knees. "No idea how James' father knows you, sir."

Wide-eyed realization crept over James' face in increments, blooming color over his cheeks. His emerald eyes snapped in sudden understanding, and, without realizing it, he stood from his seat. "You were best mates." He turned from his father to Matthew, and back again. "And you were more."

Matthew returned to John's side and sat next to him, the beatific smile of a saint curving his full lips. "I never prayed in my life," he said. "I thought God never wanted me. But if I had, I would have prayed to see John, if only once more, before I close my eyes for the last time."

"It's a miracle." Lance reached out and gave Arthur's shoulder a light punch of delight.

"It's a legend." Arthur grinned at James.

Chapter 28

Matthew graciously offered Mrs. Wylit his bed when she complained of a headache. Soon enough she was snoring in the shady interior of the bedroom, the handmade curtains drawn over the windows to block the late afternoon sun. With Lance and Arthur gone to the village for their luggage and some provisions, James, his father, and Matthew were alone. They sat on a blanket in the shade of the small tree and played with the dogs. The friendly creatures romped about in the grass, intent on chasing their toys or engaging in tug-of-war with anyone who was willing. A good stiff breeze came from the water.

"Please," Matthew said, as James raised the jelly jar of water to his lips for another sip. "Could you tell me about when you lived in Willowind House?"

"Of course." James set the jar back in the grass, and exerted effort not to make eye contact with his father. "Arthur and I were in the same class in school in '42 and we were evacuated to Willowind House together. I've never been able to hide who I am with any degree of success, and the students all knew I was different. I was the class queerie, and some of the boys made it their daily occupation to beat the stuffing from me."

Matthew put a sympathetic hand on his shoulder and gave it a gentle squeeze. Then, his hand shot away as if he'd set it on a hot stove. He shifted awkwardly and apologized. "I'm not used to..."

"I understand." James continued at Matthew's behest, retelling the familiar legend of how he and Arthur had come together, about Mr. Marlin's role, and how much they'd loved Nim. "She missed you very much," he finished. "The reason she helped us was because she felt like she'd been unable to help you. Mr. Marlin thought it was important that at some point, you visit her grave. And understand how much she meant to us."

Matthew looked at the water. The smaller of the two dogs wandered over, exhausted at last, and settled down on the blanket next to him. Matthew stroked its ears, his eyes distant and unfocused. "I think of her often. I always knew that she loved me no matter what. But she couldn't find it in herself to stand up to my father. At the time I thought, well, if she *really* loved me, she would have put her foot down in some way. It's a mother's job to protect her child, even if that child is..." his voice dropped into a whisper, "a disgrace. A criminal, no less."

"Don't talk about yourself like that." John moved a few inches closer to Matthew on the blanket.

"I know what it's like to feel unsupported by a parent." James had almost said "abandoned" but the word was so poisonous on his tongue that he held it back. There was something about seeing John and Matthew together that bashed against his walled-up heart, a battering ram against its defenses.

John looked at the dog at Matthew's side instead of anyone else. "I tried to be... normal. But I couldn't. I left him and his mother. I fled like a coward instead of telling them the truth, or at least staying close enough to try and support them. And then the war came, and I..." He sighed, and Matthew's hand touched his as they both stroked the dog. "Then I saw him on the street in London, and I knew I had to try and fix things. That's how I ended up here. I followed him to you."

"Well, it's a good thing you did." Matthew's eyes twinkled, and he let his lined face turn into a very Nim-like smirk. "I'm broke, you see, and so is your son, it seems."

"We have money in the bank," James huffed, "but not with us."

"Mr. Marlin sent me enough to get by," Matthew explained. "I use errand boys to purchase what I needed. I grow most of my own food, and the waters are full of fish, but I was worried for the winter.

I have to pay for my stovewood. Mr. Marlin must have stopped sending me letters when he became ill."

"I'm sure that's part of the reason he sent James and Arthur to find you." John held out his hand, and the dog licked it. "They were the only ones he could trust with your secret." He looked at Matthew a long time as their hair waved in the breeze. "It's like you've come back from the dead," he murmured.

"I have. And I'm never letting you out of my sight again." Matthew turned in time to catch James' pucker-mouthed expression. "James, I know it's none of my affair, and that John's decision to leave hurt you immensely. I haven't had many experiences in my life from which to gain wisdom, but I can tell you this — now that my parents are gone, I realize that there were so many things I wish I could have said to them. I never got the chance to try and fix things, to have any kind of relationship with them. Then one day, it was too late. I can't imagine what kind of pain I caused them when I arranged my death. At the time I thought it my only option besides actual suicide. But I was young and impetuous, and after doing what I did, how could I go back? And now it's too late."

"I think you're a bit biased in your assessment of this." James crossed his arms over his chest. "Of course you're going to take *his* side."

"Perhaps I am. But what I wouldn't give to have my mother appear here, right now, as if by magic. To have a second chance."

"He can't fix it." James stood up. The dog shot up also, in the hope that he was about to throw a stick. "We can't pretend that nothing happened."

"I'm not asking you to." John stood up as well. "I hope you never forget, because I want you to hold me accountable for what I've done so that I can work toward a way for you to understand. And let me — be with you. Sometimes." He smiled as tears glinted in his large eyes. "Maybe just at Christmas, even," he finished.

"I'm not the only one you hurt," James tossed back.

"I promise, I give you my solemn vow." John reached for James' hands. James flinched when they touched, but he didn't pull away. "I will find a way to make things right with your mother. First of all, I'll pay her restitution. I'm comfortable now in my career, and I know how you two struggled without my income. And when she's ready, perhaps she'll... sit down with me. To talk."

"Think you'll be able to?" James sneered, though he still did not take his hands out of his father's grasp. "After all those hang-up calls? She thought you were some kind of pervert, you know, a heavy breather."

"I know I can find the words, now that I've found you." John squeezed James' hands in his own. "Will you let me try? That's all I wish. That's all I request. Your permission to *try*."

James wanted to pull his hands away and laugh; let that laugh slice his father to the quick. But as his father's green eyes stared into his own, a matching set, and the sea breeze ruffled their hair, he remembered the old brown coat, the familiar smell of his father's aftershave he could smell even now. He remembered how safe he'd felt in those arms so long ago. He wanted to feel that again. When John pulled him into an embrace and put a hand on the back of his neck, James did not resist. "All right." The words struggled to the surface against a tide of emotion. "You can try."

After a time, James pulled back, embarrassed at the wetness on his cheeks. "I should check on Vi."

"She's an alcoholic?" Matthew's observation more of a statement than a question.

"She started drinking when she lost her daughter in the Blitz." James was surprised when an amused half-smile crept on to his face without him willing it. "But she's really rather magical."

"Doesn't she have any family?"

"She does now." James went back into the cottage.

Mrs. Wylit was awake, though still reclined on the white-painted metal-framed bed, her body spread atop the patched quilts. The tuxedo tom had crept inside and lay next to her. He purred enormously and kneaded the flesh of her stomach while he pushed his nose into the fabric of her blouse. "He's looking for a mummy," she explained as James came in and sat on the edge of the creaky bed. "Look at him. He thinks he's nursing. Weaned too early, I'd wager."

He reached out and scratched the cat's waiting tummy. "How are you, Vi?"

As usual, she didn't answer his direct question. "Matthew can't simply... come back to London, you know. He's lived in this cottage all alone since he was fifteen. What is he now, in his forties?"

James nodded.

"He'll be overwhelmed. He's going to need to stay here awhile. With John; no matter his career obligations. And me too, I think."

James' eyebrows rose. "You're staying here?"

"For a time." She ran her fingernails over the cat's stomach. He arched his back in delight. "I can't get to much liquor out here. Maybe a bottle or two with the groceries. But after a bit, I feel I shan't drink anymore. Besides." She curled her lips beneath her wild brown curls. "Once they taste my cooking tonight, they won't want me to leave."

"You're a wonderful cook." He patted her ragged stockings. "Somehow."

She gave him a playful slap on his shoulder. "The two of you will have to care for the house while I'm away. But there isn't much to do. Pay the bills and such."

James nodded.

"Lance will go with the two of you, of course." The cat put a little bit of her blouse into his mouth and chewed on it. He purred madly and bashed her with his paws. "Look at you, a grown man acting like this." She stroked his head.

"You think he will?" James toyed with a stray string that had unravelled from the bed quilt.

"Do you think he can go back to his parents' house now?" She grunted. "No. It's London for him. Or beyond. Beyond, I should think. Considering."

James hung his head. "I don't want him to go. He's my friend. He's *our* friend."

"Not everything broken can be repaired easily." She scratched the cat on his head, between the ears. The beast was dumb with pleasure. "Things take time. You wouldn't expect things between you and your father to mend overnight, would you?"

"I suppose not."

"Time. And distance."

He nodded.

She brushed her hair back and tried to get it behind her ears. He took up her combs from the small wooden bedside table and helped her put them in. She looked healthier, he thought. Less ethereal, and more human. "There's only one thing left to do," Mrs. Wylit said.

"What do you mean?"

She looked at him from beneath wisps of her escaping curls. "You know what I mean, James."

He didn't answer, so she reached out to take his hand. This upset the cat, who stalked over to the other side of the bed to lay down again. "I'm scared," he said.

"I know." She squeezed his fingers.

Just then, they heard Arthur's deep rumble and Lance's infectious laugh coming over the breeze that blew in through the open window. James got up and pushed the curtain aside to see them coming around the hill, sweaty and dusty, laden with bags and sacks. "They're back."

"Sorry, luv." Mrs. Wylit gave the cat a farewell pat and got out of bed to slide her shoes back on. "Mum's got to go to work now."

John's money had funded a feast — sausages and eggs and bread, and soda pop that Matthew had never tasted. There were bottles of wine, tins of beans, a few sweets, and a sizeable box of tea, which was the most treasured thing and the item Matthew had missed the most.

Matthew and Mrs. Wylit turned it into quite the banquet, and everyone filled their noisy stomachs as the sun at last decided to set. They laughed and talked until it became late and they were tired. The dogs slept on a rug near the door, each huffing little canine snores through their wet black noses.

"D-dad?" The word tumbled awkwardly out of James' mouth before he could stop it, like a stone he'd fumbled through his fingers.

John's head whipped in his direction, and Arthur raised his thick, dark brows.

James cleared his throat as his cheeks burned. He took a sip of water from the mason jar at his feet. "I thought perhaps you could tell us all more," he said, "about you and Matthew. From before. I still have..." He swallowed. "There are questions," he finished.

John nodded with understanding. "I grew up on a farm outside the lands owned by the Barlow family," he began, "and I used to go exploring."

"Trespassing." Matthew's eyes glinted with humor.

"One day I found a boy weeping by the edge of the pond. When he saw me he tried to pretend he hadn't been crying. I didn't know what to do, but I had some hooks and line in my pocket, so I asked him if he wanted to make some fishing poles. So we did."

"We spent more time digging for worms than we spent actually fishing," Matthew recalled, and they both laughed.

"And by supper time, we were mates. It's that easy with children." John squeezed Matthew's knee. "I went to the pond the next day 'round the same time, and wouldn't you know it, there was Matthew again, but with a smile on his face this time."

"The day before, I'd run away from home and vowed never to return," Matthew explained, "after a row with my father. He caught me playing with an old baby doll I'd found in the attic. But then I came home that night and told him I'd made a friend, a boy from a farm, and we'd gone fishing. Well, that was a fine, manly activity, and with all of my brothers being so much older, I think he and Mum were glad I'd found someone to play with. Little did they know." He winked.

"I don't know how we both knew." John nibbled a crust of bread from the plate on his lap. "We simply did."

"I was never able to hide it." Matthew crossed his legs into a figure 4 and put his hands over his knee. "Everyone knew, even when I tried to act differently... *normally*."

James felt something lift off of his chest like a bird alighting to another tree. "I'm the same way."

Matthew gave him a knowing smile before he went on. "John was the only boy I'd ever met who didn't seem to care one bit."

"I think we were twelve when we had our first kiss," John recalled, and Arthur reached over to squeeze James' hand. The memory of their own moment exploded over James' brain and radiated against the guilty stone still lodged in him.

"And it was a few days after my fourteenth birthday when they caught us." Matthew's face went grim, and he looked ten years older in a sudden moment. "My brother's prize Corgi escaped out into the woods and he and the staff were out chasing it. We were so entrenched in our own little world that we didn't hear them coming."

"I'd never been beaten so hard in my life." John shifted uncomfortably and the loveseat groaned beneath him in solidarity. "After that, we were forbidden to see one another. I never saw Matthew again, except occasionally when the Barlow family came down to the village church."

"Christmas service. 1923. That was the last time I ever saw you." Matthew wiped a stray tear from his cheek. "That's when I decided to kill myself. During that service. Here was the vicar spouting off about brotherly love and eternal peace, and the two of us, in the same room but never allowed to touch or speak to one another again. I couldn't bear it. I began writing my final note and coming up with my plan. But Mr. Marlin found some of my drafts in the dustbin. He'd been there that day in the woods and seen me lying on the blanket with my arms around John. And he was one of the only staff who never treated me any differently or whispered about me when he thought I couldn't hear. And it was he who came up with the plan to save my life when he realized that I meant to commit suicide, and no amount of convincing would sway me from my plan."

"Then my granddad and Mr. Blanchard, his friend from the war, spirited you away and faked your death." Lance lit a cigarette. The smoke curled lazily toward the ceiling and hung there like the weight of his words. "And you mean to tell us you've been living in this cottage ever since?"

"Indeed. This was the first place I ever felt completely safe." Matthew patted his lap and the tuxedo tom jumped into it. He and John took turns stroking its black fur. "I had my books and my painting to keep me company. After a time, the animals began to gather as well, cats and dogs and birds. They were my friends. People from the village know about me. They call me the hermit. The children would sometimes bring me an injured animal and leave it with the hopes I could nurse it back to health. I was able to avoid going into the village altogether by leaving notes and money for the children to do my shopping. They were always honest, because I told them to use the change to buy themselves sweeties and things. When I was a younger man, I thought about leaving. But I never could find the courage. Besides, I was supposed to be dead. When the war started, I thought about joining, but it simply didn't feel like the world had anything in it for me to defend. And I knew how it was for men like me. For," he coughed into his fist, and said it, "homosexuals."

"Do you think you'll ever be able to leave the cottage?" James asked as he looked at his father.

"I'll go wherever John goes," Matthew promised. "We have a lot of lost time to make up for. Though I will admit, I've been outside of the world for so long that navigating it does seem rather terrifying."

"I'll take care of you." John leaned forward, and they shared a quick kiss, the first one in decades. Mrs. Wylit applauded, and Lance joined her, laughing.

"I'm sorry I'm not more equipped for company." Matthew in particular seemed exhausted, his voice creaking with overuse. "There are quilts in the trunk next to the desk, but I'm afraid that's all I can offer you."

"We'll make do," Mrs. Wylit promised. "I think that black and white tomcat wouldn't mind being my pillow tonight."

Lance leaned back with a satisfied sigh, and picked his teeth absently for a moment. "I suppose it's best to sleep on it, but I wonder — what will tomorrow bring? Now that the quest is over?"

"Happily ever after, of course," John said.

They all agreed. Except James, who hung his head in silence. There was still one thing he had to do.

Chapter 29

The laughter and voices in the cottage faded as the sun set and the night insects began their inevitable hymn. Matthew and John disappeared into the bedroom together to share the small bed, grateful, perhaps, for the forced closeness. Mrs. Wylit curled up on the loveseat, and Lance did his best to make do with one of the armchairs. That left Arthur and James, who decided to drag a couple of rugs and blankets out onto the heath and build a fire. The breeze from the cliffs kept any troublesome gnats away.

In the bright light of the unfiltered moon, they collected stones and arranged them in a ring, and then scoured beneath the trees for kindling. A couple of stove lengths gave them a fire, built more for the bug-battling smoke than to keep them warm. And so Arthur and James sat cross-legged on their bedding and watched the flames as they danced against the deep blue-black of the rugged Scottish sky.

Usually, Arthur waited for James to speak first. And James always spoke first. Arthur often joked that he was deathly allergic to silence. He watched his love, his best friend, open his mouth a few times as if to speak, only to pick up a nearby stick and stir at the fire instead. Sparks crowned their vista, and settled into the firmament as stars. And the silence was loud, roaring above the ocean rattling against the cliffs far below. And so, Arthur began.

"Beautiful." He nodded toward the starry sky, so bright compared to theirs at home with its brilliance muffled by city lights.

"Yes, it is," James agreed.

Arthur thought if he could put a crack in the dam, that the words would come out of James in a flooding torrent. They did not. So, Arthur said, "We did it. Found Matthew Barlow, that is."

James was quiet a minute longer. "I'm... glad. And I'm glad my father was here. It seems like too much of a coincidence not to be a fated reunion. That gives me strength."

"Why?"

"Because it means," James stirred the fire again, "that some things really are meant to be."

Arthur waited for him to go on. Within, his heart swelled and beat against his insides, insistent — *now, let him speak now!*

But still, there was the creeping silence, the fire-stick, the crash of the waves.

Well, perhaps a joke would help. It's what Lance would do. Arthur could think of Lance now without pain, because there was only one thing left to put to rest. "Want to tell ghost stories 'round the fire?"

James tossed the stick in the flames with an air of finality. He turned to Arthur and sat facing him, legs crossed. "I don't need to hear a frightening tale," he said, "because I'm living one every day, Arthur."

"What do you mean?" Arthur turned his body to fully face James' as well. The fire crackled, forgotten, at their side.

"Every day," James repeated, "every day I wake up terrified that you're going to leave me. I go to sleep every night thinking you're going to stop loving me. And I can't live in a world where I don't have you."

Arthur kept his mouth shut, in the hope that James would continue. After rubbing the heel of his hand against his eye, he went on.

"You know what happened between Lance and I, don't you?" he asked softly.

Arthur nodded.

James sighed, weary and watery. "I thought so. You've known since that very night."

Arthur said, "I wasn't asleep. I was watching. I thought... something might happen. And it did."

James erupted in words, but Arthur used his deep voice to overcome them. "Wasn't hurt by the kiss," he insisted. "Not that. I understand Lance. This was a new world for him. He wanted some of what we've got, isn't that it?"

"Yes, he did. He does. But he apologized to me. And it sounds like to you as well, though he never told me about it." James hugged his knees closer to his chest, as if he could curl into a ball and disappear. On one hand, it was such a relief to speak of it, but on the other, he had no idea where this conversation led. There was no map to follow. His eyes burned with the woodsmoke and tears, and his stomach yawned a pit.

"James." Arthur folded his hands together into almost a prayer, palm-to-palm. "You went all this time and you never said a word. Lance and I settled up before you and I did. D'you see the fault with that?"

Of course he did. "But I was—" he tried. James took a breath, and started over. "I was so afraid of what would happen if I told you. You have to know that I couldn't face my life without you in it."

"You think I'd *leave* you?" Arthur's voice was so low a popping log in the fire muffled two of his words. "Really? You thought that? After everything? That I'd walk off because of some silly kiss or two?"

James' fear blanched his face. "I don't know," he mumbled.

"Because that says you don't trust me." Arthur's hands went into fists at his sides for a moment before he exhaled and relaxed them. "Or that you don't really know me. You really think — that I wouldn't die for you? Haven't I proven that I would?"

James said nothing, and let the silent tears drip from his nose.

"That's the thing." Arthur burst up from his seat to pace, the lines of his muscles straining against his shirt as he stalked a few feet one way, then the other. "That's the thing. It's not that it happened. Do you understand? It's that you wouldn't tell me. You were afraid of what I'd do, instead of knowing, *knowing* how much I love you." He put his hand to his eyes for a moment, and then flung it to the side.

"What do you think of me, that I would walk away from you after all we've been through?"

"I'm sorry," James wept into his knees. "I should have told you that morning, the second we woke up. I regret it all — I made a terrible mistake." He sniffed back a sob. "Whatever you want me to do — I understand. I'll go away, if that's what you want, disappear—" *What will it be,* he thought, *the pyre or the nunnery?*

Arthur's shoulders relaxed. "You aren't listening to me," he said and knelt down next to James. He reached out with his massive paw and lifted James' tear-streaked face so they could stare eye to eye, green to green. "Or else you are still so daft that you don't understand what I'm saying? You and I are going to be together forever, no matter what comes. But you have to fully and truly believe that for this kind of magic to work. Understand?"

James threw his arms around Arthur. Arthur stood and picked him up into a mighty embrace and held him there for a long time before putting his feet back on the earth. "No more secrets," James promised. "Ever."

"I promise, too." Arthur used his broad thumb to brush James' tears away, and they both laughed through the pain that must come with such a healing.

"Starting over," Arthur suggested, as they walked hand in and toward the cliffs to look at the ocean.

"The old order changeth, yielding to new."

They stood in the moonlight, their feet inches from oblivion, and sealed it with a kiss.

Epilogue — Glastonbury, 1983

Of course, Joe thought. *Of course it's raining.*

The second he stepped off of the bus at the car park next to Glastonbury Abbey, the skies opened. The rain soaked his short-cropped hair, turning it from dyed platinum to soggy yellow. He cursed and pulled up his hood. The rain pelted his black leather jacket and dampened the backpack he carried that contained everything he owned.

Tourists scuttled for shelter or whipped open their umbrellas. Most were too preoccupied with staying dry than staring at him. Good. The last thing Joe needed was trouble. He paused for a moment beneath a tree near the entrance to the Abbey grounds and took a moment to pop on his earphones, press play on his knock-off Walkman, and light a cigarette. "One Hundred Years" pounded into his head and he made tracks for the address written on his forearm in Sharpie pen. 2 Dod Lane.

His path took him through the Abbey grounds, past the ruins and the tourists gathered around the alleged tomb of King Arthur. *Bollocks,* he thought. That was a lovely bit of chicanery whipped up by the monks in the 1100s to do what the city of Glastonbury was doing to this day — making money off of the legend. He snorted and shook his head at the idiots taking pictures of the resting place of some anonymous, unimportant dead person. What were they, or any human beings, except future unimportant dead people?

He was thoroughly soaked by the time he found the house. It was gray, with two levels and a built-on carport. The numerous, multi-panelled windows were all shrouded against the bleary afternoon with heavy curtains. It seemed quiet, abandoned, almost. This was in direct contrast to the yard, which grew lush with plants, shrubs, and flowers of every color. The small stone wall topped with wrought iron that surrounded the property could barely contain the vines and blossoms that spilled out onto the sidewalk in their summer glory.

Joe's steps were unsure in their big black boots as he went up the flagstone path. But there, next to the doorbell, there was a small embossed plaque: AVALON HOME FOR WAYWARD YOUTH. He snorted. Like everything else in this tourist trap, it had a stupid King Arthur name. He paused, considered his options, and rang the bell.

Second ticked by. He felt each muscle bunch and coil. Would he need to fight? To flee? What was taking so long?

At last, a woman in jeans and a burgundy turtleneck answered the door. She had the same haircut as his mother, he realized with a recoil of revulsion, but where his mother's perm was a mess of Aquanet, this lady's hair had a natural curl to it that made up for its mouse-brown color. Her face was young — not as young as his, surely, but she couldn't have been over thirty, and something about its innocence and warmth, brought out by her minimal eye makeup and peach blush, exuded health and goodwill.

"Hello." She pulled the door wide. Behind her, he could see a short hall that opened up into an airy sitting room, and a staircase that led to the second floor. The windows in the back of the house were open to the light, as they weren't visible from the street.

"Uhm, hello," said Joe.

"I'm Rowena. Welcome." She stepped back from the door, and raised her hand to wave Joe inside. Just like that, no questions. With a smile, even.

Joe tromped inside, and tried his best to wipe his boots on the rug near the door.

"You're soaked. Back in a tick." Rowena disappeared down the hall and made a right, and then returned a few moments later with a fluffy bath towel. "There you are. I'll put the kettle on as well."

"No milk, please," Joe found himself saying, nice as you please, as normal as ever, as if he weren't a stranger on the street. "I'm allergic."

"Noted," she promised. She looked at his backpack, which he had removed and clasped in his hands before she lay the towel over his shoulders and head. He thought she would offer to take his backpack, but she didn't. He placed it securely between his feet, and rubbed the towel over his wet hair, neck, and shoulders.

"All right, I think the dripping stopped. This way." She led him back into the house, past a country kitchen, and through the sitting room, which was done up in cottage style. She turned toward a white-painted door inlaid with glass panels and opened it a bit before she stopped herself.

The room beyond was some kind of study. Though the shag carpeting was unfortunate, at least it was a dull beige color. The walls of the comfortable room were lined with seven tiers of thin wooden bookshelves affixed to the wall with minimalist wire frames. Books crowded most of the space, but there were vases and little bits of art, as well as potted plants that trailed their vines down to the floor. These were especially prominent near the windows, where some of the shelves extended even over the glass. The room also had a plethora of photographs in frames, whether on the walls or sitting on the shelves. In the center of the room stood a rectangular table which served as a desk, a chair, a small shaded lamp, a typewriter, and a telephone. Before the desk sat a comfortable-looking houndstooth loveseat.

There was an antique sword mounted against the wall above the largest window. The thing gleamed as if it was polished every day, its blade and pommel reflecting every bit of light that could travel through the window on such a gloomy day. The weapon was strange, out of place, really, with the modern decor. *Well, as modern as the early '70s would allow*, Joe thought.

Two men sat on the loveseat, their backs to the door. One was bulky, with wide shoulders. His curly hair was grown out into a ponytail. His strands ranged from deep black to light gray inter-mixed. This man had his arm around a smaller chap, whose auburn hair was silver at the temples. He wore spectacles and a tweed suit jacket. The large man's deep voice rumbled through the crack Rowe-na had made in the door. "And the result?"

"Lance said it was completely negative. He's going to be fine. It really was only a nasty cold. But so many of his friends." The smaller man shook his head sadly. "I wish he'd come back for a visit. Should I tell him to bring Eddie and come for Christmas?"

As the hulking form with the ponytail nodded, the smaller man leant forward and gave him a peck on the cheek near the corner of his mouth. Joe was so startled he almost dropped his bag, and flushed scarlet as if he'd seen something he should not have. He looked at Rowena, who did nothing except reach out and knock gently.

The two men sat up on the loveseat and looked at her, and then moved to stand. Joe thought they would be embarrassed at having been caught in such a compromising, private moment, but they on-ly smiled and waved Rowena and Joe inside. "Sorry to interrupt," Rowena said, "but did you hear from Lance?"

"Affirmative...and negative," the smaller man smiled to assure her, as he removed his glasses to polish them.

"Oh, thank God." Rowena's relieved hand flew to her breast-bone. "That's so wonderful to hear. I'll ring Mum here in a minute after I get the tea going." As if it was nothing at all, she said, "And this is Joe."

"Welcome, Joe. I'm James Wilde, and this is Arthur Pensinger." The man put his spectacles back on, smiled, and extended his hand. Joe gave it his tightest squeeze, but was rewarded not with intimida-tion, but good humor. "What a grip. You must be an athlete."

"I box." Joe wiped his nose on his sleeve. "And I been in loads of fights."

The large man nodded knowingly at him.

"*Arthur*?" Joe asked irreverently before he could stop his mouth. This is what he always did — spoil things out of nervousness, the bitter words escaping before he could stop them. *Hurt them before they hurt me.* "So you match the rest of this tourist trap shite, eh? That why you moved here?"

Instead of scolding, instead of staring at him in shock, everyone in the room broke out in waves of laughter.

"You have no idea." Arthur turned to the one called James. "Thought I'd pop out with the lads. Take 'em to the cinema, seeing as it's too soggy to dig today."

"Home for supper?"

"Aye." They squeezed hands together, another gesture that floored Joe, and the large man left. Rowena disappeared as well. This left Joe with the professor, who removed his suit coat, draped it on the back of the desk chair, and rolled up the sleeves of his light blue shirt.

"I'm glad you've come." He turned the fabric briskly past his elbows. "Rowena will be up with tea and sandwiches in a few minutes. She doesn't simply fetch the tea, though; she's our substance abuse counselor."

Joe nodded. He felt rooted to the spot a few steps inside the door, and he clutched his backpack tighter against his chest.

"You can stay as long as you need to." James shoved his hands into his baggy trousers' pockets. "All we ask is that you comply with our house rules and attend your therapy appointments. We do expect our residents to pitch in with the chores, too, so I hope you aren't allergic to a bit of work."

"No. Only milk. And cheese. Cream. Er — dairy," Joe mumbled.

"Of course. I'll be sure to let everyone know. In fact, why don't I put you on kitchen duty tonight and you can help cook supper? That way you can help us understand what you can and can't eat."

Joe's eyes swam for a moment, and he blinked rapidly. "This is — all — fast."

"Of course, I'm sorry. Would you like to sit down?" James sat at the desk and offered Joe the loveseat. Joe sank down onto it. James took out a legal pad, and a pencil, which he patiently sharpened. "Where are you from, Joe?"

"Bath."

"And how old are you?"

"Eighteen."

"And how did you hear about us?"

"In London." Joe chewed his lip, unsure what to reveal. "At a club. Voxhall."

"One of my favorites." James grinned and his eyes went distant for a moment. "Then I suppose it was Howie who sent you."

Joe's eyes bulged. "You really know Howie Yourfather?"

James nodded. "Old friends. We met at the Royal Voxhall years ago. And I know him as Angela, too." He smiled. "I know it's hard to believe that an old man like me ever had a wild streak and went to the cabarets, but Arthur and I always enjoyed them. That's something I miss since we've moved out here." He tapped his pencil's eraser a moment against the legal pad. "But that's a lot about me — can you tell me more about how you came to us?"

They were interrupted by the tea tray which came to rest on the desk between them. There were sandwiches and biscuits. Joe audibly snorted at the traditional pot, cups, and saucers, and grandmotherly spread of edibles. Rowena fixed him a cuppa and handed it to him. "No milk," she promised, and shouldered her purse. "I'm off to the market. We were going to have alfredo tonight, so I need to grab some tomato sauce as well."

"Right. Ta, dear," James said as she left.

"Mum's relieved about Lance," she called over her shoulder.

"Aren't we all." James leant forward to pour his own cup, and then sat back to watch Joe as he wolfed down the food and slurped his tea. When he'd finished, Joe was surprised to see a blue glass ashtray had appeared, as if James had read his mind. "Just so you know, we don't allow smoking upstairs in the bedrooms, and we encourage it on the patio outside if possible. But I think that was thunder I heard." He nudged the ashtray closer. Joe patted his satisfied belly beneath his Cure tee-shirt and lit up.

"So," he said, "who's Lance?"

"Come and see." James waved him over to a cluster of pictures that sat in simple frames on one corner of the bookshelves. Joe left his backpack on the loveseat and joined him. "This is Lance, and his partner Eddie." James indicated a professional portrait of two men. One was Black, with close-cropped hair faded on the sides. The other was white, with a feathered haircut. They stood back to back like they were in an ad for some kind of network TV sitcom, maybe a buddy cop comedy. Both wore matching gray suits with blue and white ascots. "They run a law firm in glamorous Los Angeles, if you can believe that. Lance went there as a young man hoping to work in the movies. He had a few small parts, but what he wanted to do was represent the performers and the crew working on films to make sure they were treated fairly. So here they are — Lance and Eddie, lawyers to the stars." He made a small dramatic gesture with his hands, and Joe felt laughter snort out through his nose. Then James' face, lined but not without its youthful qualities, went sober. "Lance wasn't feeling well, and he was afraid he'd contracted HIV. I assume you know what that means."

"Of course," Joe snapped. He hadn't meant it to come out that way, but fear drove his voice to a higher pitch. He coughed and masterfully lowered it again. "But you said he was tested."

"He and Eddie both were, just to be certain. Negative for both, thank God, or whoever is listening." James made a prayer motion with his hands before he dropped them to his sides again.

Joe puffed smoke out of the side of his mouth. "Who's this?" He used the end of his cigarette to point to another photo. It showed a man and a woman in casual attire standing in front of the ruins of a castle. A little girl leaned on the woman, who was obviously her mother, a well-loved stuffed Pooh bear tucked under her arm. The mother's waved bouffant suggested the late 1960s.

"That's Rowena, and her mum and dad, Viola and Silas. Viola, believe it or not, was my landlady before we became friends. She and her husband live in London, and they still rent out the apartment upstairs, even though they've purchased several other properties to let."

"She *looks* like a landlady. Wouldn't want her asking after the rent." Joe moved on to another framed portrait. This one showed two elderly gentlemen, one in a wheelchair. They were in a garden, surrounded by a kaleidoscope of flowers. Joe realized it was the garden in front of the house.

"That's my father, John Wilde, and his partner Matthew Barlow." James gave a sad smile beneath his glasses, the curve of his mouth wistful.

"Partner?" Again, Joe felt the molten words slip out before he could stop them. "Must run in the family, yeah?"

"One could make that argument." James seemed completely unfazed by Joe's insistence on pushing his boundaries. "I've met many young people who have told me that they suspect one of their family members may also be homosexual. Of course there isn't a study to prove such a thing. I think it's best to keep away from being studied like specimens, at least for now, don't you agree? Times have changed, but not much."

"I think they should study it," Joe argued, as smoke curled up from his hand. "Because if it's biological, then it isn't anyone's fault, is it?"

"An excellent point." James put a brief hand on Joe's elbow, and to Joe's surprise, his body did not immediately recoil. "But can love really be scientifically calculated? Can science explain how, when Matthew had his heart attack, that my father, seemingly in good health for his age, died the next morning?"

Joe had no answer, so he instead motioned to a section of the shelf near the pictures that was crammed with slender volumes. "You wrote those," he said.

"I did." James glanced over the book spines. "Poetry, mostly. Of course, I never became famous, though critics seem to like my work. And I do know a few university faculty members who use my King Arthur sourcebook in their medieval literature classes."

"Makes sense now why you moved here."

"I think the legends have something for everyone. You have to rethink how you interpret them."

"It's not for me," Joe argued around his cigarette. "Chivalry, true love, all that shite?"

"Well, my Arthur is a gay man, and that is his Excalibur." James gestured to the sword. "Given to him by our own Lady of the Lake, if you will — Matthew Barlow's mother. We even had our spiritual guides along the way." James' hand went out to lovingly touch a frame that contained the army portrait of a WWI soldier with familiar eyes — shaped like those of Lance, the Hollywood lawyer. "Legends are written down by the victors, or the ones with the most power, but that doesn't mean that there isn't room for the rest of us if we allow ourselves to believe."

"You actually *believe* in true love and destiny and all of that?"

"I don't simply believe, Joe. I'm living it." James' gentle hand guided Joe over to another picture of two boys in their school uniforms, standing next to a tree. "Arthur's mother took this one. She lives up the road, tough old bird — in her own house, independent like you wouldn't believe. I'm trying to convince my mum to move down here, too, but she's just as stubborn. Says the only way she'd leave London is in a casket or an urn."

"That's you and Arthur." Joe's dark eyes went wide. "You were only lads."

"That was about a year after we fell in love," James explained. "We went to the same school in the same class. In '42 we were evacuated in Pied Piper and were sent to a country estate. That's how we met Lady Barlow and Mr. Marlin, and when we inherited Excalibur." He smiled at Joe's confused face. "But that's a long story for another night, best told 'round a fire." James guided Joe back to the loveseat, and sat down at the desk again. "That's enough of my blathering on about myself," James said. "Why don't you tell me more about you?"

Joe thought for a moment, and then dug into his bag. He came up with a laminated ID card and handed it to James. James adjusted his spectacles and examined it. It was a school identification card from 1981. On it was a picture of a girl with wavy dishwater hair and blunt bangs. The name on the card was Josephine Karen Hawkins. James' eyes travelled from the blurry picture to Joe's face. The wide dark eyes were the same, as were the arched brows beneath the wild, short-cropped platinum hair, framed on either side by many-times-pierced ears.

"I see," James said.

"Do you?" Joe challenged.

"Explain it to me." James put down the pencil and folded his hands over the notepad.

Joe said nothing, and stabbed out his cigarette into the ashtray.

"Joe."

Joe slowly raised his eyes to meet James' green gaze.

"You are *safe* here."

Haltingly, Joe began. Part of the way through, James fixed him another cup of tea, and then another, as well as passing over a box of tissues at the perfect moment. Joe spoke of how, when he was young and running around with the lads, that he was simply a tomboy. This became something else as Joe grew up, went through puberty, and still felt most comfortable in trousers and men's shirts. He cut his hair short and only seemed to have male friends. "I thought I was a lesbian. I fancied girls. I still do. My family chucked me out after they found me with Sara... I started going to the clubs, even had a girlfriend or two. Howie took me under his wing and showed me how to dress. In drag, I guess. And I can. Go as a man, that is. People can't always tell. That's when I feel most like me. Mostly." He heaved a great sigh, and rubbed his forehead. "I can't explain it, but—" He coughed. "Some days I really do feel like a woman. But others, I'm so sure, I'm so comfortable as a man. Do you understand what I'm saying?"

"Yes," James promised. "I absolutely do. You're not the first that I've met, Joe, and you certainly won't be the last. There is a condition in the psychological literature called gender identity disorder, though I don't like the term disorder — it implies there is something broken about you, which there isn't. The problem is with a society that can only see gender in binary terms."

Without warning, tears cascaded from Joe's eyes. "There's — nothing *wrong* with me?"

"No, there isn't. Of course, there isn't. You're on a journey now, to becoming the person you feel you are on the inside. And we can help you as much as we can with that journey. For now, that means a safe place to stay until you're on your feet. In the future, it may mean hormone therapy or other medical procedures, or just learning to think about your identity differently." James sipped his tea, and dabbed at his own eyes with a tissue. "Now you've gotten me started," he laughed through his tears. "It happens every time. Ask Arthur."

Just then, there was a gentle tap on the glass of the French door. James stood up and waved Rowena back in. She smelled like Estée Lauder and summer rain.

"Having a good talk?" she asked.

Joe nodded.

"All right, Joe, it's time to start on supper, so I was wondering if you could give me a hand. Arthur and the others aren't back from the cinema yet. I think they've gone to see that *Mr. Mom* show of all things."

Joe wiped his nose and shoved the tissue into the pocket of his now-dry leather jacket. "All right," he said, and followed her to the kitchen.

As the office door swung shut behind them, the phone on James' desk rang. It was Arthur. "How was the film?" James asked.

"Dreadful. The lads had a good chuckle here and there, though. After, we were passing by the school. Found a lad walking home, followed by a couple of boys who reminded me of Morgan and his lackeys."

"Oh dear." James sipped his now-cold tea. "Did you handle it?"

"They won't be coming after him again," Arthur promised, "but he's a bit shaken up. I've invited him home for supper. He called his mum, and she said it was all right. She's actually Trudie, one of the ladies who gives tours at the Abbey."

"I saw Trudie this morning," James exclaimed. "I didn't know she had a son."

"Hope there's enough to eat. Need us to stop at the market?"

"No, there's plenty." James smiled as the sun broke through the clouds outside. The rays glinted off of Excalibur's mirror-like surface. "I'll set an extra place at the round table."

Arthur laughed, and rang off.

THE END

All passages from "Idylls of the King" were obtained from the Project Gutenberg free online library.

About the Author

Amelia is an author, freelance writer, and secondary educator. She was born, bred, and corn-fed in the great state of Iowa. Amelia's short stories have appeared in several anthologies, including the pro-human sci-fi collection Humans Wanted and My American Nightmare: Women in Horror. The literary journals Saw Palm, Quantum Fairy Tales, Wizards in Space, and Intellectual Refuge have featured her work. She also blogs for the parenting website mom.me and at akibbie.wordpress.com. More information can be found at ameliakibbie.com. She lives in Iowa City with her husband, baby girl, and three spoiled cats. They share the condo with a shy ghost.

Past Titles

Running Wild Stories Anthology, Volume 1

Running Wild Anthology of Novellas, Volume 1

Jersey Diner by Lisa Diane Kastner

Magic Forgotten by Jack Hillman

The Kidnapped by Dwight L. Wilson

Running Wild Stories Anthology, Volume 2

Running Wild Novella Anthology, Volume 2, Part 1

Running Wild Novella Anthology, Volume 2, Part 2

Running Wild Stories Anthology, Volume 3

Running Wild's Best of 2017, AWP Special Edition

Running Wild's Best of 2018

Build Your Music Career From Scratch, Second Edition by Andrae Alexander

Writers Resist: Anthology 2018 with featured editors Sara Marchant and Kit-Bacon Gressitt

Magic Forbidden by Jack Hillman

Frontal Matter: Glue Gone Wild by Suzanne Samples

Mickey: The Giveaway Boy by Robert M. Shafer

Dark Corners by Reuben "Tihi" Hayslett

The Resistors by Dwight L. Wilson

Open My Eyes by Tommy Hahn

Christine, Released by E. Burke

Upcoming Titles

Running Wild Anthology of Stories, Volume 4

    Running Wild Novella Anthology, Volume 4

    Legendary by Amelia Kibbie

    Recon: The Anthology by Ben White

    The Self Made Girl's Guide by Aliza Dube

    Sodom & Gomorrah on a Saturday Night by Christa Miller

    Turing's Graveyard by Terry Hawkins

    Running Wild Press, Best of 2019

    Tough Love at Mystic Bay by Elizabeth Sowden

Running Wild Press publishes stories that cross genres with great stories and writing. Our team consists of:

    Lisa Diane Kastner, Founder and Executive Editor

    Barbara Lockwood, Editor

    Cecile Sarruf, Editor

    Peter Wright, Editor

    Rebecca Dimyan, Editor

    Benjamin White, Editor

    Andrew DiPrinzio, Editor

    Amrita Raman, Operations Manager

    Lisa Montagne, Director of Education

    Learn more about us and our stories at www.runningwildpress.com[1]

    Loved this story and want more? Follow us at www.runningwildpress.com[2], www.facebook/runningwildpress, on Twitter @lisadkastner @RunWildBooks

---

1.   http://www.runningwildpress.com/

2.   http://www.runningwildpress.com/

CPSIA information can be obtained
at www.ICGtesting.com
Printed in the USA
LVHW051247031119
636167LV00015B/60

9 781947 041325

7